≪FOOLS≫

PAT CADIGAN

BANTAM BOOKS
New York Toronto London Sydney Auckland

FOOLS

A Bantam Spectra Book / November 1992

ISBN 0-553-29512-8

Published simultaneously in the United States and Canada

Bantam Books are published by Bantam Books, a division of Bantam
Doubleday Dell Publishing Group, Inc. Its trademark, consisting of the
words ''Bantam Books'' and the portrayal of a rooster, is Registered in
U.S. Patent and Trademark Office and in other countries. Marca
Registrada. Bantam Books, 666 Fifth Avenue, New York, New York 10103.

PRINTED IN THE UNITED STATES OF AMERICA

RAD   0 9 8 7 6 5 4 3 2 1

This one is for
George and Marguerite Fenner,
my parents-in-law,
with love and thanks

Special thanks to:
Sheila Williams, Gardner Dozois and Susan Casper, Ellen Datlow, Cheryl Cordes, Jim Cappio, Dwight Brown,
Lawrence Person, Glen Cox and Jill Engel, David Gar-
nett and Frances Jobling, Mike Resnick, Malcolm
Edwards, Merrilee Heifetz, Beth Meacham, Lisa Tallar-
ico-Robertson, Jeannie Hund, and the Delphi Wednes-
day Night Irregulars.

An additional round of thank-yous to Jim Brunet, Allen
Varney, Laurie Mann, Carl Fink, Larry "Wombat"
Hammer, Katherine Lawrence, Lenny Bailes, Tappan
King, Connie Hirsch, Rick Wilber, and Nathan/EVPA,
for their suggestions and commentary about word-
processors.

≪ FOOLS ≫

PART I

FOOL TO ≪REMEMBER≫

Everywhere I looked in Davy Jones' Locker, I saw me, or people who wanted to be me. And the club wasn't even half full yet. I knew I was going to love being Famous.

The holo fish floating through the deep blue holo water flickered, vanished, and then reappeared more vividly than before. I could relate; I'd just flickered into existence myself, it felt like. A small price to pay for being Famous, these little lapses. Happened whenever I had to fine-tune the system, nothing terribly serious. All I had to do was give myself a few minutes to get oriented, take a few deep breaths, and it would all come back to me. It always did.

I caught sight of my new manager on the other side of the club, talking to some of the employees. I gave him a cheery wave to cover the fact that I could not, at that moment, remember his name. Post-mindplay amnesia can be *so* embarrassing.

He froze in midgesture, both hands spread in front of him, and stared at me as if I had two heads or something. Migod, I thought, what was *his* drama? Had I come out too early, should I have still been in back putting on another coat of paint for La Grande Entrance later?

I gave a big, exaggerated shrug à la Constanzia, the role I had just finished playing at Sir Larry's. It would have been just like Constanzia to jump the gun this way —maybe I could blame it on leak-through. For all I knew, it *was* leak-through. My manager started to take a step toward me and one of the employees pulled at his sleeve. I was pleased to see that she had already been made over with the Look, though I doubted she had been enfranchised completely. It wouldn't have been much like me to be serving refreshments in a club, even a club like Davy Jones' Locker.

She said something to my manager and then pointed toward the back room. He looked torn, turning from her to me and back again, long white hair swinging with the movement. I made a dismissing gesture to tell him that he didn't have to worry about me right now and went for a stroll to admire the decor. I'd been to Davy Jones' plenty of times, but tonight, it was all mine, hired for the debut. My manager certainly knew what would make me happy. I was going to have to figure out some way to keep his name from melting out of my memory all the time. It was the least I could do.

The club was starting to fill up now, but for some reason, nobody seemed to notice me wandering around. Maybe because I wasn't really dressed up—I still had on my street clothes, which were as nondescript as a person could get and still remain visible. Well, I'd just have to rely on my manager or my valets or both to drag me back to the dressing room at the proper time. After all, what was the point of being Famous if you couldn't leave the little details to the people who were supposed to take care of them?

On the other side of the main room, the funhouse mirror was already running and drawing a crowd, so I decided to go over and have a fast look. Once the party really got going, they'd be lined up half a dozen deep and climbing all over each other for a turn in front of it.

An oyster bed faded into existence in front of me on the floor. The jeweled shells opened to disgorge pearls that rolled into the golden sand. It was very pretty, but I'd seen it about a million times before. Not so much pearls as chestnuts; I'd have thought I rated something a little less overexposed. I tiptoed through it so as not to spoil the illusion. Hackneyed or not, there was no reason to be rude.

I was a good ten feet away from the mirror when I suddenly got the strangest urge to turn around and run for the nearest exit as fast as I could. More than an urge —it might have been some kind of inner alarm going off. Mi*god*, I thought, I wasn't getting one of those tiresome body-image problems where you get all mirror-phobic and start starving yourself, was I? I'd heard that sometimes happened to people after they became Famous— something about seeing yourself in so many different places that you developed some kind of aversion. I'd have thought that I would have been the last person to suffer from something like that.

Then I saw the more likely explanation for my sudden case of dread—i.e., Em-Cate, big as life and twice as gruesome. She was actually *preening* in front of the mirror, admiring her reflection, which had come up as a silvery-white shark. Typecast again, I thought, feeling nasty. Why on earth had she come here? She'd known as well as I had that the invitation had been only a formality. I couldn't imagine Em-Cate wishing me well under these circumstances or any others. There had never been any love lost between us at Sir Larry's but now that I was going to be Famous and she wasn't, she had dropped all pretense and had been openly displaying her revulsion for me.

Well, the timing on this thing could have been a lot better, too. My manager could have made the franchiser wait until I'd finished with the role at Sir Larry's before announcing I was under contract. But the contract with the franchiser wasn't going to interfere with the play—I had promised Sir Larry's. Of course, as soon as the last performance was over, I'd be lucky to get fifteen minutes to gather up my personal belongings and clear out, probably with Em-Cate dogging my every step to make sure I didn't make off with something that belonged to the theatre. And like what—a jar of pancake, for God's sake?

Professional jealousy was a monster. I hoped to *God* that it would never happen to me. I liked to think that if they'd gone for Em-Cate instead of me, I'd have been big enough to hold my nose, grit my teeth, and say, *Congratulations*. Or maybe just *Good-bye and good luck*. Or, okay: *Good-bye*.

She'd been such a pig about things that I would have sworn she'd have flung herself off the tallest building in Commerce Canyon sans parachute before she'd attend a party in my honor. But it had been an open invitation for anyone and everyone at Sir Larry's; no other polite way to handle it, really. Almost everyone had told me they planned to come, though the director had begged off, claiming artistic differences. Just what I would have expected from a man who mainlined Fosse, but at least Bayles wasn't a hypocrite.

If Em-Cate thought I was going to let her presence sour things for me, she could write up her own scenario and stick it in her eye. I sidled up next to her and said, "Enjoying the show, Em-Cate?"

She turned away from the mirror and blinked up at me. (She also hated me because I was taller. Tonight, she must have forgotten her stilettos, which would have brought her up to about the level of my nose.) "Pardon?"

"I *said*, 'Enjoying the show, Em-Cate?' "

She blinked some more, a habit Bayles had practically had to beat out of her, since it tended to leak through to her character. "Why, yes. Yes, I am. Thank you." She gave me a puzzled smile and went back to admiring the shark.

Mi*god*, I thought, the bitterness of her jealousy knew no bounds—now she was pretending she didn't even know me! I felt so bad for her. Well, for a second, anyway.

On Em-Cate's right, Twill Carstairs—of *course* he made it up—paused in his admiration of his own reflection, a stingray wearing a bow tie on the stinger, to look at me curiously. Twill and I had always been on good terms, even though I knew he really didn't approve of what I was doing, and probably wouldn't have accepted an offer like it himself. Which was too bad—with the right ad campaign, lots of people would have wanted to be him.

"Looks like another satisfied customer already," he said, glancing at Em-Cate.

Was he referring to himself or Em-Cate? "Well, I'm still an entertainer, Twill," I said. "Even when I'm just helping you entertain yourself."

His square face took on a wary expression, as if I had

said something patently untrue. Maybe Em-Cate's rotten mouth had finally gotten to him and he had decided I was scum after all. Or had he and Em-Cate hit up the pharmaceutical buffet early and scrambled their brains? I smiled at him and turned to the mirror.

Oh, *very* clever. Instead of a shark or a stingray or some other fish, I had an aquarium filled with all sorts of exotic-looking fish. Em-Cate and Twill were staring at it curiously.

"If you're thinking something about small fish in a big pond," I said, "keep in mind that it's *my* pond." I gave them both a farewell salute and moved off.

"Was that . . . you know," I heard Em-Cate ask as I moved away.

"If it is, I don't like how much she's giving away with it," Twill answered.

Well, *that* made *no* sense whatsoever. Maybe they hadn't waited to hit up the pharmaceutical buffet and picked up some cheap risers before they got here. Best to get back to the dressing room and stay out of trouble, I decided. I looked for my manager—dammit, what *was* his name?—but I couldn't see him or any of the employees he'd been talking to. Davy Jones' was getting more crowded by the moment; he was probably searching for me even more frantically than I was searching for him.

"I thought they'd sent you home."

I turned around. Sovay's bleached face had soaked in every bit of blue light. It made him look slightly luminous. "Are you *serious*?" I said. "Go home and miss my *own* de*but*?"

His expression went from wary to openly amazed.

"Mi*god*," I said wearily, "is everyone on some kind of new drug that makes everything I say sound astonishing?"

" 'Migod,' indeed," Sovay said slowly. "I suppose what I really find astonishing is what some people will do to other people for the sake of a profit."

Given our history together, Sovay was probably the most entitled to a say about what I was doing. But mind-to-mind contact hardly meant that he owned me, not as a fellow performer, and not personally. After all, he was married full-time, a fact he had gone to great pains to impress on me.

"I don't see where the choice I made constitutes my 'doing' anything to you or anyone else at the theatre," I said. "So I decided to pursue the franchise rather than continue onstage—so what? I didn't try to force anyone to go and do likewise. I didn't even suggest anyone for the recruiter to talk to, though I'm sure if I told him *you* were interested in a no-obligation interview, he'd be happy to meet with you. He's a great recruiter and an even better manager."

"Who do you think you are?" Sovay said, that fragile, bleached skin wrinkling with concern. He should have taken a semi-immobilizer to prevent overexpressing before he was repigmented. Unless he actually *wanted* his face to look like crumpled paper for some reason.

"Okay, okay, I know," I said, "you're getting little flashes of Constanzia, aren't you? It's not really leak-through, just a little flashover, and that's quite normal, nothing to do with the franchising programs. It's just that she's the freshest portrayal and, frankly, she's my favorite." I spread my hands and wiggled my fingers. "It's a tickle to have a grand gesture for every occasion."

Sovay put a finger to his mouth, caught himself, and

stroked his chin instead. "Do you know," he said, "tickling is actually a very sadistic thing to do?"

I rolled my eyes. "Even if you tickle yourself?"

"You can't tickle yourself."

We stared at each other for a long time. Mindplay amnesia had not affected the memory of how he had felt mind-to-mind and how I had felt to him. He had been as surprised as I had; Sovay, the man of stainless, no-rust virtue, devoted to his plump little drab of a wife, discovering love-at-first-contact.

There hadn't even been time for second thoughts—when you're mind-to-mind in a system, the speed of thought makes the speed of light look like a snail's pace. Perhaps if there had been time to consider, my nobler instincts might have won out, but I hadn't had that option and neither had he. Personally, I'd always thought we'd done the best thing for everyone. Some things you just have to get out of your system. Once it had happened, we'd gone on with the character interplay and it had been the best session I'd ever had with anyone.

Thank God his guilt-storm hadn't hit until after we'd disconnected—I couldn't have taken such an onslaught myself. I'd told him over and over that his wife needn't ever know, that it wasn't as if he'd been unfaithful to her in fact or in act. A fantasy for two is as unreal as a fantasy for one, after all. But he just couldn't seem to allow me to reassure him; it was something he had to work out to his own satisfaction by himself and I supposed he had. I didn't know for sure because we'd stayed out of each other's head after that, and he never discussed it with me.

But though he seemed to return to normal, there were times when I would catch him looking at me in an odd, almost suspicious way, as if he were sure that whatever I was thinking threatened him in some way. I figured he was just afraid that if I went mind-to-mind with anyone else, the whole dirty little story would spill out into the middle of whatever scene we were working on. I wanted to reassure him, tell him I could keep a secret and that just because I was mind-to-mind with someone didn't mean I felt compelled to show everything I had. But I had never been able to bring myself to say anything at all to him. His whole being, which I knew better than I'd ever planned to, warned me to keep my distance.

Now he was probably afraid that someday, someone would run up to him on the street, declare undying mental lust, and demand to relive the entire experience.

Poor, silly scared boy. Part of me wanted to tell him his fears were groundless. Another part of me said to let him suffer. That he didn't seem to understand me as well as I understood him was a pretty telling thing.

"You know," I said after a bit, "if you devoted a little cold rational thought to things—just a *little*— you'd be a lot better off. But as long as you drag around all that sad baggage, I can't help you. You can't even help yourself."

"That's all right," he said. "Maybe *I* can help *you*."

I laughed and moved off toward where I thought the dressing room might be. Sovay helping me—what a novel idea. The man was fine as long as he was pretending, but put him in a real situation, even an unreal-real situation of the strictly mental variety, and he fell on his face.

A bright yellow fish with spines all over it sailed by me and then circled around for another pass, closer this time. I was appalled to see that it had the Look, too. Mi*god*, I thought, club employees were one thing but the party decorations, too? Whose brilliant idea had *that* been, the club's or my manager's? The price of being Famous, I supposed. I made a shooing motion, hoping that whoever was on the holo controls was paying attention and would send it away or make it disappear altogether. I was going to have to have a little talk with my manager about this. Franchises were one thing, but fish seemed just a little undignified.

The fish hung there in midair, staring at me with its freakish human eyes. Then it blew a kiss at me. Heart-shaped bubbles floated upward. I had to laugh out loud in spite of myself—never let it be said that *I* couldn't take a joke—and looked around to see if anyone else was catching this little encounter.

Only Sovay, still staring after me with a forlorn, pitying expression. Mi*god*. Who did he think he was feeling sorry for, anyway?

Maybe only himself, I thought suddenly, watching the fish blow more heart-shaped bubble-kisses at me. Its face looked even more human now. I stepped back; having to focus on it at such short distance was making me dizzy. I hoped my eyes hadn't picked this moment to go glitchy on me. Scant minutes before my actual debut, I didn't need my eyes spinning like loose marbles. I had to find the dressing room and my manager *now*.

There was a slight commotion across the room and I saw the employee who had the Look, surrounded by a number of other employees. She was upset about something. My manager was bent over her; when he moved away slightly, I saw it wasn't the employee after all, but someone else who had the Look. Enfranchising on the premises tonight? Quite a vote of confidence in the product, though rather unorthodox.

Well, if they were going to pull out all the stops, they could have at least changed her clothes. She looked like she'd spent a bad week with ragpickers turned fashion terrorists, and they'd won. I'd have been upset in that outfit myself.

Faint snatches of what they were all saying to each other came to me through the underwater sound effects, which had come on without my noticing. ". . . clothes . . ." she was saying. ". . . itch *stole my clothes!*"

I couldn't help laughing a little. If fashion terrorists really want you, they'll get you, no matter how careful you are. It was funny, even if she couldn't really be expected to see the humor in it.

". . . *can't* . . . stampede her . . . won't . . . clean wipe . . ." My manager was physically restraining her and she was practically hurting herself, trying to get away from him.

". . . *me* . . . derstand that? . . . thinks . . . *me!*"

My manager had both arms around her and was trying to drag her into the back room. Forget the fashion terrorists, I thought, nauseated, this had to be an enfranchising gone wrong. How *awful*; especially the timing. If this hurt my image, I was going to sue the pants off everybody, including my manager, who apparently didn't have the sense to carry emergency tranks.

The sight was making me even more nauseated. I turned away and found the fish had moved up even closer. Its face was even more human and for a dizzy moment I thought I was back on the other side of the room, looking at a reflection in the funhouse mirror.

That face was *definitely* in the wrong place, I thought. The dizziness intensified.

• • •

Okay, the last thing I remember is throwing someone off a cliff.

Now I am standing in the bottom of a swimming pool filled with holo water and fancy holo fish and a couple hundred souls who are getting a lot more out of this experience than I am, as most of them probably remember how they got here and those that can't don't care anyway.

This, they say, is the lot of the memory junkie: bad living, bad cess, tough stuff. I know I am not exactly in a position to complain to karma-rama, but who ever sets out to be a memory junkie on purpose? Ten thousand people buy and sell memories every day. Me, I'm the ducky luck-out who gets the thunderbolt in the head: junkie-junkie-junkie. The crazy side effects are just another fringe benefit. But what the hell, I always did say that anyone who wasn't pulling a fugue state here and there just wasn't trying.

The light in the swimming pool is the appropriate underwater mood-indigo murk, but my eyes are adjusted, which must mean I've been here awhile. I glance around in what I'm hoping comes off as casual, trying to get a feel for the social climate in my immediate vicinity. Apparently, I have not been throwing money, marriage proposals, or punches around carelessly, since nobody is looking except a weird, puffed-up fish with prickles all over it, floating in front of me and glowing like a radioactive yellow ghost. It's got eyelashes about an inch long on its bulgy eyes, and instead of a standard fishy mouth, there's a little Cupid's bow, red lipstick and all, blowing fishy kisses at me in tiny, heart-shaped bubbles—yow! Isn't *that* a hell of a thing to find coming after your bait. But what's worse is, the face is familiar.

The thing darts right at me. Instead of letting it swim through my head, I dodge to one side and it sails up and away, twitching its tail fins. Not that it would have hurt or anything; I just didn't like the idea.

A few feet off, I see this guy watching, and he's got kind of a fishy look himself, like he disapproves but he's too prim to say so. He's wearing one of those lighter-than-air sacsuits, the kind that billows out if you even twitch, making him look like he really is underwater. His skin is all bleached out, prepped for a tint—I can tell by the way it glows blue. The chin-length hair is a darker blue blot around his head. I don't know him. Maybe he's the fish's friend. So let *him* pucker up.

Then I realize there's some kind of something going on behind me, and that's what he's really looking at. Yah, that makes more sense; I can't be important enough for anybody to disapprove of. But then, who knows what kind of changes have been playing while I've been fugued out?

Whatever the big attraction is over there, it's drawing people and holo fish from all over the pool. Angelfish are swimming through me before I can get out of the way, and I hate it. I've heard about this kind of thing, this is how they throw a party uptown—if you're some kind of high-power celebrity priv, they send all the party decorations your way so you can make La Grande Entrance. I'm not sure what I'm more curious about, who the celebrity is, or why I'm in on it.

There's a break in the crowd all jockeying for position and I see her. It's that bad old kissy fish! Or rather, it's the person the fish was modeled on. She must be Famous. I wonder if she knows what they've been putting her face on around here. Pretty good face; if I had those custom cheekbones, I'd show them off, too. But jeez, on a *blowfish*? At least they didn't try putting the hair on, too. I guess a hairy fish was too sprung even for the priv'd-out joychildren who run this place. Whoever that might be.

The people around her are all working hard to get noticed and she's looking a little shaky about it, like she's not so sure she wants to be there. One woman wrapped in scarves keeps moving back and forth in front of her like she's dancing. Boy, I've heard about professional pests, but I never saw one in action before. If it was me, I'd just relieve her of the waking state and use her ass for a footrest, but Miz Famous looks too blown out to blow up. There's a guy in a chef's outfit and a lady angler complete with a fishing rod and waders, somebody else dressed like a court jester, two Madonnas, one pre-Raphaelite and one postmodern, a human torch whose holo flames have a bad case of static, the fakiest-looking samurai I've ever seen in my life, and, all told, a lot more horse's asses than there are horses. Suddenly, I get this very loony flash that all these people are holos, just like the fish, and Miz Famous and I are the only real people here.

And then I think, *No, that's some other place*, but I'm god*damned* if I know what place that could be. But I *almost* know. It's on the tip of my brain. Maybe some old memory I bought to feed my beast of a habit, repeating on me like bad chili.

Miz Famous turns and sees me then, and there's no doubt from the look on her designer face that she knows me. *That's* a good one—*nobody* Famous would know me or anybody like me. I sure don't know her. I don't know her name, I don't even know what she's Famous for. Whatever it is can't be anything to do with me.

So what am I here for anyway?

Abruptly, the image of that cliff pops into my head again, a memory of looking over the edge into some foggy nowhere. Can't be her I threw over, unless she can fly without a plane.

A tall guy with sanitary white hair puts a hand on her

shoulder, telling her something he obviously thinks is very important. Now, him I *do* know . . . but that's all I know. I don't know if I like him or hate him or owe him money or worse, so I step behind a big underwater plant. A memory junkie can't be too careful.

Then this other guy in a purple satin tuxedo steps in front of her and I get a real funny feeling. Something about him makes me think I ought to go home to the Downs where I belong as soon as possible. I'm not sure where this place is, but from the look of the crowd, it's a long walk home if I can't catch a freebus.

I have *got* to tell Anwar about this. I don't think he'll believe me. He'll think I've been feeding the beast again and he'll start telling me how I'm gonna have to do something to take care of what I owe.

Of course, if I hang around here long enough, I can maybe build up a memory I can pawn. Any pawnshop'll pay more for firsthand stuff like this. Not enough to take care of the whole debt, but maybe enough to keep me out of any immediate trouble.

I look over at the Famous person again. She's turned out in full Brain Police drag—grey tunic over jumpjohns, visor cap sitting on the back of her head, even a trank-pak clipped to her belt. Jee-zuz, how did I miss *that*? Everybody else must be in on the joke, but I personally do not find a whole lot of humor in it.

Well, I was leaving anyway. I turn away and almost run right into the guy in the sacsuit. By the look on his face, I can tell I was right the first time after all, he definitely does not approve of me. And then I wonder if he meant to cut me off, and maybe that Brain Police getup on the Famous person isn't a joke. But when I look back to see if she's coming for me, she isn't wearing it anymore. She's wearing some bad designer crap that's supposed to look like something you fished out of the trash. Figures; the guys who put the Emperor in his new duds are still getting rich these days.

I ain't laughing. I throw someone off a cliff and then I'm hallucinating Brain Police in water over my head? Even if it's just holo water, that sounds like a karma-gram to me.

I move away from the guy in the sacsuit, looking for the exit. It's slow going, what with all the marine and other life I don't care to get interactive with. I get to the far side of the pool and there's another big group of people jamming things up, except they're all mostly side by side, with other people trying to wedge themselves in between them. Stupid party games of the privs and Famous? I go back and forth trying to find a way around them and then some fool of a priv in mink shorts, so hyped out that his moonstone eyes are practically spinning in two directions, grabs my arm and says, "Here, let's check what *you* look like, game-girl."

I'm just about to smack him and tell him *I'm* no game-girl when I see what's really going on. The whole wall is one big funhouse mirror, hottest toy of choice for the filthoid rich. Whoever's running the mirror controls tonight must know these people, because the reflections look pretty pointed. One woman reflects as a shark, and the resemblance is too good. Another woman gets an octopus, and I can see the family resemblance in that one, too. One guy's a sponge, and the one holding my arm is some kind of tube-shaped worm thing. There's a few eels, another sponge, a stingray with a bow tie on the tail, a giant sea-horse (with studded bridle and bit, yet—wonder what *he* does for fun), and a lobster with only one claw.

This is all supposed to be real big fun, but for some reason, seeing myself in that mirror is 'bout the last thing I want to do. But then Mink Shorts shoves me out in front of him, yelling, "Squid! Squid! Squid!"

Now, I never thought I was the squid type, but what I see in the mirror doesn't make any more sense. I'm an aquarium, filled with assorted fishes I don't know the names of. This is supposed to be clever?

Everybody's staring. Then there are two new reflections on either side of me. Not fish, people wearing the same outfit. I turn to look at each one, thinking maybe the mirror operator is witty enough that I'm going to find I'm standing between a couple of holo fish. But no, they're people on this side of the mirror, too, and the twin outfits are uniforms, not acute fashion-itis. At least they're not Brain Police uniforms, just hired help doing security duty.

"Madam, you'll have to go now," says the one on my right.

Which is exactly what I figured he was going to say, except for the *Madam*. That's a bonus.

I pass the sacsuit on my way to the egress. Now he looks almost happy.

When we get outside, I see I'm on the rooftop of the Royale Building, in Commerce for-God's-sake Canyon. I also see that I have just been thrown out of the legendary Davy Jones' Locker, which I should have figured was where I was. Where else do they have holo water over everybody's head? An old-fashioned marquee card on an easel informs what part of the world that can read that it's closed tonight for a private party. Jee-*zuz*. What am *I* doing *this* far uptown? When I get fugued up, I get damn-the-torpedoes, no-prisoners fugued up.

The security guards walk me over to the transit area and ask me which do I prefer, the freebus pad, the air-taxi, or the valet-service salon for owners of private vehicles?

"What do *you* think?" I say, and they take me right to the freebus pad, sit me on the bench, and practice their servants' bows. In lieu of a tip, I look impressed. A very hotwire private club, Davy Jones' Locker, so exclusive and fancy you're supposed to tip the guards when they throw you out. I was on the lookout to buy a memory from anyone who'd been to it, but I never ran across anybody who had one to sell. Made sense; the type of clientele the Jones' got wouldn't be out selling their memories. And even if they were, I probably couldn't afford to buy.

And *then*, just as if my karma's getting all kittenish and contrary, I stick my hand down in my pocket and my fingers close around a wad of currency that is definitely more money than I am supposed to be able to ever hope to see.

Wild.

But what's even wilder is that I have a matching wad in my other pocket. Good thing, I'd probably be walking lopsided if I didn't.

This is not exactly the place for an audit. But I've got to have at least a hint, so I pull just the very top of one wad out of my pocket and peek at the number on the outside bill. The light from the overhead floodlamp shows me the figure real clear: $100.

My head begins playing Sousa victory marches, all brass. I push at the corner of the top bill with my thumb, trying to flip it up and see if the one underneath is the same nice round number. The wad shifts and I see that I was mistaken. It's not $100. It's $1000.

I slide over to the darkest end of the bench and try to think. Lotteries don't pay off in cash, and if I've inherited a fortune from some rich relative I didn't know I had, I wouldn't have been thrown out of Davy Jones'. So who did I kill?

The memory of the cliff blooms in my mind like a

dandelion on fast forward. My inner eye can see the grassy edge, and the foggy nowhere below. If I could just make the picture in my head a little bigger, maybe I'd see who I threw over it.

Then I'm off on a fast hope trip. Memory junkie, yah, maybe I've been feeding the beast after all and this is somebody else's memory. Two seconds later, the trip's over. This can't be something I got from someone else because I didn't get a rise out of it. The only memories I get junked up on are someone else's, no matter how dull they are. Someone else's vacation at the shore, someone else's wedding, someone else's frigging trip to the grocery store and I'm totaled, buzzed and rebuzzed. But the day *I* killed somebody—ha, and ha. Doesn't even raise a blip.

Across from where I'm sitting, the overhead rail lights up and I can hear the freebus droning in the distance like a bored hornet. Better hurry home now and see if I'm hiding bloody clothes in the shower. After all, who says this is my first kill? Maybe I *really* screwed up and got myself a murder jones from somewhere.

The freebus pulls in and the few souls peering out the windows at me look a lot more murderous than I feel. Even the stick-tender looks like a thug and that's just a holo, one of those cosmetic urban improvements they put in to make you feel like you're getting personal service from all the impersonal automateds.

Yah. Who else is gonna be on a freebus this time of night, Brain Surgeons For Jesus? They're all gonna figure anyone who climbs aboard at the Royale is a priv and they'll pick my bones clean before we hit upper midtown.

Instead of getting on, I walk over to the air-taxi pad, feeling everyone on the freebus staring daggers into my back for causing an unnecessary stop. But us killers don't sweat that small shit, ha, and ha, I think to myself, and that gives me that old sick feeling of impending doom in the pit of my chest. Anwar's always telling me that's just being short on potassium, and a banana a day keeps impending doom away. Ha, and ha. But not if that feeling of impending doom means impending doom, which it sometimes does. Anwar always covers his ears when I say that.

The freebus drones away. The backwash of cool night air feels prima, which causes me to take a better look at how I'm dressed. Normally that rooftop wind would go right through my quik-wear and chill me to the bone.

Yow . . . none of *this* stuff came out of a vending machine, not even recently. I was so blown out about the wads, I never even noticed the quality of my frigging pockets. I have to stop, close my eyes for a second, and look again, just to make sure this isn't another hallucination like the Brain Police rags.

Nope. This is what *real* people put on their real bodies. Black tailored jacket that feels like velveteen over a silver Latin Revival shirt, and black don't-care pants, one size covers the earth. The shoes are standard shitkickers, but they're *new* shitkickers. Now that I'm aware, the shirt is just a little tight under the armpits, and the sleeves on the jacket fall short, but Jee-*zuz* all the same. On me, these are not clothes. They're a disguise.

So what am I disguised as?

As *not-a-killer, what else?* says that voice in my head, the one everybody's got that tells them what a fool they are. Well, yah, of course, this ought to fool whoever I meant to fool. I fooled myself with it. Didn't I?

"Excuse me?" says a polite, amplified voice. I almost drop dead of cheap surprise. "Up here," the voice adds.

There's a woman in a glassed-in booth on top of the taxi stand. Not a holo, but a real person. This is how they do it uptown, real people to serve their real selves.

"Hello?" I call up to her.

"No need to shout, I can hear you. May I summon a taxi for you, madam?"

I stick my hands in my pockets and grip the wads tight. Just making sure they're still in there. "Yah. *Sure!*" Bring 'em on—hell, call two so I have a spare.

"At this time of night in this area, the only air-taxis available have drivers. Will that be satisfactory?"

It will be expensive is what it will be, but for once, that isn't my biggest worry. "Just what I wanted," I say, feeling extravagant.

"There will be a five-to-eight-minute wait, according to traffic patterns," she says, glancing down at something in front of her. I can see only the glow of the screen lighting her face from below. "The refreshment service is through for the night, but beverages are available from the automated dispenser-wall to your left. Complimentary, of course, for your convenience."

For *my* convenience. That's a new one, but I could get used to it. I wave at her and go over to see what the carriage trade gets for free.

No hard stuff, according to the panels in the wall—three kinds of coffee, half a dozen teas, soft drinks, fortified water, prehangover treatments, and all fancy-label. I'm getting more impressed by the second.

I decide to see if free Brazilian coffee out of a vending wall has more going for it than the poison I usually drink. When I press the panel, a screen lights up right in front of me and shows a little home movie of an antique silver pot levitating and pouring coffee into a commuter cup. A moment later a chamber below the screen opens up and I smell it even before I reach in for it. The commuter cup is identical to the one on the screen. Nice touch.

The screen says, *Enjoy the Royale's private blend often!*
Come again soon!

"Beg me," I say. And then I *taste* the coffee and I think,
fuck it, cancel the taxi, I'm going to live here, right here in
the taxi stand. Maybe I can work the booth, calling rides
for privs and making polite announcements about only hu-
man-driven air-taxis available. Us killers can do polite as
well as anybody else.

Then the taxi sets down on the landing pad and I'm
impressed all over again—it's running in whisper mode, so
as not to bother the privs with too much noise. The driver
pops the rear door for me and I climb in, clutching my
coffee with one hand and still holding on to one of my
wads with the other.

Kind of a letdown here, because the interior of the cab is
slightly on the shabby side. Privs are hard on their toys.
The clear plaz panel between me and the driver is open—I
guess there aren't too many priv stick-up artists, at least
not in this part of Commerce Canyon.

"Destination, please," says the driver politely. Yah, I can
definitely get used to this. Without thinking, I give him my
address.

He turns around and looks at me so hard that I get
scared. Maybe I'm a publicly wanted killer, with my name,
address, and description all over the dataline.

"That's a *Downs* address," he says, like he's telling me
there's shit on my shoes. I just sit there thinking it figures,
humans won't go to the Downs.

He sighs and takes off his overdecorated livery cap. Underneath, his black hair's been knitted into a dizzy herring-
bone design now mostly flattened from the headgear.
"There are only eight rooftop pads in the Downs that serve
air-taxis," he says, talking real slow, like I might not understand one word in three, "two in each quadrant. Four are

clustered near the center, four are spread out on the perimeter. If you tell me where that address is located, I can let you off at the pad closest to it."

"Oh," I say. I'm supposed to know this, except I never had any reason to, till now. "Northwest quadrant. Um, inner."

But he's still glaring at me. I try my impression of a polite smile on him, but apparently that's not what he's been waiting for.

"I have to charge you fare-and-a-half," he says sourly, "because I've got to come back from there empty."

"*Oh,*" I say again. Yah, that figures. It's not like he's just going to happen on a bunch of privs looking for a ride back to uptown after a sleaze-along. I finish the coffee and toss the cup in the suckhole. "That's okay," I tell him. "Fare-and-a-half, let's do the thing right."

Now he gives me an up-and-down, waits like he wants to ask me something else, then shrugs and turns around. As we lift, the partition between us slides shut. Maybe he thinks he's got the first ever priv stickup artist in his back seat. Nah, just a killer. In spite of myself, I feel like a rich kid on National Greed Day—the only time I ever get airborne is if I'm strapped into a showboat on my way to a court appearance. This way is definitely better.

He swings the cab around to get into the correct flight path and I have a farewell view of the Royale from the back window.

A small group of people who have just come out of Davy Jones' are hurrying across the roof to the taxi stand; one of them points up at the cab and they all look. Guess they think I took their ride. Just as they're turning toward the glassed-in booth, the taxi rises and levels off and I see only the jeweled summit of Commerce Canyon getting smaller behind me.

• • •

". . . of the line. We're here. *Hey!* Second time, end of the line!"

The driver's rapping on the partition. I didn't even know I fell asleep. Groggy, I dig around in one of my wads and find a smaller bill in the center, which I push through the fare slot. This does not make him happy.

"What is this?" he says.

"What is what?" I'm still all full of this crazy dream about an old guy falling out of a sky-island.

"What are you, somebody's pet bank robber? I'm set up for fare strips and bearer chips. What is this currency?"

Was there some kind of banking coup while I was asleep? "What's the matter with it?"

"You want to buy shoes, it's great. But I don't have an accounting system that works with it."

I start getting scared and then all of a sudden, this weird calm comes over me out of nowhere. He's telling me about his accounting system like *my* life depends on it? "I don't know accounting, I'm paying fare-and-a-half. *I'm* paying you. You work it out."

He looks like I just spit on his upholstery. Then, when I think that maybe he's going to slide back the partition and punch me, he takes the currency. "This was a lot more trouble than it was worth."

"Your accounting system is more trouble than it's worth," I say, and pop the rear door myself.

"Wait a minute!" But I'm already out and walking away. The downshaft to the street is closed, I'll have to take the outside stairs, but walking ten flights down isn't so bad. Besides, the idea of being shut up in a downshaft is enough to bring on a case of the short-breath tonight. I get to the fake wrought-iron stairs when the driver takes off. Guess he decided he didn't feel like pushing it any further in the middle of the night on a Downs rooftop. Maybe he's afraid I'd kill him; us people who use currency are probably capable of anything.

I'm halfway to the street when I think to ask myself where I'm going. It's such a good question, I have to sit down on the steps and come up with an answer worthy of it. Go home, sure, crawl onto the futon, pull a blanket over my head, and hope I wake up knowing everything-and-a-half. Except I do *not* want to be alone with *that* picture in my head. Now that I'm out of the club and back in the Downs where I belong, it's starting to give me a case of impending short-breath. Impending doom. And me without a banana.

Oh, hell, I think, getting up and going the rest of the way down to the street. I'll just go to Anwar's. His place is only about a block from where I am right now. I'll tell him about it and he'll give me a banana, or at least a place to spend the night while I try to unkink this thing and figure out who I threw over that cliff, and when, and why.

Which begs the bad old question, do I really want to know any of this?

Jeez, but I wish my mind would make up its mind. Ha, and ha.

I'm halfway to Anwar's when I'm about to pass a twenty-four-hour pawnshop.

Cause for pause. I want to get off the street as fast as possible, but I know I've done business with this place. Something of mine might still be in the inventory, and for once, I've got enough money to buy it back.

I'm thinking about going in . . . and thinking about it . . .

. . . and when I come to, I'm hanging on a parking meter at the curb, about to topple over into the gutter.

Dizzy spells now, for chrissakes. I'm getting to be a real hazard to navigation here. I've got half a mind—ha, and ha—to forget the pawnshop and just run off to Anwar's, get indoors before I pull a really big blank and wake up in a crib or worse.

And then I think, hell, I'm here, I might as well go in. It'll save me a trip later.

Behind the counter, the pawnbroker raises an eyebrow at me and goes on combing her white hair.

"Can't stay away, eh?" she says. "What's the good word?"

Far back in my mind, something jumps, and I hear a small voice say, *Tell her*.

Tell her? Tell her what? For a moment it feels like my head is full of cotton fuzz.

"We're having one of those nights, are we?"

We're having one of those lifetimes is what we're having. But at least I can remember her name. "You got anything of mine, Ofrah?"

She looks at me for a long second before she runs one hand over the screen sitting to her right on the counter, moonstone eyes going side to side, then rolling up in her head while she consults deep inventory. This goes on for almost too long before she says, "Nothing but what I had."

"Who took it?" I ask.

Her look says I'm the craziest thing since eyes first popped. I start to reach into my pocket and something tells me very strongly that I shouldn't bother; she's not going to tell me who bought my stuff while I was off in uptown adventureland.

She notices the movement and her mouth twitches. "Void again, are we?"

I open her mouth to tell her, no, I just won the lottery or something, but I stop again. Instead, I take my hand out of

my pocket and shrug. "Even an uptown priv gets finan-
cially embarrassed from time to time."

"Privs have credit ratings. You don't even have a good
word."

I give her another bad word, wondering if I have finally
achieved the early stages of complete mental meltdown;
there's some block that won't let me tell her for once I am
holding more money than memory. I want to ask her what
I said the last time I came in, what I was doing, what I was
like, and why I didn't put in for a call-back-and-retrieve,
but somehow I know she's not going to tell me even if I
beg. She'll just keep giving me that bored look.

I turn away to leave and catch sight of a pair of bald
heads just outside the door. Great, this is just what I
needed—a pair of onionheads with insomnia, looking for
someone they can claim violated their marital space and
then stomp into blood pudding. For all I know, they've
been following me since I left the cab on the roof.
Onionheads'll do that when they're bored enough.

They spot me and grin at each other. Yah, they're ready.
They can't come in and get me because they can't claim a
challenge in a public space less than ten thousand feet
square; that's the law. I turn back to Ofrah.

"So," I say, feeling humble, "can I go out the back
door?"

Ofrah gives a short laugh; she's seen the onionheads,
too. "Yah, sure enough. For you, that's free. You don't even
need a good word." She jerks her head at the curtain behind her. "Run like hell. Onionheads got long memories,
even if you don't. Come back when you've got a good
word."

Grind my nose in it, Ofrah. I give her one last bad word
by way of farewell. The curtain takes me right out to a back
alley and I run like hell. Exactly like hell.

• • •

"Ah, Christ," says Anwar. "Do you do this just to tor-
ment me, or are you now a practicing psychotic?" In the
tiny security screen, his face looks like an unmade bed,
probably as much the fact that I woke him as the low-res.
But he buzzes me in and he's waiting with a cup of coffee
when I get up to his apartment. Sort-of coffee—after the
uptown Brazilian, I can taste every chemical and additive
they put in those instant cubes. But it's the thought that
counts.

"You're true," I tell him, sipping and not making a face.
"You're the truest of the true, and the truest one I ever
knew."

He scratches himself through his robe. "Yah. *But*—" he
yawns—"one time, Marceline. One goddam time *only*. You
either give yourself up or you don't come here anymore,
because I don't need this kind of trouble." He yawns again
and plumps down next to me on the broken-down frame-
work of cushions that passes for a couch.

My heart sinks. With the picture of that cliff in my head,
this can only mean I'm a known killer now. "Maybe I can
plead amnesia," I say. "Or being fugued out. They give you
a break for that, don't they?"

He smears his dark hair back from his forehead and peers
at me through slitted eyes. "*Who*? *Who* gives you a break
for amnesia? You *must* be psychotic, because nobody on
Bateau's payroll is that stupid."

I pause in the act of taking another sip of poison. "Bateau?"

Anwar throws both hands up and claps them over his
face. "Mother of God, she's forgotten she works for Bateau.
Shit, I might as well wake up all the way. If I go back to
sleep again tonight, I might never wake up again. How
could you do this?" He gets up and marches toward the

bedroom. "Finish that," he calls over his shoulder. "We got a fast date in a memory lane."

Jee-*zuz*, it just gets worse, I think unhappily, pouring the rest of the coffee down the sink in the kitchenette. I work for Bateau. I see the cliff again in my mind and I know what I do for him. That's a real balls-up throw-up. Anwar comes out of the bedroom buttoning a faded orange shirt and finds me leaning over his sink, spitting out the taste of vomit.

"Ah, *shit*," he says. "I want to tell you it's not that bad, but we both know that'd be a lie. Or we'll both know when you get your mind right with the lord."

"Debts got that bad, did they," I say, wiping my mouth on my sleeve, forgetting it's too good for that. I grab a rag off the counter and try scrubbing the spot I made. "Debts got so bad that I work for an Escort service. Is that right?"

Anwar takes a breath. "You'd better hope so."

I think I ruined the frigging sleeve. "Huh?"

"You'd better hope you're Escorting for Bateau. Still Escorting, that is." He comes over and flicks one of my lapels. "Because this is not what you were wearing a week ago when you disappeared."

"I didn't disappear," I say, but I don't know if I did or not. It feels like I'm lying but I can't tell for sure. That's wild.

"Oh? Vacation in Tahiti, perhaps? Or just a bender at the shore? You been *nowhere* for a solid week, and when somebody's nowhere for that long right after a job, Bateau assumes the worst."

I have to swallow before I can speak. "And what is the worst?"

Anwar looks at me hard under the kitchenette light. "You're really asking me that," he says. "You're really and frigging truly asking because you don't frigging *know*. Jesus *wept*, Jesus wept a fucking *river*.''

"If I didn't know I worked for Bateau, how could I know what the worst is?" I ask; reasonable question.

"Look at you!" He grabs my jacket and shakes me. "You're dressed like a—like a—a friggin' *taxpayer*, like some goddam day-wage priv! The clients tip, but they don't tip wardrobe, and *you* don't get enough to buy rags like this, not unless you skip and go into business for yourself!" I think he's gonna hit me; instead, he does something a lot stranger. He wraps both arms around me, tight.

Something goes *beep*. At first I think he's squeezing me so hard I popped an eardrum or something, but then there's another beep, and I realize it's him. Still hanging on to me with one arm, he reaches down and fiddles with something at his waist. "What's that," I say into his chest, "Bateau's first-alert system? Is he coming over to get me now?"

"No. It's a pump. Shut up."

"A pump? What's it beeping for?"

"Overloaded capacity. I had to turn it off. Shut *up*."

I manage to pull away from him so I can breathe. "Look, I didn't know I disappeared. I didn't know that I was supposed to appear anywhere. If I've been out for a week, someone took me out and kept me out. And what the hell are you wearing a pump for?"

"The only way you're gonna convince Bateau is to get your bad old ass to a memory lane and come up with the goods from the job. You'd better have them. Floating a deal yourself and then crapping out on the memory and claiming hijack is an old dodge. Bateau hasn't bought that one for ages."

"What if it's not a dodge?" I say, thinking about the wads in my pockets. Christ, if that's how I got them, I *must* have been psychotic and no wonder I can't remember a thing.

"Then you're twice fucked. He assumes the worst, remember? You got to get to a memory lane *now*, pull up everything you can remember and offer it to him on a silver platter. He'll still pop you out himself and take his own look inside, and that ain't gonna be the best day you ever had. But at least you'll have everything right up where he can get at it the easiest way."

He's telling me I'm gonna have Bateau running barefoot through my mind; I can't believe this. I don't want to believe this, I don't even want to think about this. I rewind a few steps. "What's the pump for?"

Now he looks as mad as some onionheads I know of. "What's it for, she says. What does anybody wear a pump for?"

"I *know* what a goddam pump is goddam *for*. What the hell are *you* pumping out?"

He makes a noise that might have been a laugh in its former life. "You," he says. "I'm pumping *you* out. And every time I come face-to-face with you, the motherfucker goes off the scale and I have to shut it down."

I'm still trying to get my mind around that one when he drags me out of there.

Predawn in the Downs is dead time. The curbside parking spaces are full of illegal doubles and triples, mostly rooster-boys and gofers, it looks like. Later, the meterheads will clear them out, hauling them off in wagons for the grievous offense of exceeding the two-hour limit. They're not supposed to do that, they're supposed to clear them out around the clock, but the meterheads get a cut of the fines, which increase with the time, and I guess that improves the quality of their shitty meter-reading lives. The offenders get several hours of sleep and free use of the jailhouse lavabo before they go to court. So maybe everybody's just doing everybody else a favor after all.

And who am I to criticize? An Escort is not exactly in a position to watchdog the public morals. And I'm not exactly in a position to be critical about Escort services, either. I can see how I'd end up like this. I can't name an addict, *any* addict, who didn't end up doing something hinky to feed the beast. Escorting is about as hinky as you can get, and if I didn't know that before, I sure as hell know it now by the way it's so solidly *gone* out of my memory. Like I deliberately threw it out.

Which was a very stupid thing to do, seeing as how I work for Bateau, and that's about the worst news I've gotten in recent memory—ha, and ha—unless it's the fact that I have also just surfaced from a week as a missing person. I don't know what was in my mind when I did that, but I hope to hell whatever I was holding is recoverable, buried safe and intact. Because even the kindest-hearted pimp—that's agent to you—will rip your brains out through your nose for freelancing on the sly.

And while we're on the subject of bad news, I'm wondering if I should tell Anwar we should watch out for incoming from low-flying onionheads. Nah, I'll just ruin his night even more. As it is, he'll probably never forgive me for forgetting his pump. I'd rather think that memory got swept out along with all the stuff about Bateau, because I wouldn't want to be the kind of person that would deliberately forget that about somebody. Just because I'm a hypehead doesn't mean I got *no* heart at all. Though the fact that he's wearing a pump and I'm not isn't lost on either one of us, even if we're not saying anything about that.

The pump has to be Bateau's idea, but we're not saying

anything about that, either. We don't have to. It tells me a
lot about what kind of life I live now. Maybe when I get
my memory back, I'll be able to figure out why I ever
wanted to live this way.

But then I don't have to worry about it because we're at
the memory lane, and Anwar's shoving me through the
front door.

You Must Remember This is one of those places privs
like to claim they've gone into on a sleaze-along. I saw
some actually come into the waiting room once, about half
a dozen of them moving like they were roped together in
some kind of onionhead-style marriage. For all I know,
they were. They looked around and then one of them said
loudly, "Dear me, I thought there was a bar at this address," before they all shuffled out again. And it's not even
that bad, by Downs standards.

There's nobody in the waiting room and the wall screens
are all blank except for one running General News off the
dataline. The guy working the front is busy watching something in his desktop. I almost know him; it's so close, I
actually start to say his name, but it vanishes off the tip of
my tongue.

When he sees Anwar, he leaps out of his chair with an
eggsucker's grin. Business must really be in the toilet.

"You got anyone for a general all-around boost?" Anwar
asks him, jerking his thumb at me.

"This is a memory lane—what do *you* think?" the guy
says, still smiling. "Sally's taking them walk-in."

Like You Must Remember This has a full appointment
book? Who are they putting on for? I glance down at myself. Maybe for these fancy clothes I'm wearing.

Anwar grabs my arm. "Go on. I'm buying. Last time ever
—come out with the goods, or don't come out."

He shoves me toward the door the guy is already holding open. I step into a long narrow hall and a woman sticks her head out of the nearest doorway.

"Booster?" she says.

"How'd you guess?"

I don't recognize her. She's got glossy black hair, golden skin, onyx eyes. The effect is heiress-with-a-bad-attitude. But then someone else comes up the hall to me and forget the heiress—this woman is starving to death. She's not just scrawny, she's bones wrapped in skin. A strip on the left side of her chest says SALLY LAZER in raised black letters. One skeletal hand closes around my arm and I have this wonky flash that *she's* an Escort and all this is just an hallucination. That hand feels real enough, but all us hypeheads know that it doesn't have to *be* real to *feel* real.

She steers me firmly into her room and the way she's got my arm, it's like she thinks I might bolt on a whim, which makes me wonder if maybe I've got cause to. Then I see the sandwiches.

Actually, I smell them first. She's got this big bad old platter of sandwiches on a desk, not edible polyester but real food. You can always tell the real stuff by the smell, and if I closed my eyes, I'd think I was in a deli. She acts like they aren't there, not letting go of me till I'm sitting on the chaise across the room, next to her system.

"Can you take your own eyes out, or shall I do it for you? No extra charge for the service."

I put my legs up on the chunky cushion before she can do that for me. The chaise shifts under me and for a moment I'm afraid I sat down on one of those live things that'll mold itself to any position, but it's only a plain old adjustable. I'm still wondering why Sally Lazer would be working in a Downs joint if she's scale enough to afford stuff like this when she comes at me with a long-handled scoop.

"Don't point that thing at me," I tell her and pop out my left eye. She's got the holding tank ready for me and I hurry up and do the other eye before she thinks I've decided to leave the job to her after all. But Jesus, what's her hurry? Does she actually have a full appointment book, or do skinny people just have to move fast before they lose so much weight they disappear altogether?

Her system connections are brand-new, I can tell by the way they latch on to my optic nerves, no pull, no jerk, just smooth. Am I the first person she's used them on? I'd ask, but the sensory cutoff's kicked in, and that's a relief, because the smell of those sandwiches was starting to get sickening.

The relaxation exercise is some kind of sequential color-building thing, simpler than what I'm used to, but I'm not too picky. The last few hours have me docile enough to be a herd animal. Any minute I'm going to be chewing my cud.

I get the space of maybe half a thought-beat to wonder if I'm going to regret this more than not. Then I'm down in it, alone in the system with fast Sally Lazer.

It's Davy Jones' Locker all over again, except all the people and fish are gone. There's just me and the mirror in the moody underwater half-light. Just me and the mirror, literally—I don't even have a reflection yet. That makes me think this was an even worse idea than I thought when I first saw old Sally Lazer.

And speaking of old Sally, where the hell is she? I wave a hand in front of the mirror to see if I can stir up an image for myself. Nothing happens in the mirror but I get a faint sensation of a distant, answering movement that might be

Sally signaling her presence. Maybe her mind's as skinny as her body. That could be me carrying over impressions from outside, or she might really be starving to death.

Meeting someone mind-to-mind in a system, even the stripped-down kind dedicated to one function, you still get a fair amount of personal stuff in the drift, snatches of the other person's inner life. But I'm getting damned fucking little from bad old Sally Lazer. She's like the first draft of a facade personality for a system, operational enough for a test run but barely there otherwise.

Some kind of time passes, hard to tell what. Time in the system is a stretchy old blob, thick and slow in some places, brittle and fast in others. That's all subjective, and only low-ballers who fell off the turnip truck yesterday believe that old story about the hypehead who died of old age in three clock-hours.

Sally Lazer—right, the name wants me to believe she's built to travel at the speed of light, but she'd have to be a machine to work at the same speed every time, even down to the way her own inner time passes.

Maybe she can't get herself in synch with me and that's why she's holding back. I wait for her to figure it out so we can live at the same pace in here. Anwar's paying for this but if I'd known she was this stumble-headed, I'd have made her pay me.

Anytime you're ready, Sally.

No answer.

. . . Sally?

It doesn't pay to get puffed up when you're on the business end of someone else's system, but it's a triple-A, all-wool bore to hang fire with minimal visuals and nothing to do.

About the time I'm thinking I'm going to envision the exit and get the hell out of here, a feeling comes over me, like dust settling. At first, I think it's carry-over from what I was thinking before about being a herd animal; the weirdest shit will boomerang on you. But this isn't me. It's Sally. Sally is . . . chewing?

Chewing. Sally's not eating, just chewing.

Come on, get it right—herd animals don't come in extra-emaciated economy size. Then the deli smell-taste rolls in at gale force, damn the torpedoes and no prisoners. Sally's chewing away, chewing and chewing and I can tell by the feel that this is what Sally *Does*. We all got one Thing we *Do*, each one of us, and this is Sally's: she chews.

I can't shake the bad old feeling that she's overridden her own cutoffs and she's really chewing. You're supposed to disable outside-world movement when you're hooked into the system so you won't sleepwalk, but Sally *Does* this so through-and-through, I swear if I put my eyes back in this second, I'd find her sitting at that desk blindly chewing sandwiches with the wires trailing out from under her sunken eyelids.

My stomach declares mutiny. The taste is bad enough, too strong to be good, but she's killing me with this not swallowing. Chew-and-swallow is how it's supposed to go, but Sally only chews. *Only*.

Talk about fed up, ha, and ha. I wish that were funny. I try to concentrate on swallowing, thinking that'll teach her to hook in with me and force her bad Old Thing on me. Sally doesn't even notice. Nothing gets her when she's in peak-experience nirvana.

I stare at the mirror, concentrating. Something's got to come up in it pretty damned soon. *Okay, Sally, let's see what you're up to.*

The mirror fogs over and the image comes in slowly. Some kind of office . . . but did anybody ever have an office like this? It's full of fat furniture, pudgy overstuffed chairs that look like they're fighting with each other for space, a desk with weird old bulgy sides—even the lights are globes with the texture of excess flesh.

Guess I found the secret Sally-land she lives in. She won't last long in this business, putting her Thing in the clientele's face, even in the Downs. Maybe she's an ex-fetishizer who can't kick the old subroutines. Fetishizers are just cut-rate neurosis peddlers with no brakes on their missionary mode. If I'd known she was one of those, she couldn't have paid me enough to come in here. And Anwar's buying.

And then I see her, crouching in the middle of all those obese chairs, too busy even to know I found her. What a *bitch*.

I start to move toward her and run a little moment of truth when suddenly there's a new image in the mirror between us, blocking Sally from me.

Her. The Famous person, the one with her face on the fish. What the hell?

No, I'm wrong, it's not her after all, it's someone else altogether.

No, wrong again. No, not wrong, exactly, just not quite right. Now, what the fuck is that supposed to mean? How do I *do* this shit to myself?

Wait a minute, says the other woman in the mirror. *This is what you're looking for.* She holds one hand out, waving me closer to the mirror. There's something shiny in her palm.

I've killed before. That's okay. That's right. The guy was asking for it.

That's how it goes when you bet your life on a roulette wheel and lose. I remember:

An antique roulette wheel in a sky-island. A *sky-island*—

if the Royale is uptown, a sky-island is like . . . heaven. They were all overdressed there, period costumes from some time in the past where everybody overdressed, and it was like they were all moving in slow motion. Who could move any other way under all those layers of brocades and silks and lace?

The guy was wearing stiff-looking black clothing, funny stand-up shirt collar, funny tie, and a coat that split into two panels—tails, he called them. Skin the shade of rich hardwood, but only here in the sky-island. Anywhere else, he was little more than a pile of dark ashes, tubes growing out of every hole he had and a few holes he never used to have.

The siege of adult-onset progeria, he told me. *Happens when the body has taken too many rejuvenation treatments— the cells suddenly react to the restoration drugs by accelerating the aging process.* Like Nature gives you only so many reversals before she slams her hand down on the fast forward button.

But in the sky-island's main gaming salon, he was in full healthy bloom in the golden light slanting through the windows running all around the place. On one side, you could look out and see the sun hanging above the cloud line, waiting; on the opposite side, the sky had deepened, evening just beginning to show itself. Also waiting.

And the roulette wheel went around with a rapid ticking sound, a ball skipping over the little holes, color changing from red to white to black on each bounce. The wheel was antique but the ball was strictly today—the old-fashioned kind didn't used to change color. He had these tokens— no, he called them chips—instead of money, and he put some on only one number for each spin. Sometimes the pile of chips shrank after the wheel spun, sometimes it grew. He was the only one playing because he was the only one who had any of those chips. Everyone else including me was watching, and waiting, just as the sun waited on one side and the night on the other.

I remember:

He was real happy. More than that; there was a place called *happy* and he was in it. *My life has been filled with many sophisticated ways to be happy and unhappy, to win and lose,* he said, *but in the end, it really comes down to some relatively simple thing like this: a roulette wheel.* I didn't know much about it and he didn't tell me anything except that sooner or later the wheel must turn against you.

I knew the moment it began stealing from him. There was nothing different about that spin, but the pile of chips never grew larger afterward. It just kept shrinking little by little, until he had just one chip left. So many numbers, and just that one chip. He picked it up, holding it between two fingers at eye level between us. I was supposed to choose the number this time.

Had to be that way; that was how he needed it to be. I took the chip from him and put it on a number right in front of me. And all of a sudden, that was the most beautiful thing in the world, that chip sitting there on that losing number.

In all the complexity born of sheer duration, he said, *that's what ultimately belongs to me, to anyone: beauty, and loss.*

And the wheel spun, the ball bounced, changing colors over and over again, and came to rest in a number I hadn't noticed before: 00.

House number. Everybody *loses.*

Everybody except me. None of the chips on the table were mine.

The windows on the sun side of the island blew open then; the wind rushed through, fluttering everybody's silk and lace and scattering all the chips, before it died. The guy got up from the table and offered me his arm.

You can . . . Escort me now, he said.

We walked over to the open window together, and there was absolute silence as he climbed up onto the sill. He looked out over the plain of clouds for a few moments before he turned and held out his hand to help me up. That was okay, I could go that far. The dress he'd put on me was heavy and itchy but I managed to get up there with him.

The sun was still waiting.

I've enjoyed every moment, he told me, stepping away from the frame behind him and holding on to me as he balanced on the thin sill. I got a good grip on the part of the window behind me. He took one foot off the sill, and he looked as if he were about to step out onto the clouds and stroll away.

Every moment, he said, and I knew I was going to have to be the one to let go. He wanted to, but he just couldn't make that last move. Lots of them couldn't. That was mostly what Escorts got hired for.

Only this far, I reminded him.

House number, he said. Everybody *loses.*

Everybody with chips on the table. That was okay, too, nine times out of ten, it came down to this. They got used to the company and forgot that the end had to be first-person singular. I didn't mind holding him there. The link between us was telling me everything I wanted to know.

Including the exact moment to let go of his hand.

There was no pause, no in-between; he just went, fell backward, straight down into the clouds and disappeared.

Like that, I was back inside the island. The rest of them were lined up at the window now, single file and in an orderly fashion. One by one, they went, too, still gliding in slow motion.

That was what they all believed, too, that it all went when they did. Even the ones that were sure they knew better. Hell, that was what it felt like, the absolute end of

. . . the line?

Good-looking guy, too much makeup and overdressed, holding some kind of skinny book out to me. He's overdone the makeup and the clothes so much that it takes a while to see he's the guy from Davy Jones', the first person I saw when I came to. *You want to check the line? You want to check—*

The line? No, I know how it goes. Except *I* don't. But somebody does. Memory junkie, tourist in other people's lives; no memory ever gets wiped clean away, it always leaves traces, associations. Associations can reconnect.

. . . feed the beast . . .

And there's Sally, chewing and chewing. Threw me a little bone I could gnaw on myself, but it's never my own memories that junk me up. That didn't even make a mouthful for me.

What else *you got, Sally?*

The other woman can't run interference for her. Sally's head snaps around as fast as a snake striking and I know down to the root that it was a bad old mistake to mix it up with this one. Her goddam cheeks are *crammed*, for chrissakes, and she's chewing, chewing, chewing like she's really just all mouth, all the *inside* of a mouth and nothing else is real to her, in here or out there.

She senses me thinking all this and the taste in her mouth goes bad. Sickening enough before, but that's too much. I move closer, trying to see what she's doing. Jee-zuz, she's got my memory loss there and I didn't even feel her working on it. I can't feel it now. She might as well be working on someone else for all it means to me.

No, now that I'm aware, things start occurring to me, some of it making sense, some not. The images come in flashes—

—check the line?

—walking along some twisty dirt road out in open country, knowing that the cliff is waiting at the end of it. I'm not alone but like in one of those silly elementary dreams, I can't turn my head to see who they are, or even how many. All I know is, when we get to the edge of that cliff, one of us is going over it.

And Sally is chewing and chewing, in time to my heartbeat. Or *someone's* heartbeat.

You want to check the line?

No, not yet. We're getting closer to that cliff. One of us is going over it, as sure as God made little green brain cells. And while we're on the subject, who *is* God now, anyway? God is

Chewing. Flecks of food glisten on the lips and I think I'm going to let fly with the bad old technicolor shout right there.

You'll get some odd effects off the mirror.

She's chewing right the hell at me, trying to block it. But I'm a memory junkie; anybody's but mine, and I'll take it. This is my life, and this is my life, and this is—

Chewing. The edge of the cliff is ragged, as if a giant hand came along and broke off whatever was there before, and this is what's left, this is—

—the line? He's stuck in my mind like a fish hook, like he's really there, too, dangling, one more filament among all those loose ends—

—in deep water, just holo water but sounds like a karma-gram to me. I can tell it's a bleach-job by the way his skin soaks up the murky blue light and reflects it. Hair like a patch of darkness—

Like a tapestry that's become unraveled. The sound of his voice is warm and textured enough to wrap up in like a blanket. *All the threads are still there, but the picture is gone. You just have to wave them all back together the way they were. Or you could make an entirely different picture.*

Memory of a smile like a blessing.

Yah. *Oh, yah.* Someone else's memory of someone else's man. Is *this* what she got Famous for? If it isn't, it's gonna be, if this is what the carriage trade gets when they come in and say they wannabee Famous, too, so strap 'er on and let 'er rip—

Does he know she kept him? Does he know it's on a hair trigger and he's alive because she put up the mirror when they did it?

You realize, of course, this means the truth is what you make it. Try not to forget that.

Lover boy, you don't *have* to tell that to a memory junkie.

Did you want to check the line?

We're at the edge of the cliff. Long walk finished, journey over, the proverbial moment of truth is at virtual hand: *my* hand. This is what I Do. We all have one Thing we Do. Chewing is Sally's, but this is mine, this is

Over.

Over the edge of the cliff, *that's* the line and that's the end of the line: surprise good-bye.

Sorry it has to end like this, but I couldn't let you stay and you wouldn't go. Better you than me, because I've got a life to go back to now and all you'd leave me is

Chewing. Sally's image gets up and comes toward me with this look on her face like whatever she's chewing is poison. Her gaze moves in a slow left-to-right scan, and I can feel the process going on inside her: reality check. I already know what the result will be. My reality doesn't fit hers, or hers doesn't fit with mine.

Chewing: her bad old Thing was a signal to something. Someone?

Someone *else*. Whoever should have been looking into this mirror at her isn't supposed to be me—

Abruptly, someone says in a cheery little voice, *What's the good word?* I was in the pawnshop twice last night, but it was me only the second time. The first time—

Sally tries to clamp down on that, too, but she's been too open to me, because that bad old Thing, her signal, got an answer somehow, the right answer, the answer that told her go ahead, this is the one.

Except I'm not the one. Mistaken identity. Except it *isn't*. I *am* the one, because I threw somebody over a cliff who didn't want to go, somebody who offered me the only thing that could have stopped the long fall and the surprise good-bye. And somebody else, the one that called me to the cliff in the first place to throw that someone over, she never knew what happened until it was too late. So now I'm the one.

I have half a moment to think Sally's one of those silent psychos, the ones who are never crazy outside where you can see it. The one *what?* Who does she think she's been waiting for, Neo-Jesus? Or just her One True Love?

The mirror goes blank. I don't have to check the line now, I know what's coming up next. It's too stupid, too sickening, and there's no way to stop it.

This is going to put me off mouths for good, I think.

Just before it happens, I finally understand that I'm not standing in front of the mirror anymore, but in it.

Sally turns her head and spits.

• • • •

You *know* it's going to be a bad day when you come to in some rude Downs joint with a famine fancier standing over you like one of the Four Horsemen of the Apocalypse on holiday, and there's some ratatat hypehead you can only vaguely remember tapping his foot for you out in the waiting room. Worse when you realize those connections the famine fancier is holding have just come out of your eye sockets. All I could think was *migod*, over and over like a mantra.

"I said, that's all." She wound the wires around one bony hand. Those skeletal fingers *touched my eyes*.

Migod, I thought, *I'm going to be sick*.

She looked pretty amused, touching either side of her mouth daintily with her little finger, as if she'd just finished a hearty meal. Christ, what *could* she have eaten? I didn't want to think about *that*, nor about how I could have possibly thought letting someone like this run around in my head was a good idea.

Well, it hadn't been *me*, of course. That was just one of the hazards of being a Method actor. Without warning, you could fall into character and run off, especially if you were close to a performance date, when a character was always on a hair trigger.

Normally, though, Sir Larry's had some of the staff on wrangler duty, ready to flip us back to normal with a code word if it looked like a character was getting out of hand. Sir Larry's was terribly conscientious about that these days, ever since the time Em-Cate's game-girl character had achieved escape velocity and hid out at the shore for three weeks. They'd finally found her working out of a house of ill repute that she'd set up all on her own and which had been responsible for a minor crime wave at the very height of the vacation season. What a monster hue-and-cry there'd been about *that*. I smiled at the memory, though I shouldn't have—if any of the subsequent lawsuits had gone to court, Sir Larry's would have been wiped out. It couldn't have happened to a nicer person—just a nasty bitch like Em-Cate.

And so: what had happened to the wrangler who should have been watching *me*? And what had I been doing the night before? I was wearing my party clothes, so I must have been out somewhere. But the last thing I remembered was—

—*throwing someone off a cliff*—

I winced with annoyance. The damnedest associations can trigger leak-through from a character.

"Something wrong?" asked the famine fancier.

"If you actually *meant* to scramble my brains, no," I said, a bit snappishly.

"Oh, you'll be spotty for an hour or two, till it really takes," she said, tucking the connections into the top of her system. "Don't try to worry anything into coming up. After the associations resettle, things will start occurring to you all on their own, without any prompting."

"Oh, *very* comforting," I said. "You won't mind, then, if I sit around here till things start popping."

She found that pretty amusing. "There *is* a back way out of here, you know."

"How considerate."

She laughed. "You're not the first person who's gotten her memory back in here and decided she didn't want to go out the same way she came in. Go all the way down the hall and turn left. If you change your mind again, though, you'll have to come around the front, because the back door won't open from the outside."

I put the turbo on my exit, swerving around a desk with a mostly empty platter on it.

"See you around the ward," the famine fancier called after me. One of those *witty* farewells. I shuddered at the idea that she'd been touching my mind. Famine fanciers had to be the most obscene creatures on God's green earth, and they proliferated only in lands of plenty. *Migod*, I thought as I pushed out the back door into a narrow alley, *don't let me have come in to get a diet from her*.

No, the hypehead I was dodging had brought me in here. Or rather, he had brought my character in. That much I could remember, thanks to leak-through, but not much else. Except that he wasn't the type who would just fuck off quietly, even if I showed him that the person he'd thought I was, was just a character from a play. Maybe *especially* if he knew—

I'm pumping you out. And every time I come face-to-face with you, the motherfucker goes off the scale and I have to shut it down.

That had to be a line from the play. Migod, I *hoped* it was.

You want to check?

Sovay's image floated in my mind. I didn't know why my mind had seized on him to play ringmaster for my associations. Well, actually, I did know; I was just surprised, even now, that he'd been the one to stick.

Mi*god*, I thought suddenly, looking back at the exit I had just come out of. I hadn't done *that* with that hypehead, had I? Or, well, not *me*, but my character. That would have been just like Marceline, but I couldn't get enough leak-through to know for sure. The things I endured for my art.

The alley ran the length of the block and came out on

a side street. I wasn't sure exactly where I was, and it was obscenely early in the morning besides. Didn't I *ever* sleep when I was in character?

I felt in my pockets. Mad money still there—what a relief. I'd be able to take a taxi back to Sir Larry's. And wasn't I going to nuke somebody when I got there. At least one wrangler would be looking for a new job by lunchtime, and a certain director was going to lose a lot of sleep worrying about a lawsuit.

The thought of lunchtime made my stomach turn over. There was nothing in it except for that minor burning sensation you get from drinking poison like cube coffee. Now that I was aware of it, the minor burning blossomed into a full-scale ache, most of it hunger. No pleasure in that, thank God, which meant I hadn't caught the famine fancy from that awful woman.

What I should do, I decided, was find some place to sit down, get something to eat, and let my spotty memory un-spot in peace. Then I could go back to Sir Larry's and read the riot act from a more informed position. In fact, the more I thought of it, the more I thought it would be better if I *didn't* go rushing back there as fast as my little legs would take me. They couldn't do the play without me—I'd made sure that was written into my contract—and my prolonged absence would definitely throw the fear of God into some people.

And all I was really suffering from was a little characterization amnesia. Some people, like Twill, who was always so wound up he had to have his reality affixed after every performance, or Sovay, who was almost too serious even for me, would have panicked if they'd found themselves in a Downs hypehead joint *sans* a chunk of memory. But I'd always said that if you were going to work the Method a hundred percent, you couldn't let a little thing like a blackout stampede you. After all, whatever you didn't remember the character probably did, and you just had to get the leak-through reenabled.

Which was not to say that it didn't *feel* funny, and I'd seldom felt funnier than I did right then. Not to mention being too hungry to think straight. I went over a block on the vague recollection of having been to a video parlor/doughnut shack there, but when I got to what I thought was the right place, there was a dreamland there instead. They weren't open for business yet, but they were testing their sidewalk holo display and there were unicorns and gryphons and djinn and exotic dancers flickering in and out of existence all over the sidewalk.

I stopped to watch. It wasn't like I hadn't seen the same kind of thing a hundred billion times before, and very few of these places ever showed much in the way of originality—I mean, mi*god*, if overuse of gold-scaled dragons were a felony, a lot of people would have been doing life without parole. But it was diverting to see the place running through its catalog, promising all sorts of inspirational visions and signs and wonders and whatnot. All you could really get in there were your own boosted dreams, of course—if you wanted *real* visions and signs and etc., you went to a dreamfeeder and paid real money for the good stuff. But few people in the Downs could afford that kind of freight—if they could, they sure wouldn't have been living in the Downs.

I became aware of the turn of my own thoughts. Watching the sidewalk show was helping to unbind my mind and reenable leak-through. That was just the way I'd been taught to do it, of course—you keep yourself

distracted with something attention-getting but not too
demanding and pretty soon the gears of memory would
engage. And if mine didn't, I thought smugly, Sir
Larry's Storefront Theatre would be out-of-pocket for
the patch job, not me. They were notoriously stingy
about that kind of thing, but they'd have to take respon-
sibility this time.

"Cuba?"

I jumped. The pimp had materialized at my elbow as
if he were a holo himself. For a moment I thought he
was a holo. He was a wiry little man in scream-green
ersatz-angora, the kind of fuzz that ought to have bal-
loons stuck all over it.

"I said, 'Cute, huh?' " He jerked his head at the
display. I looked; a gryphon was preening itself on its
hind legs.

"Never really thought of gryphons as 'cute,' " I said,
"but as they go, it's not bad."

He stroked my arm and I drew away, resisting the
urge to wipe the place where he'd touched. "I didn't
mean the gryphon, I mean the *real* animal. Wait for
him, he comes back any second now. *There.* Don't miss
him."

A well-developed exotic dancer dressed (barely) like
Hercules with cheap gilt on his hair and some genuine
dancing ability did a turn around the projection area,
threatening to remove his loincloth.

The pimp nudged me and I drew away farther. Now I
was hugging the wall. "So? Cute?"

"Cuter than the gryphon," I said. "Go away, I'm
null-and-void."

"Sure you are." He felt the material of my jacket
between his thumb and finger. "That's why you dress

uptown and cruise downtown. Come on, taste the good life. Don't miss that train."

"Told you, I'm null-and-void. Really. Spent the trust fund in a thrillsville. I'm on my way home to beg Mommy and Daddy for a loan." My character would have handled him much better, I was sure, but it seemed like I could never fall into character when it would have been most advantageous. Offstage, anyway.

"Sure, and I bet your taxes must be killers. Deduct it, business entertainment."

I brushed his hand off and walked away. Hercules danced across my path and I veered around him, even though it's really nothing to walk through a holo image, or have one walk through you. But I never could stand it myself. It made me feel like a ghost.

"Tonight you'll wish you did it!" the pimp called after me. I didn't doubt it; I was always rather suggestible when I came out of character.

I spotted the video parlor/doughnut shop several doors down, next to a soundtrack shop that promised *ZILLIONS of GREAT TUNES To Enhance Your Holiday or Your Day-2-Day—Or Let Us CUSTOM-COM-POZE The **PERFECT SCORE** For YOUR Life, From REAL COMPOSER ANALOGS!!!* Today's specials, I saw with some amusement, were Bernstein, Mozart, and Elfman.

Right. They were probably holding hands under the table with an obsessive-compulsive clinic. Doctor, I just can't get this damned tune out of my head. All right, just hold still, this won't hurt a bit, one thousand dollars please, next. I could hear a little of the Elfman as I went into the parlor; it certainly was catchy.

The doughnut aroma hit me like a fist in the face; a moment later, my mouth was watering so much that my

salivary glands stung. Totally illegal, of course. Appetite
gas was against the law in establishments that provided
any kind of entertainment or diversion, even just video,
the idea being that the entertainment was enough in-
ducement for the customers to stay and eat. And even if
it had been legal to gas the trade here, the concentration
had to have been about five times the limit allowed in
the available space. God, I thought, living in the Downs
was like living under siege in a minefield.

I went over to the doughnut counter anyway. The gas
was active in my system now and if I didn't eat here, I'd
end up somewhere else, pounding down a dinner for
eight or worse.

I took a tray from the dispenser and lined up behind
a scruffy local in one of those technicolor quilt-suits everyone had been wearing last year. The colors were
barely moving; it needed a recharge but quilt-suits were
so passé, I couldn't think of a single place that would
have done the job.

As if that were *my* worry. Well, when you were waiting for a memory boost to take, your mind *would*
wander. A bit of the old carbo express was probably just
what I needed. Or what I thought I needed. I chose half
a dozen assorted artery-killers from the counter, three
of them dripping custard. But I also managed to force
myself to take one edible poly. *Damn* that gas.

I dug a couple of small bills out of my mad money
without displaying the wad and stepped up to the collection box, looking for the cash slot.

"Won the lottery, did we?"

The local in the quilt-suit was eyeing the money with a
half smile that had more in common with rictus from
nerve damage than it did with any real expression. I

made a polite noise and pushed the currency through the opening on top.

"You know, that don't give change," she said, brushing at strawlike hair the exact shade of chicken gravy (*damn* that gas).

"It don't? Doesn't?"

"'Zack change for cash customers or losers-weepers. That's how they make up the overhead and pay for friggin' *gas*. *You* oughta know that." Her gaze went to her own tray and then to mine. She had one doughnut.

"If I'd known that, I'd have gotten three more custard-filled," I said. "And I think I'll just go back and get them right now."

"Can't do that," she said, catching my arm. "Go through again, they charge you again. You must really be scorched this time." She pinched my sleeve between her fingers. "Musta really been worth it, too."

"Thanks for the tip." I pulled away from her as politely as I could and walked toward the rear of the place, where a tall skinny man in a stained duster was wiping off an empty table. I hurried over and slid into one of the two chairs, flicking on the tabletop screen.

"Chit?"

I paused with a doughnut halfway to my practically drooling mouth and frowned up at him. "What?"

He tucked the end of his washrag into a band around his arm and held out his hand. "Chit. *Chit.* Freelance worker here. Extra service not provided by shitty bad-food-dealing owners. Come on, gimme a chit, baby needs a new pair of nose-filters."

"*What?*" I said again.

He turned and made a beckoning motion; a boy about eight years old sidled up to him and pressed close. He had his own washrag.

"Baby of the family. Nose-filters wearing out, can't work in family trade without nose-filters. See?" The man tilted the boy's head up to show me his nostrils. "Go crazy, eat till stomach explodes—"

I was already shoving a small but overly generous bill at him. "Here, *please*. Thanks for the service, buy that kid a decent meal, too, while you're at it."

The man took the bill and held it as if he'd never seen such an outlandish thing before. "Chrissakes, she doesn't got a chit." He gave the bill to the boy. "Tell Mom to stash, try to convert later. And *you*," he added, leaning over me, "you go home. No place to be spending *cash*."

The kid had run over to a corner booth where a woman and three other children had apparently taken up residence. I saw the boy say something to the woman, who looked over at me with a disapproving expression on her tired face. As I watched, one of the other kids slid out of the booth and hurried over to a table that had just been vacated, pulling a washrag out of his back pocket.

"So?" the man said, as if I had spoken. "Good luck. Could have been you." He moved away, scanning the room for anyone about to leave.

"Fortune really smiling very good on you, I guess." The local in the quilt-suit plunked herself down at my table and folded her arms expectantly.

I transferred two doughnuts from my tray to hers. "Okay? *Now* will you leave me alone?"

She shook her head at my largesse, laughing a little. "Here's what they gonna carve on *your* tombstone: 'All balls, no brains.' What I get for callin' you in feeds me here for a *year*." She picked up one of the doughnuts I'd given her and took a large bite. Custard flowed over her fingers and I winced. I hadn't meant to part with one of the custards.

I turned to the screen and was annoyed to find that it was jammed in browse mode. That figured; once you stopped eating, they didn't want you taking up a table because you wanted to watch some program all the way through.

"So now that you in thrill-and-chill for yourself, where you gonna run your stable from, uptown?"

I didn't look away from the news footage. "I don't know what you're talking about."

"Sure can't run 'em from here, unless you plannin' the violent overthrow of the crowned head."

"Look," I said wearily, "I had a bad night and a badder morning. I just want to eat my doughnuts and go home. Please leave me alone."

"Marceline, Marceline," she sang, wagging her finger in my face. "Don't *tell* me you got no clue."

I frowned. How could *she* know the character's name? Well, how else, I thought suddenly, feeling uneasy. Obviously this was another friend Marceline had made while she'd been on the loose. When I finally did get some leak-through from the character, I was probably going to want to forget it all over again.

"Marceline, you know what your agent says about you?"

"*You* talked to my agent?" I said, surprised.

"So? My agent, too."

Mi*god*, I thought; that was a possibility I hadn't considered—not a friend of Marceline's, but another actor.

"Your agent says you been dead for a week."

I couldn't help laughing bitterly. "I'm not surprised. Half the time he can't remember my name. Especially when he talks to casting directors. So you're with him, too? Which theatre are you with? I don't remember you from Sir Larry's.''

"Theatre." Her pasty face broke into a broad grin. *"Damn.* That's *good.* When it's an act, it's theatre. Sure, *I* shoulda thought of that. This Larry got any slots to fill at his place? Maybe I'll chuck our agent, too.''

"The troupe is full up right now," I said carefully, "but without an agent, you couldn't get an audition anyway.''

"No? All-poacher, all the time? That's the best one I've *ever* heard, and I've heard them all. Hope they put some bodyguards on you, because Bateau says now that you dead, you got to lie down and be quiet.''

"Sorry, but you lost me completely," I said.

"Yah, I know. Bateau's sorry about that, too.''

"Bateau who? I have no idea who you're talking about.''

Her face lit up even more. *"Shit!* You don't! You wiped!''

"Actually, it's just a little characterization amnesia. I didn't really get my memory wiped. In fact, I just had a boost and as soon as the right associations connect up with each other, I'll be back to normal.''

Her head wagged from side to side. "Doping works maybe two times if you're desperate. After that, there's no fooling yourself. Thought you knew that.''

" 'Doping'?''

"You know, pull the memories out and then have them put in again. So you can get a rise. Like blood-doping, pump the blood out, pump it back in again, makes you feel like Super-Duper-Man. Never had to do that after a hard week, I'd be surprised about it.''

I spread my hands. "Oh, you've got *me* confused with the character. That's not actually who I really am.''

"No? Who, then?"

"My real name is Marva. And *I'm* not the memory junkie, *she* is."

"Who?"

"Marceline," I said patiently. "Apparently, you've always met Marceline, and not me. *I'm* Marva, and the *character* is Marceline. Got it? Marceline is a character in a play."

She clapped her hands, producing a cloud of powdered sugar. "Ha! *Now* I got it! Some very nice people! They're *too* good, make a memory junkie go all the way! *Damn!* But, okay." She used her sleeve on her mouth and sat up straight, squaring her shoulders. "So, *Marva*, you like being Famous?"

I used a napkin to brush powdered sugar from my jacket. "Oh, I'm not Famous yet, though I have resume'd a couple of franchisers and there's been some interest. No offers yet, and it's something I'd have to think long and hard about . . ." My voice trailed away. Even as I was saying it, it didn't sound right, for some reason. The gap in my memory yawned like a bottomless pit, but for the life of me, I couldn't imagine what was supposed to have been there. Except that I was pretty sure, now that I'd said the word, it had something to do with a franchiser . . .

The thought blossomed in my mind like a poisoned flower. Had I done some kind of business with a franchiser while I'd been Marceline?

Some instinct was screaming yes. But what reputable franchiser would do business with someone who was obviously not herself?

"Still thinking?" said the woman, amused. "Well, this must be a test run, eh? How you liking it? Ah, dumb question, you don't even know you like it or not. Because *you* think you're true."

You're true . . . the truest one I ever knew. Another line from the play? I remembered saying it to someone . . .

You want to check the line?

"I want to check my brain," I muttered.

"Check your brain at the door when you see Bateau. Easiest way to go, save him the trouble of pulling it out your nose." She got up. "Thanks for the doughnuts. And try to remember, if it was you, you'd have done the same as me, even for a friend." She sailed away, swerving around tables while I blinked after her.

Theatre of the absurd, I thought, glad to be left in peace. The appetite gas wasn't working as hard on me as it had been, so I could nurse my last two doughnuts.

On the screen, an androgyne was gesticulating earnestly and silently in front of an enormous product map of Wisconsin. I pressed for volume up; nothing happened. Figured; of all the tables in the place, I'd had to pick the one with the malfunctioning screen and now there were no other tables vacant. Oh, well. Twill always said the dataline was nine times more entertaining with the volume off anyway.

The androgyne got more and more exercised until I thought s/he was going to start trashing the set. A small legend appeared at the bottom of the screen: Cheese Advocates Join Dairy Strike. It made me wish I'd thought to get some coffee to go with the doughnuts.

I started to bite into the edible polyester when my gag reflex suddenly came to life. *Damn* that famine fancier. Before I could work up a good mad, the screen gave a jump as the channel browser kicked in again and suddenly I was looking at my own face.

Migod. It wasn't any still I remembered posing for. As I stared, the pov pulled back from the head shot to a three-quarters body. The still began gyrating in melty near-animation through several different poses and costumes—all the roles I'd played at Sir Larry's. I'd seen similar things often enough to know that it was an ad for a franchise, but I couldn't tell which one.

Damn. I banged on the volume button and then the speaker, but to no result. My image was replaced by that of a large man in a chef's outfit doing a jerky dance while he flipped a pancake in a frying pan. Dammit, why weren't these things closed-captioned? I tried to pull down a menu and got a message telling me I couldn't have a menu in browse mode.

Shitty cheap public screens—I gave it a last hard slap and the image disappeared under an onslaught of static.

"Perfect," I muttered, sitting back and looking around. The place was not full of people I'd have felt comfortable asking to share a table and screen with.

Hell with it, I thought. Time to go home and find out what I'd gotten myself into. Or what Marceline had gotten me into.

You want to check the line?

Yah, I sure did want to check the goddam line.

The skinny guy's youngest kid started working on the table before I was all the way out of the chair.

"Sovay's in rehearsal."

Apparently, today was my day for bad hardware karma; Rowan's pearlized brown biogems were the clearest things on the static-filled phone screen. From what I could make out, she was as impassive as ever, as if she had no idea who I was. So like her. She was always detached, remote. I'd thought it was because she didn't really approve of Sovay's career or any of the people around him, but someone—Twill? Sovay himself? I couldn't remember that either—had told me that she was that way about everything, which made me wonder how she and Sovay had ever met, let alone married.

"Would you give me the number at Sir Larry's?" I asked her, squinting through the static. "I don't have it on me at the moment, and I seem to have misplaced my memory as well."

"Um," Rowan said. I waited, thinking she might be looking it up.

"Don't put it on the screen," I said. "I've got a blizzard on this end."

"Oh? I can see you fine here, but I wasn't going to. I really don't think Sovay would want to be disturbed right now. If you want to record a message, I'll see he gets it when he comes home later."

I almost bit a hole in my lip. Weren't we high-handed these days! Maybe Sovay actually *had* told her what had happened between us, a very stupid thing to do unless he really *wanted* a lot of domestic problems. Or maybe it had something to do with my selling out to a franchiser—if I had. I must have; no franchiser, no matter how sleazy, would dare advertise anyone it didn't own the rights to. And we'd just see about *that*. They could plead innocent and we-had-no-idea-*really* all they wanted to, but if Marceline had sold me out, the contract would be invalid.

"If it's something urgent," Rowan added, "you could leave me your number and I could call Sovay for you and see if he could call you back right away." She paused. "How did you know he'd be at the theatre this early?"

"Look," I said, trying to stifle my impatience, "I

know the routine at Sir Larry's, we're about to go from preproduction into full rehearsals. For the last few weeks, I've been preparing with the Method and I've been a little out of touch. All I need is the number of the direct line into the rehearsal hall and then I'll leave you alone."

She blinked. "The Method?"

"Come *on*, Rowan," I said, and she jumped a little. Maybe Her Majesty wasn't used to being addressed so casually. "I've been having what we call a less-than-perfect day. I'm running on no sleep at all, so give me some cush here. I wouldn't have bothered you at home if I absolutely hadn't had to."

The static thickened enough to obscure her so completely that I was afraid she'd hung up on me. Then a small red light blinked in the lower left corner of my screen, indicating everything in her phone buffer had just been saved for later replay. Fine by me; maybe Sovay would find her attitude interesting. Her image faded back in again and to my surprise, she gave me the number at Sir Larry's.

"Thanks, Rowan," I said, and she winced at the use of her name. Migod, what *was* her problem anyway? We'd only met about six dozen times and I'd called her by her first name without getting that kind of reaction. Maybe that silly Sovay had told her.

"D-do you want to leave a number where you can be reached?" she asked.

Migod, what did Madam Cool-And-Remote have to be stuttering-nervous over? Maybe something that had nothing to do with me, I thought—maybe Sovay had gotten a Call, the kind of Call we all wanted to get, from Somebody Big. *Loved you in your latest, darling, how would you like a slot with a national company?* Yah, I'd have been breaking out in hives myself about something like that.

"Same number I've been using," I said, "but I wasn't planning to go back there yet. If I can't get through to anyone at Sir Larry's for some reason, tell Sovay I'll keep checking the various message boards and services. Thanks again, Rowan." I reached for the hang-up button.

"Wait." She leaned toward the screen. "*I* don't know what number you've been using. You'll have to give it to me."

"Sovay knows," I said.

"In case he's forgotten, then. Or lost it."

She waited and I restrained myself again. Treating me like a stranger wasn't going to change anything that had happened between me and Sovay, so what did she think she was accomplishing? Maybe just a little self-gratification; maybe that aloofness was her way of hiding a childish streak as broad as a full moon. I shrugged and gave her the number at my apartment. "See you around the Storefront," I added. Through the static, I could see her staring at me openmouthed as I disconnected.

The first time I tried Sir Larry's, I was bumped to call-waiting limbo. Somebody was tying up the line talking to an agent, probably. The second time, I got the recording from the box office giving an abbreviated schedule and the proper hours to call for tickets. That bitch Rowan had given me a number I could have looked up myself, not the rehearsal studio's direct line. I was so frustrated, I hung up and fumed for five minutes before calling back and punching in my bypass code. Probably there'd be no one in the office and I'd have to record a message.

No static this time; the words came up quite readable:

INVALID SEQUENCE . . . REPEAT ENTRY: _____

I wanted to scream. Damned cheap public phone was probably garbling the numbers now instead of the visuals. I tried again anyway. I got the INVALID SEQUENCE message twice more and then Sir Larry's hung up on me.

I tried again on another phone, with the same results. I started to move to a third telephone and then hesitated. It could have been some kind of technical problem in the area node, I thought uneasily, or my bypass code might actually have been invalidated.

I decided I didn't want to know. Calling for a ride was just a big waste of time anyway, I thought, lifting the privacy hood and stepping away from the phone. I'd just spring for my own cab, go right to Sir Larry's, and get this whole mess straightened out.

The comm center was starting to fill up with odd types who seemed to be less interested in the phones and message boards than in who was using them. One free soul was using one of those illegal line-biters to collect any leftover time-credit previous callers might have left behind—just right out in the open, not even trying to conceal what she was doing. Yah, this was the Downs, all right, and I'd be damned glad to be back uptown where I belonged.

He must have spotted me as soon as I stepped out onto the sidewalk. I was scanning the street for a cab and there he was at my elbow, spitting little glittery stars into the air from the corner of his mouth. Street vendors did that all the time in the Downs, but for some reason, it really turned my stomach this morning.

"'Ey, ya noya-nuff?" he said, sending a cascade of stars over my shoulder.

"Yah, I'm annoyed enough. Now skin off," I said.

"Unless you want to earn a fast tip by telling me where I can get a taxi."

"Not *annoyed*," he said, chuckling out more stars. "*Paranoid*. Are you *paranoid* enough?"

I looked at him, making a face at his smelly leather armor. "For one day, yah. Now, *skin off*."

"Heya, day's young. *Very* young. How do you know *They* won't be coming to get you by lunch? Gotta think ahead. *They* know all about *you*—why shouldn't *you* know all about *Them*?"

I groaned. There wasn't a single taxi in the thickening vehicle traffic. "All I want to know about are cabs. Why can't you get one when you want one? It isn't even raining."

He put a dirty hand around my upper arm. "*They* took all the cabs. And if you were paranoid, you'd know where. And why." He wiggled his tangled eyebrows at me and blew out another stream of stars. My stomach did a slow forward roll. "Come on, it's a done deal anyway, ain't it? You know there's something going on, you just can't figure out where-to. You buy some paranoia from me, you'll be so here-and-now, you'll be reading the future in the traffic patterns the way happy idiots read what happens in the daily news. Live hot, only the dead are cool. Whaddaya say?"

I jerked away from him. He took a step toward me and then jumped back. I was holding a steel comb, sharpened points aimed at his face. He raised both hands, blew a star-laden kiss at me, and hurried off.

He wasn't half as surprised as I was. I examined the comb. Everything had happened so fast, I couldn't even remember doing it. Obviously, the comb had to have come out of my hair. Except I never wore combs, my hair was—

I caught sight of my reflection in the tinted window of the comm center then, and I had the *weirdest* flash that it wasn't a window at all, but a funhouse mirror. I went over to it, ignoring the derelicts making faces at me from the other side. Mi*god*, the street vendor had been right —obviously I *wasn't* paranoid enough. Even worse, I thought, touching that round face and the brown rat's-nest that was supposed to be hair, I had absolutely no sense of design.

Characterization amnesia was one thing, but I'd never in my life forgotten that I'd gone into full costume. For that matter, I'd never gone into full costume while I was still working on a character. Sir Larry's costumers wouldn't even look at a design sketch until the week a production was scheduled to open, much less execute something.

So what did this mean . . . had I jumped the gun for a reason I couldn't remember anymore? And something this extensive—migod, no wonder Rowan had been acting so strangely. I was completely unrecognizable.

A hand clutched my upper arm again. I turned away from the window and whipped the comb up. "I told you to skin—"

Green fingers plucked the comb out of my hand, flipped it over and around like a magician's prop, and made it vanish into a matching green sleeve. "Very dangeroso," said the green man, still holding my arm. His hand felt strong enough to snap the bone if he'd cared to. "I keep saying you shouldn't be allowed to have things with sharp points on them, Mar, but nobody listens to me."

I tried pulling at his fingers and he tightened his grip so much I could feel the muscle bruising. "Nah-nah-nah." He grinned. His teeth were a lighter shade of the same green, a kind of rain-forest emerald. I made a mental note never to dye my own teeth if I went color-mental. "You've got an appointment you're long over-due for. Bad to be any later."

"You've got the wrong party," I said. "I'm just pass-ing through here—"

He grabbed my other hand and took a long, hard look at my fingertips before seizing my chin and taking an equally good look at my eyes. He had telemicro; very pricey feature. I was impressed, not to mention relieved. My finger- and retina-prints would tell him he'd been fooled by a chance resemblance and that would be that.

It seemed like ages before he refocused on my face. "Same old mess, eh, Mar? Let's go."

"*Wait* a minute," I said as he dragged me up the sidewalk.

He laughed and kept going, much to no one's dismay except mine. I barely got a glance from the gofers shar-ing a parking space and a bottle. This was the Downs, after all, people dragged each other away on a regular basis. I had to dance along with him in double-time or fall down and let the pavement sand my skin off.

"Please," I said, "you're hurting—"

He swung me around square-dance style and I saw the side of a van coming at me. I closed my eyes and felt someone catch me just before I would have hit.

"You *really* stunk it up, running out the back door like that, Mar."

I opened my eyes. My friend the maniac who had taken me to the memory lane a thousand years ago this morning. His name popped into my mind out of no-where: Anwar.

"I don't know you, either," I said, without much

hope. He kicked open the side door of the van and tossed me inside.

"This is a mistake," I said into the carpeted floor as the green guy drove us away from the curb. Anwar was sitting on my back. "Whoever you think I am, I'm really not. I'd know if I were, really—"

"Thou shalt not fucketh around," laughed the tint from the driver's seat. "But if you do, don't be stupid about it."

"But I'm not—"

Anwar gave me a glancing swat on the back of the head. "No more garbage, okay, Mar? I bought amnesia before breakfast, but it's closer to lunch now. Nobody runs out the back door of a memory lane because they can't remember anything. *You* wouldn't cover for me for the same thing and you know it. So do me the service of not trying to bury me up to my eyes in bullshit. Just as a thank you for the coffee, if nothing else."

I had a vague memory of drinking a cup of coffee-flavored chemicals last night while in character. "Not *that* coffee," I said.

He gave me another swat. The van accelerated.

We didn't travel long before the van went over a bump and began descending. The light coming through the windows faded, leaving the interior in near darkness. I kept telling myself that this was good, the sooner we got to wherever they were taking me, the sooner they'd find out the tint's telemicro had malfunctioned. Then they'd kick me out and my worries would be over.

By the time we stopped, I almost believed it. But as the tint got out and walked around to open the side door, I decided Plan B was better—the moment I was out, kick him in the crotch and run for it.

The door slid back and I tensed, waiting for Anwar to pull me up. Something cool touched my upper back, spreading out to my shoulders, up my neck, and around to my face. There was just enough time for a regret before the Vitamin Q in the transcutaneous patch Anwar had stuck to me took over.

Q-up and calm down, a billion strung-out hypeheads can't be wrong, as the saying went. I calmed way down, beyond the level of bothering to notice what I was doing or where I was. The buzz had it that you could counteract Q by sheer force of will if you really needed to, but that had always sounded like pharmaceutical folklore to me. Even if it was true, my will just wasn't up to the dosage.

I began to notice the world again just as we stepped off a lateral or elevator (I had no idea if we'd gone up, down, or sideways) into an immense, airy-looking space, with a sunken area in the middle of it. Sunken living rooms had been all the retro-rage last year, I thought idly, still too Q'ed to care, but they'd always looked like furnished swimming pools to me. Which reminded me of *something*, but all I could think of for some reason was a fish and a line . . .

"Well, another country heard from," someone said from across the room. Part of my mind knew it should have been panicking; another part was trying to log the memory of the disconnected feeling exactly for possible later use. You can't take the woman out of the Method or the Method out of the woman.

On the upper level directly across the sunken area a small man in white pajamas was standing in front of a desk. He pointed at the couch lining the sunken place with a careless gesture.

As soon as I stepped on the carpeting, I knew for

certain that I was still heavily drugged—no power on earth could have made me walk on it otherwise. It was one of those crawly, half-alive things that's supposed to feel so good on your feet, though I'd always thought people bought them to have sex on. And then there'd been that kinko guest director from last year, who had bought one to have sex *with* . . .

Pajamas did a slow walk halfway around on the upper level, passing out of my peripheral line of sight. I was staring at the carpet fibers, working away on my shoes in a vain attempt to stimulate them.

"This wasn't *my* idea," the tint said.

"I was afraid she'd panic and try to run," Anwar said defensively. "So I dosed her."

"Quite all right," Pajamas said breezily. "I think you did the right thing, Anwar." I hadn't seen him come down into the sunken area but suddenly he was bending down and looking into my face. "I even think I like her better this way. Not so prone to trivial debate." Pajamas looked up and to my right. "Though I don't imagine she does much for *you* like this. Does she? Or does she?"

Deep in my mind, something stirred, as if there was some part of me that hadn't been affected by the Q. I had no feeling one way or the other about that, either. The sensation of alertness was a strangely isolated thing, like an air bubble going from deep under the ocean to the surface.

Abruptly, my vision gave a jump and something happened in my left eye. No, in the left side of my field of vision. It was like seeing through a window with a crack in it . . . a window, or a mirror, where everything on one side of the crack was slightly displaced, so that it didn't match up with the other side.

Interesting, I thought; was I falling into character, or just having a stroke? I was still too dosed to be any more than mildly curious.

Pajamas took hold of my chin and lifted my face, frowning.

"What?" said Anwar.

Pajamas turned my face one way and then the other. "Something just happened in there." He let go of my chin but I held the position, not really wanting to look up at him but not having any reason to move. "This is the last time I ever put a memory junkie on the payroll. Much too unstable."

"I don't think—" Anwar started and Pajamas made a cutting motion at him.

"That's good. Because thinking's not what I pay you to do, Anwar."

The left side of my vision became unusually vivid. I could feel a sort of mental searching or groping, as if I were trying to remember something. Except I wasn't.

Aliens, I thought, bombarding my head with thought-control rays. So this was schizophrenia. And even *that* didn't feel like my own thought. Maybe this *was* schizophrenia.

"—no surprises," Pajamas was saying. "What I always liked best about you, Marceline. In the six months you've been in my employ, you've never *once* surprised me. Until now. And that makes me feel"—he looked pained—"unhappy." He picked up my hands and held them. "Now. I have to have what's mine, dear. The good girl you used to be would understand that."

Marceline. Well, that explained it; the character had slipped the leash, achieved escape velocity, and formed some liaisons without my knowledge or cooperation. God only knew what she'd been up to—

I had a sudden absurd flash that God had chewed me up and spit me out before the rest of what Pajamas had said registered on me. Six months? *Six? Months?!*

Impossible. I never worked on a character for that long; nobody did. Let alone in full costume for the duration—

Unless Marceline really had managed a complete break with my life. But that would have meant I'd been a missing person for half a year with no one looking for me—even more impossible. Even if the rest of the troupe had hated me as much as Em-Cate did, none of them would have let me go missing for six *days* without pursuit—the lawsuit for negligence would have left me owning all their sorry asses. These people, Pajamas, the tint, Anwar, they all had to be crazy, or their minds had been tampered with—

Well, of *course*, I realized. We'd *all* been tampered with. This had to be an improvisational exercise—long and involved, but an improv just the same. The scene at the memory lane must have been part of the scenario and I must have been playing it just fine until I'd fallen out of character, thanks to a certain ham-handed famine fancier.

And so Anwar must have given me the Q to try to induce the character to resurface. But he'd overestimated the dosage and turned me into a zombie. No real harm done; the Q was starting to wear off now. My alertness was increasing, except it still felt strangely distant . . . as if the Q were wearing off my body, but not *me*. But wasn't that impossible, too? I'd have to ask someone.

You want to check line?

Check the reality, Sovay, I thought. Pajamas let go of my hands. They fell limply onto my thighs. Anwar and the tint got me up on my feet. I was at least a head taller than Pajamas. He folded his arms and looked up at me, still with that pitying expression.

"For all your faults, Marceline, you were really a damned good Escort. I'll miss you. Your technique was—" He kissed his fingertips to the air. *Ham*, I thought at him. I felt like laughing out loud, never a good sign. If we didn't break within the next minute or so, I'd have to disrupt things and tell them I still wasn't back in character. They'd all probably have a group tantrum over the wasted time and effort, but it wouldn't have been fair to let things go on any longer if I couldn't react properly. Out of character, I was just *terrible* at improv.

I concentrated on making my mouth move to produce the words *We have to stop*, saying them over and over in my head. Then I cleared my throat, and my voice slid out thick and low, like a slowed-down recording.

"Jee habba cop."

Pajamas blinked at me. "Pardon?"

Migod, I thought, exasperated. The split-vision effect intensified. Whatever was doing it was now affecting my speech center as well. I'd have to warn Anwar not to give me so much Q in the future.

I swallowed and cleared my throat again for another try. Before I could make a sound, the left side of my vision gave a funny jump and I could no longer remember how to talk. But my voice came out anyway.

"She had a cop," I heard myself say. "She was a cop. She was Brain Police in deep undercover."

Pajamas looked from Anwar to the tint and back to me. "What *are* you talking about?"

I'm *not talking*, I tried to say, but my voice went on without me. "That last trick . . . *client*. The actor.

She was Brain Police in deep undercover. That was why she wanted an Escort. To kill the cop. We killed a cop."

Pajamas took a step back as if that would somehow help him see me better. "To refresh what seems to be your suddenly failing memory, the client is a silly stage actor who couldn't purge herself of some useless character she'd made up for some stupid flop of a play."

Migod. This fool of a scenery-chewer was actually so caught up in the improv he was going to fit whatever I said into the scenario without questioning it. "That's what she told *you*," I continued, unable to stop myself. "And me. But she was Brain Police in deep undercover. The cops set her up with a life and if she had too many personalities, well, who's counting anyway? She wasn't even supposed to find that one, but she did. Or rather, her lover did. I got the whole story when I threw the cop over the cliff."

Pajamas' face was wary. "All those silly stage actors are multiples, and they're all Method actors. They believe they're whoever they're supposed to be. That's not *our* problem, unless you start believing it, too."

My head went from side to side. "The cop was the real thing. And—"

—and she's still here.

I finally managed to will my voice to shut off but the unspoken thought burned slowly into my mind like a shot of absolute truth. It didn't make any sense whatsoever. The character was a memory junkie, but unless there had been some kind of major script rewrite while I'd been unconscious, Escort services and Brain Police didn't figure into any part of the plot. Unless Marceline . . .

But then, that would mean this wasn't an improv.

Just how out of hand had things gotten?

"That's got to be horseshit," the tint was saying. "Stupid delusions. She's a crunching *memory junkie*, she's got a whole head full of horseshit. She wants to be somebody else anyway, she probably believes she's God on the even-numbered days."

Pajamas gave him a look. "Today *is* an even-numbered day." He frowned at me and then went up to the upper level to fiddle with something in his desktop. "Hm. The client's mailing address has changed from that dreary storefront theatre to some very nice people. Moving up in the world. Perhaps Souse was right and our girl here has just been indulging in a little persona pattycake." He chuckled. "Dear Souse. I'd give her a raise, but it would just go to her head, and she'd waste it all on bad doughnuts, anyway."

"Should we go get the trick?" asked the tint.

Pajamas rubbed his palms together slowly, as if he were mashing a bug between them. "Yah," he said, coming back down to stand in front of me again. "I think we should talk to her. It might have been just some silly character, or it could be our girl here got all mixed up and she's having a delusion or two from the persona overlay. Or it might be the real thing. There's no way to tell without having a look at the trick. Maybe she'll tell us where our girl has been for the last week."

"And what'll we do with *our girl* in the meantime?" The tint gave me a hard poke.

"Hold for later disposal, of course. I want to get the both of them together. If the trick actually conned our girl into dumping a cop, there should be a lot of very interesting information locked up in here." He tapped his index finger on my forehead. "Box her at three-quarters capacity. That ought to keep her motor idling well enough without anything wearing out too soon.

Most of them don't even realize they're in a system when you run them at seventy-five percent.

"Then go visit some very nice people and bring the actor in. *Alive.* But fast. If it's the real thing, it'll take time to jigger her memory. I don't plan to go down for a cop-kill." He pinched my cheek. "If it comes to that, that's what *you're* here for." He made a brief dismissing gesture.

I waited for everyone to break out of character. Instead, Anwar and the tint walked me out of the sunken area and back into the elevator/lateral. Elaborate, extended exit, I thought desperately. They weren't *really* going to drop me on a slab, pluck out my eyes, and plug me into a system . . . were they?

The door closed. Anwar gathered my hand into his as the lateral began moving to the left. I started to shake. The Q had all but worn off now and I knew it wasn't an improv.

"Aw," said the tint. "Lovers' farewell? And here I thought you were off the stuff, Anwar. Maybe we oughta stop at supply and get you a bigger pump, eh? Just to keep you honest."

"Sure," said Anwar. "Let's do that. I don't think this one's working right and I've had all I can take of her."

The tint chuckled. "Gotta cancel out those nasty old brain chemicals that make you think you're in love before they make you do something everybody'll be sorry for. Maybe you oughta go all the way and get your blood changed." He turned to the control panel.

I started to say something. Anwar gave me a hard shove. Then the tint was lying on the floor of the lateral with blood welling up from the gash in his forehead where Anwar had slammed his face into the wall.

"This'll buy you two, maybe five minutes," he whispered to me, pulling me into a far corner of the lateral, which had begun to descend now. "You're a big pain in the ass, Mar, but I can't let them do this to you. Supply's on an exit level. You shove us out there and take this thing to the out-door. Then run like a rabbit. I'll tell a story."

"Where do I go?" I said, feeling helpless.

"How should *I* know? Go back to where you've been for the last week, I don't know!" The lateral came to a stop and the doors opened. Anwar hauled the tint up and threw him out bodily before turning to me and pointing at his chin. "As hard as you can."

I didn't get it.

"*Punch* me, goddammit!"

I'd never punched anyone in my life. My fighting experience was limited to stage combat, showy stuff that wouldn't even smear anyone's makeup. Then the funny vision on the left flared suddenly, spreading over to the left and I felt—

sorry, this is all for shit and it isn't even my own fault except for taking the job. But there was no choice about that, either, Bateau doesn't exactly let us pick and choose the clientele. I want to tell Anwar to keep wearing a pump because feeling like you can't let something happen to somebody in this business is pretty goddam inconvenient. He's better off pumping out whatever that funny stuff is that makes him think he loves me. And I want to tell him I'm sorry that I don't need a pump myself, and whether it's because of something that being a memory junkie did to me, or whether it's that fatal flaw that makes me a memory junkie in the first place—none of that makes any difference. But maybe that I can feel sorry

about it counts for something. Maybe being sorry makes me
a better person than when I was just someone who couldn't
feel too bad about anything.

Above all, though, I'm sorry I'm hitting him instead of
anyone else. And if you always end up hurting the one you
don't want to hurt, then maybe that means I lo—

                                                    He was
staggering backward out of the lateral. I saw him start
to fall over the tint and then the door slid shut. The
flavor of whatever thoughts had just been in my head
was still whirling around but I couldn't catch the sense
of it. My hand slapped the exit button without any
prompting from me and the lateral started moving
again.

I must be of two minds about this, I thought giddily,
holding a hand over my mouth. I wasn't sure whether I
wanted to laugh or cry, but I knew if I started either, I
wouldn't stop until Pajamas caught up with me again
and finished me off. And maybe not even then.

—*two minds about this*. No, not really. Not anymore.
The funny split-vision effect was all gone now, leaving
me with a strange, off-balance feeling. I thought I'd go
crazy waiting for Pajamas' voice to come out of some
hidden speaker and tell me there was a reception com-
mittee standing by, but the lateral kept moving in silence. Then it began to slow and I had a fast flash of
panic until I saw the words STREET EXIT flashing on the
control panel. I hugged the wall next to the door and
held my breath.

The door slid open; nobody barreled in to grab me. I
risked a peek. The small, enclosed vestibule was empty
and the out-door, plain, grey, blinking FUNCTIONAL in
bright green at the access panel, looked so unremark-

able, I suddenly wasn't sure that the last few minutes hadn't been some kind of delusional waking dream.

No; the hand I'd used to punch Anwar hurt too much for a delusion. I rushed for the out-door.

"You'll need your keystrip to reenter."

I whirled around, flattening against the out-door, but there was still no one in the vestibule.

"Weather and traffic patterns are available from the wall console to the left of the exit," the voice added politely. Standard canned exit message, I realized, and looked for the console.

The compact screen was displaying a short menu, but there was nothing on it about me. Glancing nervously at the lateral, which was still standing open as if it were waiting for me to change my mind and get back in, I tapped the access panel.

"You'll need your keystrip to reenter," the voice reminded me, and that was all. The exit swung open silently.

Run like a rabbit.

I tried, but my hand was throbbing so much, all I could manage was a peppy dogtrot. But at least I found a cab before my endurance gave out.

The driver charged me fare-and-a-half because she wasn't licensed to pick up anywhere higher than lower midtown and so would have to go back empty. I'd expected that, but I didn't like it anyway. The pickup boundaries were supposed to be for the benefit of the populace and the ground cabs alike, to keep the drivers from stepping on each other's toes and spread service evenly throughout the city. But people seldom took cabs within a service district, so now it was just half again as expensive to get from one part of the city to the other.

I wasn't in complaint mode; I just paid the extortion, added a barely acceptable tip, and climbed out. The sight of Sir Larry's Storefront Theatre would have been reassuring if I hadn't been so drained. I didn't even want to flay anyone alive anymore. All I wanted now was a few answers and twenty-four hours of undisturbed coma. Then I could get back to my real life.

Or not. I was about to punch in my entry code when I caught sight of the mini-marquee on the front door. The schedule for the season was scrolling along at a leisurely, readable pace, but it was the time/date display, blinking in alternation with the box office phone number, that got my attention. I watched it through five cycles, just to make sure I hadn't picked up some kind of reading deficit. The date given as today's was a week later than it should have been.

Go back to where you've been for the last week. I remembered the phone rejecting my bypass code. "Shit," I muttered and tried my entry code anyway, hoping that wasn't out-of-date as well. Damned memory lane, damned famine fancier; my brains were probably scrambled so badly that I'd have to see a doctor.

By some miracle, the entry code was still correct. I went through the empty lobby and stopped in the open doorway leading to the theatre. There were half a dozen people on the large, in-the-round stage. Rehearsal in progress.

Em-Cate spotted me first and broke out of the group, moving to the edge of the stage as I came down the center aisle. Her hair was stoplight red now, or maybe arterial-bleeding red; it matched the angry flush coloring her cheeks. Em-Cate hated being interrupted even more than she hated being called Catey. The rest of them turned to look at me, but the only one who showed any sign of recognition at all was Sovay. His skin was all bleached out and under the soft yellow lights, it was the exact color of urine. Very unfortunate, I thought.

"Deliveries in the rear," Em-Cate said snappishly, fists on her hips. "How many times do we have to tell you people that? Who gave you the entry code, anyway?"

In spite of everything, I couldn't help chuckling. "I'm not here for a delivery."

Twill moved to her side and said something in a low voice. All I caught were the words *Davy Jones'*. Em-Cate gave him a disbelieving look and then turned to me again. "Sorry, but the troupe's full up now, no vacancy. Whoever you think you are."

"That's an interesting way to put it, Em-Cate," I said, boosting myself up onto the stage. "But what I'd really like, among other things, is a new bypass code for the phone so I can call in the next time I need a ride home. The cab from the Downs cost me a fortune and a half."

She turned to the others, who all looked bewildered. I was rather bewildered myself. Except for her and Twill and Sovay, I only half recognized most of them and there was one woman I couldn't place at all. I wondered if I'd be able to get Sir Larry's to foot my restoration bill.

"It's a situation for certain," Em-Cate said, "and it's all yours, Sovay. You're the one who said it was just temporary and if she was removed from the context, it wouldn't happen again. But look, here she is, all pumped up and ready to play the part. What about *that*, Sovay? What do you think we should do, throw a welcome-back party?"

Migod, I thought; had I gotten so badly messed up that I'd crapped out on a performance and been fired?

"Em-Cate," Sovay said warningly.

She gave him a dirty look. "It's a *situation*. How do you think we should handle it now, Eisenstein?"

"Einstein," Twill muttered.

Em-Cate gave him a swat. "*Eisenstein*. The great director. Sovay must think he's another one."

"Shut up," Sovay said. He was staring at me with a pained expression. Abruptly, I realized I was biting my nails.

"Well, obviously, I've had a fairly serious glitch," I said. "All I'd really like to know at the moment is why I was just left to stumble around in somebody else's life instead of being rescued and treated. Is the competition around here getting that cutthroat?"

Sovay's pained look intensified. Migod, I thought, I *had* been fired. Fired and—I glanced at the woman I didn't know—replaced. The woman looked away from me and I realized I was biting my nails again. What an incredibly vile habit. Leak-through from the character, perhaps? Just my luck—when I finally started getting something from her, it wasn't anything useful, just disgusting.

"Do you remember anything about being at Davy Jones' Locker last night?" Sovay asked me. "And getting thrown out?"

"*Thrown out?*" I gave a humorless laugh and held out some of my disastrous hair. "Looking like this, I'm not surprised I got challenged. But didn't any of you very nice people bother to tell the bouncers I was in costume?"

There was a short but heavy silence. "It was a private party," Em-Cate said snottily, "and it was for some

very nice people, not for us. There are still those who
won't sell their souls to be some very nice people."

"Shut *up*," Sovay said. "Can't you see she doesn't
get it? It doesn't mean anything to her."

"Nothing ever meant anything to that woman," Em-
Cate said. "She was always just out for what she could
get and this was the only way she could ever get anyone
to say anything good about her, going off to be one of
some very—"

"Turn it off!" Sovay barked.

Some very nice people . . . suddenly, it was starting
to make sense.

"Please," I said, taking a step toward him. He looked
as if he wanted to back away and if he had, I'd have
fallen apart right there. "I think I'm in some kind of
serious trouble with this character, but I can't remember. I woke up this morning in a memory lane in the
Downs and I was missing a week. Then I saw myself in a
dataline ad—" I lowered my voice but the acoustics
were too good. "I think for a franchiser. I think I did
something, made a deal or something, in character. And
I think the character did something else as well, because
a green guy and another guy kidnapped me and threw
me in a van and took me to—"

"Don't," Sovay said.

I pulled my fingers out of my mouth and wiped them
on my pants. "Sorry. They—"

"I mean don't tell me anymore. Just *don't*. I don't
need that kind of trouble. The only thing I can tell you
to do is go back to the memory lane you woke up in and
have them finish the job."

I stared at him. It would have been a pretty bad joke,
but he wasn't kidding. "Have you lost your mind? Or
am *I* short in that department?"

"Good question, don't you think?" Em-Cate was standing right behind me now. "Whose mind got lost? And is it finders-keepers?"

Sovay let out a noisy breath. "We can't just leave her to—"

"Oh, yes, we *can*," Em-Cate said. "We are *not* responsible. This is *not* our business and I refuse to be a party to anything even remotely connected with it." She gave me a hard look. "Regardless of who suffers."

"She's right," said Twill. "If we put ourselves in this, we all might end up in a van. If you want to take that ride, fine. Not me."

"Or me." Em-Cate turned her back abruptly. "Rehearsal's scrubbed. Everyone out of the pool."

They all jumped down from the stage, rushing for the stairs down to the dressing room as if they were running from—well, whatever I'd just run away from. Except for Sovay. Em-Cate looked back at him, shook her head, and followed the rest of them.

I waited for Sovay to do something or tell me something, but he just stood there with that pained expression on his no-color face, as if he were the one in trouble.

"Well," I said with a weak laugh, "I guess I can assume I'm fired, too. On top of everything else."

"*Christ*, I feel so bad for you." It burst out of him like he was confessing a secret sin he couldn't live with a moment longer. "And for me. And for everything that happened. I wish I didn't know. I wish I didn't know *you*."

"Quite an extraordinary expression of sympathy," I said after a long moment. "Thanks, I don't know where I'd be without your friendship and support." I turned away from him.

"Where are you going?" he asked quickly.

"Well, let's see. Unemployment office should be my first stop, I guess. I take it my termination notice is on file? Then I guess I'll get my resume rewritten, put my name in for next season's cattle calls—" I pretended to think hard and then snapped my fingers. "Oh, yah, guess I'll hit a body clinic and get out of this ridiculous costume since it tends to encourage kidnapping."

He caught my arm before I could jump down off the stage. "Listen, M-mar . . ." Pause. "Marva. *Marva.* I can't get over it. It really *is* you. Isn't it."

The expression on his face was startling; it was as if he were transfixed. "Is *that* what this is all about—Em-Cate and Twill and everyone else *just don't recognize me?*"

Now he looked as if he were on the verge of tears. The boy always could run an emotional gamut on short notice. "*I* recognize you. I remember . . ." His voice died away.

"Yah, I remember, too." I shrugged. "But not as much as I've forgotten. Which I don't think was by choice."

"No, it wasn't." He took a breath. "If I could figure out some way to help you—to help *you, Marva*—I'd do it. I miss you."

This was a light-year and a half from the never-again-I-love-my-wife agonizing I was used to hearing. It threw me so much I almost missed the strange emphasis he'd placed on my name. *You, Marva.* What in hell was *that* supposed to mean?

"I still care," he went on, embarrassed. "I couldn't let it continue between us. Not because it didn't mean anything but because it *did*."

I waved his words away. "Me, Marva as opposed to

me, *who? Who*, Sovay? Me, the character? Me, Marceline?''

"Marceline's—'' He cut off so sharply that he didn't even breathe. But I could hear the rest of the sentence so clearly in my head that I wasn't sure that he hadn't said it after all.

Marceline's not a character.

I had the sudden wild notion that I hadn't really gotten away from Pajamas and this was my mind chugging along at seventy-five percent of capacity in a box.

Marceline's not a character.

Like a shot of absolute truth . . . like *another* shot of absolute truth, straight to the brain . . .

. . . and the cop's still here.

Marceline's not a character . . .

. . . and the cop's still here.

You want to check the line?

Marceline's not a cop . . .

. . . and the cop's not a character . . .

. . . and Marceline's still here . . .

My head was full of noises and voices and a jumble of pictures that didn't make any sense—Sovay, Sir Larry's, Davy Jones' Locker, the Downs at three A.M., Anwar. They whirled around and around like leaves in a cyclone, blurring, melting into each other to form a new image, unfamiliar but vivid and detailed and unmistakably mine:

The edge of a cliff, high above some enormous, vague space. I felt a flash of something like agoraphobia, except that wasn't quite it—this was more than being afraid of too much open space, this was a fear of nothingness, of nonexistence—

A hand clamped onto my upper arm on the exact spot where the green guy had grabbed me, putting bruises on my bruises. The pain cleared my vision and I saw I was teetering on the edge of the stage.

"Easy," Sovay said, pulling me back a few steps. "You looked like you were going to faint."

"Not faint. I was going to do something, but it wasn't faint." I stared at the edge of the stage, seeing the cliff superimposed on it.

"Ah, the prodigal has returned!"

I looked up; the man coming down the aisle toward the stage had a thousand-watt smile, but as he got closer, I could see it didn't really fit him. He had a long, bony face surrounded by a lot of wiry white hair so dried out, I was afraid it would catch fire from the scented cigarette he was smoking. His expensive clothes didn't really fit him, either, as if he were wearing a costume put on in a hurry. I almost placed him . . . something about last night and Davy Jones' Locker . . .

The woman walking behind him didn't flick any switches, either, but she was wearing one of those don't-recognize-me getups, a floppy hat and sunglasses big enough to cover the upper half of her face.

Somebody Big, I thought, replete with Mrs. S.B., or maybe Somebody Big and *Mr.* S.B. Come to Sir Larry's to give some actor the Big Break everybody was praying for. I looked at Sovay. His gaze was locked on the guy, who was now climbing up onto the stage as if he owned it.

"There's no smoking in here," Sovay said thinly.

"Sorry." The guy dropped his cigarette on the stage and stepped on it. "You've no idea how glad we are to see *you* again. What a *dreadful* mistake last night."

He was talking to me, I realized, and thought of the ad I'd seen in the video parlor. Still smiling, he reached for my arm. I stepped back, shielding the sore area, and he gave Sovay a murderous look.

"I didn't say a thing," Sovay told him. "Talk to her. You'll see."

I rubbed my bruised bicep. "Are you the one running that commercial?"

"Commercial?" the man said, trying to glare at Sovay and smile at me all at once.

"Word is out now," Sovay said. He walked over to where the woman was waiting, one elbow leaning on the edge of the stage and her hand cupping her chin, ostentatiously bored. She reminded me of someone. "You know, I almost wish I could hear you explain."

She refused to look up at him. Speaking of explanations people wanted to hear, I thought; whatever had happened between them must have been pretty poisonous. Apparently Sovay's virtue wasn't as stainless-no-rust as he wanted the world to believe.

"I think I can figure it out myself," I said, ambling over closer to Sovay. "You people made a franchise deal with me, or rather, someone you thought was me. It was actually one of my characters. Maybe she really fooled you, or maybe you just let yourselves be fooled, but it doesn't matter now anyway, because the whole deal's invalid."

"Ah. Is that how it is." He glanced over at the woman.

"Erase the contract and we'll call it an honest mistake," I said. "No lawsuit, no charges. I'll even give back fifty percent of whatever you paid me for an advance. You can think of the other half as a rental fee."

"That's generous of you," he said.

"I'm a generous person. But I don't want to be a franchise."

"Are you sure about that? Maybe you should read the contract you signed. That *she* signed, excuse me. It's a very sweet deal."

"I'm sure it is, but it's not for me, thanks all the same. All I ever wanted to do was act in legitimate theatre."

"Now that's dedication," the man said. "If you insist. Come back to the offices with us and we'll take care of it immediately."

"Thanks, but you can just zap it to me net-mail," I said. "I'll trust you."

The man hesitated and glanced at the woman again. "You did leave some personal property with us. We'd like to return it to you."

"You can mail that, too," I said. "I don't mind. Or I'll pay for a courier."

"Against our policy. We have to put it into your hands personally."

"Then *you* pay for the courier."

He was struggling like mad to hang on to his patience and losing. "Look, it won't take you any time at all."

"Do as he says," Sovay said suddenly. He was pointedly not looking at the woman now, though he was still standing over her. Migod, did I want to hear *that* story. "Go with them. They'll take care of everything. They have to; there's a witness."

I didn't like the sound of that and it must have showed—Sovay suddenly gave me a quick hug around the shoulders. "Go ahead," he said in a low voice. "After, you'll remember everything."

"Suppose you just fill me in and I take your word for it."

"I can't," he said heavily. "I don't know anything."

He stared down at the woman. "All right? *I don't know anything.*"

She nodded without looking at him. "Yah. I heard you." Her voice sounded extremely familiar, but, as usual, the memory was just out of reach. It was maddening.

"Okay," I said to the white-haired guy. "But I want to come back here afterward."

"We'll take you anywhere you want to go," he said.

I moved toward the edge of the stage and damned if he didn't grab my sore arm. I tried to pull away but he insisted on helping me down from the stage. The woman was already heading back up the aisle as fast as she could go.

At the doorway, I paused to look back. Sovay was still standing there on the empty stage, staring after us. Or staring after *her*, except she was already gone. I wanted to call out to him that I'd be back, but the white-haired guy was already pulling me through the doorway to the lobby.

There was a private little-stretch humming at the curb, complete with driver. I started to hang back, trying to think of some excuse to go back into the theatre, but the guy hustled me into the back of the stretch. The woman was hugging the far end of the forward-facing seat, staring out at the traffic as if it were the most fascinating sight she'd ever seen. The guy planted me on the opposite seat, still hanging on to my arm as if he thought I might try to dive out the other door.

I leaned forward and looked at the entrance to the theatre, hoping like mad that Sovay would come running out, yelling for us to stop.

Yah. Maybe tomorrow. The guy pulled the door shut

and there was a hiss as freshened, scented air blew into the interior. Suddenly, I had the strongest feeling that just as we went airborne, I was going to discover I was getting sleepy.

But nothing of the sort happened. Nothing happened at all, except that the guy finally let go of my arm. The woman didn't even take off her sunglasses.

The room would have made *prima* rehearsal space. It was twice the size of the warm-up room at Sir Larry's, with plenty of pads for floor work, freestanding exercise barres, and a lavabo with more attachments than I could identify functions for.

"Nice?" the guy said as I looked it over.

"Yah." I pulled my head out of the lavabo and slid the door shut. "I've never seen a five-speed pulsator before."

"The item most requested by our people," he said. "We have about two dozen installed all over the building, so no one ever has to wait."

"Very considerate." I stepped away from him. "And thanks for the tour, but let's get this over with. I don't want to be Famous, and I wouldn't want it even if you had three dozen lavabos on this floor alone. I don't want people walking around thinking they're me."

"Maybe they aren't." The woman had come up next to me without making a sound, so close that I could see twin reflections of my startled face in her big, stupid, dark glasses. Smiling, she plucked the floppy hat off her head and dropped it on mine.

I knocked the hat away, irritated.

"Maybe that's not who they think they are at all." She pulled off the glasses. It took me about five full seconds to realize I was looking at my own face. My *original* face.

Freeze-frame.

Somewhere, that cliff is still waiting for me. Waiting for someone. If you put in a cliff at the beginning of Act I, someone has to go over it by the end of Act II. Chekhov's Law, isn't that how it goes? It applies even more in here than on any stage out there.

In here. That's a strange way to think of it, really; sometimes the strangeness jumps up and hits me full on. Only in my line of work does the mind become imbued with such essence of *place.* Well, my line of work and Marva's. Marceline's, too, I guess, but I don't know as much about her. Yet.

But that Marva—talk about self-destructive. Ha, and ha, as Marceline would say. She hasn't been saying much of late. My conscience is bothering me about her, in spite of the fact that I had no choice, not if I wanted to live. I had no choice, and now she has no chance. I outnumber her.

But there is no time for the contemplation of moral dilemmas, even one as critical as this is. The lights are going to come up soon and we have to give the performance of our life . . . lives? We have to get out of this intact before we can figure out what to do about Marceline's stolen life.

Not that I'd call her an innocent bystander. After all, she came to kill me. Even after she realized who and what I was, she was going to go through with it, fling me over that cliff. Marva's cliff.

Should have seen that Marva was too good . . . too *real.* The hazards of being multiple sometimes overwhelm even the most rigorous Brain Police training. But I should have seen it coming, been prepared for it.

In legitimate theatre, they're prepared for it. A hazard of Method acting, it's called *achieving escape velocity,* which gives it the sound of true accomplishment, worthy of awe. Is that what really sells tickets—a freak show? Come see the human who dreamed so hard of being a butterfly that she sprouted wings and flew away?

In the old days, Method acting had nothing to do with multiple personalities. Not so overtly, anyway. In the old days, there were two kinds of actors: the ones who disappeared into their roles, and the ones whose roles disappeared into them. But maybe in the end, it was just as hard to tell which was which.

Marva found out. She shouldn't have been able to; she wouldn't have, except for Sovay. He was the one who came upon me unawares in the depths. Maybe *he* was the one who was too good, not Marva; too good at delving the layers of personality, identity. He was too good, and Marva wanted him too much.

Being in deep undercover, I couldn't do anything about it. She had to live what she would, after all, if I was ever going to get a lead on the bootlegging operation. And that was what I'd thought was my greatest danger, that in the process of delving her mind, bootleggers would come across that closed-off room that she had no knowledge of and no access to, and they would find out she was a Brain Police officer in deep undercover. I had never thought it would actually be her lover who would find me and give me away to her.

I don't think he meant to. From that moment to this, I really don't think that was his intention. But as soon as he knew, she knew; they were hooked in mind-to-mind, after all. They shouldn't have been, given her enormous attraction to him and his own infatuation. People who want each other so much shouldn't get too much of each other. The knowledge gave him a trauma, but that was nothing compared to what it did to her.

She shouldn't have been able to initiate a split but, as I say, she was too good. She had already achieved escape velocity, she was Marva and she loved it. She wanted to go on being Marva, not some nobody Brain Police officer.

So she split off her new, more aware self from the old Marva character and if she hadn't, I'd be dead now, long gone over the border that divides life from death. Courtesy of the Escort she hired to do exactly that, take me over the border.

But just because she had achieved escape velocity didn't make her the original. That was still me, always me, and I wanted to live a lot more than she wanted me to die.

In my more generous moments, I admire her ingenuity in hiring an Escort to get rid of me. It was a true Method solution: If a character can believe she's alive, then she must believe she can die.

But here's something she didn't consider: There's life after death, if you want it badly enough.

Lights coming up. It's showtime.

The show must go on.

I was belly-down on the stage at Sir Larry's. Mostly Sir Larry's—some of the details were different, or missing altogether, little textural things tipping me off that they'd taken the liberty of relieving me of my eyes as well as my conscious state.

I should have been upset, but whatever it took to run

the emotional generator was missing. That wasn't an effect of whatever drug the guy had used to knock me out—I could feel the drug wearing off, but the sensation was distant, like the vibration of water running down a drain in another room. This had more to do with why I was flat on the floor of the stage . . . *flattened* on the floor of the stage . . .

You're getting warmer.

The words were neither thought nor voice; more like something I was remembering, vivid but definitely in the past. Information at one remove; remembering my lines, except this time I had no lines. I wasn't flattened on the stage, I *was* the stage . . .

No, I was the whole damned theatre, including the stage.

Em-Cate would love this, I thought, walking over a rival's back to do a part.

Em-Cate is not your rival, memory said, if memory it was.

Who, then?

And there I was. No, not me; the woman with my face.

Some very nice people . . .

Some Very Nice People.

Of course. Rather a cutesy name for a franchise, but the type of people drawn to franchising love that kind of cheap cleverness. It's part of what makes them crave a persona overlay. There must have been some complementary quality that makes an actor want to be Famous —i.e., get franchised—but I had no idea what it was. I'd never wanted to be Famous. What I wanted was—

—to stay in existence. To live.

Obviously. All right. Nothing like starting at the basics.

The rival for your existence. Think.

The woman with my face started to move around the stage in a series of warm-up exercises I recognized as my own—a little yoga, a little t'ai chi, a little ballet, and a little kitchen sink. I could see her from any and all angles now, and it was like watching a burglar enjoying stolen property.

Now I got it: she was really here. This wasn't an image or a memory, we were hooked in together mind-to-mind. She didn't know I was aware of her because I wasn't supposed to be. I was supposed to be—

—standing on the edge of the cliff.

Escort/memory junkie, just doing my job. This one was pretty unusual—Escorts didn't get many calls from actors asking to be rid of a troublesome personality. But what the hell, it was work. Didn't much matter as long as somebody died.

No. For the millionth time, no. That was Marceline, the character I'd been developing. Sorry, the name of the play and the general plot seems to escape me for the moment, but that's just a memory glitch, probably brought on by a stupid famine fancier in a cheap memory lane who insisted on work with her mouth full. But anytime now, it was going to come to me, I was going to remember everything about Marceline—

Marceline's not a character.

Marceline began to fade in on the stage, the image of how I looked now in full costume. Except if she wasn't a character, how could this be a costume?

She was materializing in response to the movements of the woman with my face, I realized. Like a conjuring trick . . .

Or like the creation of a character for a play, except

the character was someone who really existed and play was my life . . . my *new* life . . .

I hadn't been franchised—I'd been bodysnatched.

Is that the way it was? A lost-soul memory junkie with a yen for more than a persona overlay. *Give me a whole new life, give me somebody else's life because I'm sick of mine. Give me her life, yah, that one there. The actress. I'll take her. I'll be her.*

They'd given her my personality in an overlay and then given her my appearance as well, while they'd made me over to look like her, imprinted me with her—

Even as I thought it, I knew it wasn't quite right. Bodysnatchings weren't unheard of. There were plenty of sad cases walking around looking to hijack someone else's life and leave their own bleak existences behind, and changing their own appearances to match wasn't beyond most of them.

But surgically altering the *other* person . . . not to that extent. It was easier just to suck the mind out, scramble the finger- and retina-prints, and dump the rest in a cipher ward.

The cliff reappeared with the three women and my attention zoomed in on the one in the middle, the woman that the Escort was there to kill.

Me?

She looked like me, but there were differences.

A new image blossomed in the middle of the scene: one of us—me? the bodysnatcher?—standing in the semidark of Davy Jones' Locker, wearing a Brain Police uniform. Me? Or some character I couldn't remember creating?

The memory hung in midair just beyond the edge of the cliff. I couldn't touch it without going over.

I turned away and found myself looking at the

funhouse mirror in Davy Jones' Locker again, except it
was a million times longer than the real thing, stretching
as far away from me as I could see. Farther than that. I
was alone, but the mirror had plenty of reflections anyway, side by side by side, reflections with no one to cast
them, reflections waiting for someone to claim them. Or
waiting for someone to claim?

The reflection I was supposedly casting turned to face
me. *The mirror is in the eye of the reflected.*

What?

*We're going to find out how good an actress you re-
ally are,* she said. *In the old days, they didn't use
imprints to create characters. People just did imperson-
ations and tried to be convincing. How convincing can
you be?*

How convincing can I be as what?

She gestured at the image next to her; how I looked
now, the Escort's original appearance.

My point-of-view moved closer. Her features showed
more clearly, that round, homely face surrounded by
that terrible faded brown frizz passing for hair, that
bulky body dressed in ragpicker *du jour*, and not the
chic *du jour*, either. This was stuff that stronger, faster
ragpickers left behind.

*Can you convince them you're her? Because unless
you do, you'll really be her. And no one will ever believe
otherwise. Can you convince them? Can you convince
her?*

What, in here? The Escort's reflection was aligning
herself with me now. I couldn't move away.

*In here, out there . . . everywhere. She can't stay
in contact with you while this one takes control—too
risky for her. She could get herself confused with you.*

You have to keep this one from taking over and then convince them she has. So they'll let you go.

Oh, was *that* all. And how did I manage this minor miracle? Was there a miracle kit in here somewhere?

Abruptly, I was back in Sir Larry's again—*was* Sir Larry's again. The Escort's image was standing in the middle of the stage, a marionette sans strings. Somewhere in the theatre—in me—was the remote control for her. I let my awareness spread itself out as if I were doing one of those full-body relaxation exercises where you concentrate on each part of yourself . . .

Found it. With the control came a small flood of information, names, faces, locations, and a flash-shot: the sight of my own face rushing at her, pulled by some tropism from the empty space beyond the edge of the cliff one scant moment before the fall.

More images came up in bursts, scenes from the area of the Downs where I'd been doing characterization research. She knew them all as if she had seen them with my own eyes . . . or as if I had seen them with her own eyes . . .

Onionheads, rooster-boys, street-corner neurosis peddlers, sidewalk holos meant to jump-and-jive you into the dreamlands for a cheap dose of REM-pix, and the featureless one-roomer where I'd been staying on a short-term lease. Hustlers passing off cheap fixations and compulsions and calling them real neuroses, dreamlands fronting for chop shops that sold stolen memories and the last scrapings from sucked-out minds to hungry junkies (like me?). Anwar, who had suddenly had an attack of something like decency. Bateau sending (me) on another out-call, saying, come back with something good, come back with something I can use, that's what I keep you for, come back and I'll fill your head with all

the things you can't get enough of and can't have for
real, but most of all, come back. Come back.

*Yah, I'll come back, if I have to walk through a hail
of fire, if I have to kill them instead of just taking them
to the edge and letting them go over themselves. And
whatever I find in the lives they leave behind is mine to
take with me, at least until Bateau takes it from me,
and sometimes I call him a pimp instead of an agent,
but I ain't no uptown day-wage priv. I got less than
nothing but other people's memories make it like there's
something. And in here, who knows the difference?*

The vertigo of being in two places at once was almost
overwhelming. I wanted to stop and reach for the
Method instead, but something held me back until I got
used to what I was doing. It felt so strange. How did
those old-time actors do it, how did they become other
people and still know that they weren't?

My eye sockets hurt, so I know I'm not in the system
anymore, but where I really am I want to find out without
anyone knowing. I've got this crazy memory of being at
Bateau's and getting away, but I was delirious or something . . .

Shit, the damned memory lane Anwar took me to. That
skin-and-bones bitch must have shot me with a bad load.
She used me for a dump, scraped out the bottom of the
barrel of whatever chop shop she was fronting for, and
while all the junk she shot into me went playtime, I fugued
out. Christ knows who or what I've been claiming I was.
My memory's all jumbled up, I remember things about a
theatre and someone named Sovay and some other guy
with white hair—

And her. The client. No, fuck Bateau's fancy talk: the
trick. Much better word for her, trick. She was a trick, all

right, they're all tricks in the end. Especially in the end, where they always try to drag you along with them. They can't help it, drowning people will do the same. But that's not *my* problem, my problem is getting out of the thrill-and-chill alive and in one piece. That's the *real* trick.

Well, I'm alive, but I don't know how many pieces I got now. Worst thing I could have done was take that job. I tried to get Bateau to let me out of it, but he was all excited. Go on, go ahead and kill that personality for her and while you're in, grab for all the goodies you can, let's see what we come up with while the client's still alive and maybe of some use.

And what do you know: she didn't have much, not the one who hired me. It was the one she wanted to kill who had all the goodies, because she was the one in charge after all. Surprise good-bye, followed by a surprise hello. I got a little more than anyone figured I'd get, and all I have to do now is unload it without getting chilled myself. If Bateau knew she was a cop—

Jee habba cop.

Shit, did *I* say that? Does he believe it?

And the cop's still here.

He doesn't know *that* yet, but if he gets his hands on me again, he'll find out, and I'll get the chill with no thrill.

Unless I can make him think it was all just runaway memory after the fact. Then give him some cop stuff. She must have had plenty when she sank her hooks into me and reeled herself in off that cliff, and it must all still be there—

"Are you awake?"

I was still too drugged to startle. The trick leaned over me looking all you-poor-baby and I was supposed to buy it. "You can sleep a little longer if you like," she went on, too friendly. "The operation was a success, the patient died, and all's right with the world."

I get it. I'm supposed to think it just happened, what we did last week, I'm supposed to think we're just finishing up. The game is, I pick up and go home, walk right into Bateau a week or more out-of-date. He takes a can opener to my head and that's *my* problem. And their problems are all solved, because when I go, the cop goes with me and no one's left to tell the tale.

And a tiny little voice in my head says, *Sovay*. For a moment I get him confused with Anwar and I can't remember which of us had who, or, for that matter, how. Was he there, too? Was he there, watching from a safe distance while we balanced on the edge of the cliff?

No. I know that one for sure, he couldn't have hidden from me. But he'd been there. He'd left traces. And he could claim all he wanted that he didn't know, but when Bateau took that can opener to my head, Bateau would see where he'd been and what he knew, and even if he didn't know it anymore, Bateau would make sure he couldn't know it again. Just in case.

I got to get out of here *now*. Maybe I can tell this Sovay he's got trouble, maybe not. He should know he does, just because he knows *her*, but he probably doesn't. If he were really smart, he'd have gotten himself a pump like Anwar's.

I sit up, ready to go, and then freeze. I'm back in my old rags from last night. If my fancy clothes are gone, that means my wads are gone. Son of a bitch, how cheap can they get?

"If you're all done with me," I say, "you can call me a cab. Right after you pay me."

Ha, and ha—who says I can't think up stuff? She wasn't expecting that one. She looks off to her right and this white-haired guy comes over, and I almost choke, because it's Coney Loe in uptown drag.

So *now* I get it. We *are* talking bootleggers and body-snatchers and who knows what else, if Coney Loe's involved. Anybody fooling with bootlegging and body-snatching has got to have a Downs connection and there's none better than an information junkie like Coney Loe. He lives to find out everything and then spills his guts. Got to say he looks good in uptown drag. Hell, he almost looks natural, except I think the last natural thing he ever did was breathe in for the first time.

She makes Coney come across with a fistful of currency —not as much as I was holding when I came to in Davy Jones' Locker. After having that much, I'm ruined, I want it all back, but what can I do?

"There," he says, pressing a pile of bills down on my hand and closing my fingers around it. "Your fee, and a tip you can hype out on."

She gives him a look. "Maybe we'll beat that errand boy's vocabulary out of you."

"Call her a cab," he says, jerking his head at her. They have a glare contest for a few seconds and then she stalks out of the room.

"Temperament," he says to me. "You know how these actors can be. Even after they get everything they want."

I swing my legs over the side of the bed, barely missing him as he steps back. Just as my feet hit the floor, I get the oddest damned sensation, this damned feeling that I'*m* not moving. More like I'm being steered. Used.

Sometimes, you eat a bad memory somewhere that gives you the being-used creeps. You find yourself taking a little daytrip to the scene of somebody else's crime all because you've got the memory of what happened and where. Like the memory knows somehow it's in the wrong head and it wants to get back to where it started.

I want to shut down, take a breather, and figure out what I could be remembering now, but whatever's making me move isn't in the mood to stop.

"Something wrong?" Coney's giving me a wary look.

"Hangover," I growl at him. What does he know about it?

She steps back in with this big, bad old smile. "I took the liberty of calling your agent instead of a cab. He's sending a van for you. A free ride's better than fare-and-a-half, isn't it?"

The adrenaline rush is like a punch in the gut.

"You sure you're all right?" Coney says, and for a minute there I can almost believe he wants to know.

"*Hangover*," I growl again. "Just show me the way outta here, I'll wait outside." If I can hit the sidewalk before Bateau's van shows, I can sprint for it.

"This way," she says, crooking her finger at me. I follow her through this big old empty room with a lavabo in the middle of it, to a lift that isn't much more than a cage on a pulley and a chain. Moving around still feels funny to me, like my body is an exoskeleton and it's a bad fit.

The lift is so slow it's painful. I'm slouching in the far corner and she's at the control panel like she thinks I might jump her, which reminds me of being at Bateau's in delirium. I can remember how I got out of there now. Poor Anwar, I hit him with everything I had and it must have hurt. Not likely I'll get a chance like that again.

And *then* I remember what Bateau said before that, in his office. *Bring the actor in alive. And fast.*

Oh, boy. Bateau must have wet his pants laughing when she called him to come pick me up. Do I tell her she's taking this ride with me, or do I just let it be a surprise?

"What?" she says suddenly, and I realize I've been staring at her. "Nobody can prove a thing," she adds. "She's gone, and her memories are gone. All I have to do now is purge my own memory of the knowledge that she was ever there, and I'm home free, warm, and dry."

Now, I know, I just *know* that she's talking about that cop, the one she had in her head, or thought she had in her head. Well, fuck her. Let Bateau have at her with everything he's got. What choice did I get in any of this anyway? It's not like we voted. Let *her* get the box and I'll be home free, warm, and dry for a change. Bateau will find out how things really are, and take her apart instead of me.

"You'd better purge the memories when you're through with them," she says then. "You don't want to risk getting caught with them if they actually get a search warrant. And they *will* come looking when she doesn't report in. But if they can't find a trace of her, they'll just have to give up and leave us all alone, and I'll be free to live my life the way I want to. I just hope for your sake that your pimp knows how to hide the database."

The database. That's it. That's what Bateau will want, when he knows it exists. All the Brain Police have one locked up in their minds, all the things they have to know, but that they can't get at until they really need it. The only problem is, I don't have it anymore. I used to. I can even almost remember what was in it, but I put it somewhere, and I'm goddamned if I can remember where—

From nowhere: chewing.

Oh, Jesus, *her*? Did I give it to that skinny bitch in the memory lane? Or did she just help herself to it like it was a platter of fucking deli sandwiches?

Like *that* matters. What matters is that I get it back again. It's the only thing I can offer Bateau to make him believe I'm still with the program.

"Tell me," she says, "is it hard for memory junkies to forget, or are you used to your memories coming and going?"

She's got that look, belligerent and knowing, one-up-on-the-world. The urge to gloat was going to be the death of her. "Yeah, sure," I say, "they come and go and one's as good as another if you want to get a rise."

The elevator thumps to a stop and the outer door rattles open. We're at the far end of a large, airy, glassed-in lobby and it's a mob scene, people all over the place. She starts to get off but I hang back. This tall guy in a silvery uniform strolls by and gives me a wink.

"It's all right," she says, and she looks like she doesn't know whether she wants to laugh at me or swing on me. "It's just the catalog. They're all holos."

Now I can see that. The tall guy is looking about six inches too far to my left, about the usual margin of error for guidance software. But it's still pretty great holo; no static, even though it's indoors, and real solid, you can't see through them unless you get right up close or unless there's a bright light right behind them.

"Doesn't this scare off the trade?" I say.

She's trying to pull me out of the elevator. "Don't be ridiculous. This is what everyone comes here for." I hold on to the door, trying to see if there's a van parked at the curb outside. But who says Bateau would send the same van, or any van? Maybe he wouldn't even send Anwar; maybe he figured out what Anwar did and Anwar's treading time in a box now.

"You got another way out of here?" I say. "Back door, trapdoor?"

She blows out a heavy, put-upon breath. "Look, why don't you just go back to your life? You're not me, and you'll never be me. If I'd known you were such a quick study, I wouldn't have—"

Boom—like that, I've got both hands around her throat before I even know it. Someone is yelling—

"I *know* what happened, you incredible bitch!" I yelled into that face, my stolen face. The feel of Marceline broke apart like wet tissue; so much for the masquerade. "*This* is my life and *you* stole it!" I slammed her against the wall. "*You're* the one going back to that pimp, not me! *You're* the Escort—"

She was making choking noises and pulling on my wrists. I could squeeze the life right out of her, I realized. I was bigger and heavier now, I could literally kill her in the old-fashioned, down-and-dirty way and suddenly I really wanted to do that. Let her find out what it was like to go all the way to the brink of death and be forced over it—

She's not going to go willingly.

The memory came up with such force and feeling that I thought I'd been instantly transported to some other place, *that* other place, the cliff where it had all happened—

That's what you're *here for, that's why I called you. She's just a character, just a useless character who put down too many roots and believed she was real. I can't use her anymore but she keeps trying to take over.*

I remembered; I remembered saying it. But if *I* said it . . . who was I choking?

Her face was a deep red. I let go, shocked at the sight and at myself. Coughing, she staggered away from me just as the front door slid open. I stepped into the crowd of holos as the green guy came striding in, a graft bandage on his head marring the green. Anwar was right behind him. The pump on his belt was bigger.

I slipped behind a holo of a woman in a billowy outfit of scarfs; she was swaying back and forth with her arms spread, dancing in place to whatever music she'd been hearing when they'd scanned her. With only a wall behind, it was all but opaque. Still coughing and clutching her throat, the bodysnatcher staggered through the image of some man in a glittery quasi-military costume cracking a soundless whip and directly into the tint.

"Where is she?" the tint demanded, digging a hand into her hair and pulling her head back. A sad-faced clown in a hobo outfit broke into silent laughter, holding his stomach and pointing. All the woman could do was cough and try to shake her head.

"Where?" yelled the tint and jerked his head at the holos. "Look around!" he barked at Anwar. "Keep your eyes open!"

The dancing woman made a sudden small leap to the left; I leaped with her, spreading my arms behind hers and matching her movements as best I could. The projection was so high-res, I could just barely see through her head as Anwar walked toward the center of the lobby, letting various characters pass through him as he scanned the display.

The woman leaped to the opposite side and I managed to go with her again. The long, filmy scarf around her neck flew back and ripped through my head. I felt nothing—having a holo go through you is less than having a shadow fall on you—but I was afraid of interference breaking up the image. But nothing happened, not so much as mild static, even when she took an unexpected step back and I found myself wearing the image like an exoskeleton. That was all right; I had her choreography pretty well figured out. All I could do was keep moving and hope it didn't make any sudden and dramatic changes. If she did anything even mildly acrobatic, I was finished.

Anwar continued his slow walk through the room. I was swaying in place when he stopped five feet away and turned to look directly at the holo. I forced myself to keep swaying instead of jumping out of my holo skin and bolting for the door. At that distance, he had to see me. At least, he had to see something moving inside the image like a double exposure that didn't quite match up.

Maddeningly, he just stood there and kept watching, and now his eyes seemed to be looking directly into mine. I kept moving with the image, waiting for him to reach forward and pull me out.

Instead, he reached down and shut his pump off in mid-beep. I dropped my arms and stood there as the holo woman jumped to the left, but at the same moment, he turned away.

"She must have run out just before we got here."

The tint was dragging the bodysnatcher toward the front door. "Come on, we'll see if we can catch her out on the street," he said. She was struggling, trying to pull out of that bruising grip. I actually felt sorry for her. The tint swung her around in a casual way and gave her a solid punch in the face. She went down with her mouth bloody and I heard her head hit the floor with a nasty cracking sound.

"Jesus!" yelled Anwar. "Couldn't you wait for me to patch her?" He flicked a glance in my general direction. I caught up with the holo and started dancing again.

The tint picked her up and slung her over his shoulder. "No. I couldn't. Head injury won't bother Bateau."

Anwar followed him out, glancing over his shoulder in my direction again. I danced with the holo for a full count of thirty after I saw the van pull away from the curb and then took off in the opposite direction.

It wasn't until I'd gone three blocks that I realized there hadn't been so much as a squeak out of the guy upstairs. Coney Whoever, I could remember having known the name, but it was obscured now. There wasn't any time to wonder about him anyway.

Somehow, Sovay's face in the monitor actually managed to get paler. "No, don't come back to Sir Larry's," he said, leaning forward. "That's the first place your Escort service friends'll go looking after Some Very Nice People." He paused, looking pained. "I'm going out the door now. Meet me at home in an hour." He gave me his address and disconnected before I could tell him I already knew it.

I raised the privacy hood and took a careful look around the tube station. Other than a few stragglers who had missed the late afternoon rush, a security guard relieving her boredom by zapping cockroaches off the wall with her prod, and a forlorn-looking hypehead who couldn't seem to relieve his boredom at all, there was nobody around.

No matter how far uptown you got, the tube stations were all alike, little branches of life in the Downs. The only difference was, the uptown stations closed at midnight and the security force cleared the stragglers out by putting them all on the last tube going downtown.

It wouldn't take me an hour to get to Sovay's by tube —he lived at the lower edge of what was officially an uptown district, though the property values said midtown—but I didn't want to stick around here until the evening trade started coming out.

I left the phone kiosk and went out to the platform, feeling conspicuous. The guard gave me a once-over, but apparently decided I wouldn't be as diverting as cockroach electroshock. The hype was slumped on a bench, asleep with his eyes open or having an out-of-context experience, I couldn't tell which and didn't care.

I leaned against a tiled pillar and tried to smooth myself into a state of alert calm. There was nothing else I could do, until I saw Sovay. Marceline was thoroughly dormant again for the time being. Sleeping deeply; maybe what she dreamed came to me as memory, I thought idly. Maybe on some level, she wanted her old life back as much as I wanted mine. I wondered how she thought she could have pulled it off. A persona overlay from a franchise was never as deep and substantial as the franchiser wanted you to believe; eventually, it would need to be renewed. But with me completely out of the picture, Some Very Nice People wouldn't be able to do that—there wouldn't be an original to provide the feel of growth and change that was part of the state of continued existence, and you couldn't get that from a template, no matter how richly detailed an artificial reality you kept it in. So how had any of them expected to continue any of my personas?

The mirror, I realized. She must have gotten the mirror when she snatched me.

But the mirror *still* wasn't the original. And maybe Some Very Nice People didn't care about that. Maybe they were just going to use her to grind out whatever personas she came up with on her own, and so what if they weren't exactly top of the line? An outfit that would steal someone's life probably wasn't working in terms of a standard of excellence, I reflected, feeling dour. They just wanted to sign *Marva* on the work, with or without my cooperation.

A small movement caught my eye. Someone was peering around a neighboring pillar at me, a ragged skinny guy with the face of an urchin who's been stricken with progeria. I stared back at him boldly. Something told me he was more nervous about me than I was of him and there was a sour satisfaction in being able to intimidate someone else for a change.

He circled his own pillar, glancing around furtively and pushing at the uneven shock of dull, sand-colored hair falling down over his forehead. I turned away and watched the dark hole of the tunnel for the tube.

Why had this snatch worked so well, I wondered. Why had the Escort slid into my persona with such ease, why didn't she think she needed to draw on me anymore? And why wasn't she ever confused and disoriented? Even people who bought top-of-the-line persona overlays from haute operations like Power People would get some identity problems . . .

I looked at the aging waif again to make sure he wasn't sneaking up on me. He had his back to me, busily writing something on the pillar with a marker. I had to press my fingers against my lips to keep from laughing. The Age of Fast Information, they called it, the crown of creation—technologically speaking—with a myriad of nets that would accommodate almost any form of communication and expression from facsimile calligraphy to detail holo that would fool your mother (or a pimp's hired help), and none of it had managed to displace the urge to kilroy. The virtual still couldn't hold a candle to scribbling on the walls.

The tube slid into the station with a hushed, windy

roar and the waif looked up, startled. He zipped past me to board the last car. I strolled along the platform to the next one so I could sneak a look at what he had felt so compelled to leave as a trace of himself.

The letters were a little shaky, like a child's attempt at script: *Jerry Wirerammer lives!*

The name meant nothing to me, but I felt a sudden, strong surge of empathy.

Me, too, Jerry. Me, too.

"It's not a bootlegging or a bodysnatching," Sovay said wearily, leaning back on an untidy pile of pillows. Pillows were what passed for furniture in the softly lit living room. At least, I was assuming it was a living room.

"Then what is it?" I said, trying to punch a cushion into a support for my back.

"Marva told me about it, until I made her stop telling me." He insisted on referring to me in the third person and it was getting on my nerves, but I didn't say anything. After he spat out whatever grotesque lie that woman had told him, I could bite his head off if I wanted to. He gazed at his bleached-out hands. The skin looked fragile. "I'm due at the colorist's in the morning. It'll take a few days to set the pigmentation evenly."

"That's really fascinating. And what did *that* Marva tell you?"

He ignored my emphasis. "She said she'd discovered she had a . . . an *aberrant* persona mixed in with her characterizations. She didn't give me many details about how she found it, or what she'd already tried to do about it, if anything. Just how she was going to get rid of it."

I blew out an impatient breath. "And what was that?"

He looked at me. "Hiring you. That is, hiring an Escort. It just happened to be you, and you just happened to be . . . a quick study."

I sat up straight, pushing both hands into the small of my back. "And what's *that* supposed to mean?"

"You imprint fast. And I have to say, it looks thorough. You've got her mannerisms, her vocal inflections, even her posture. Everything. It's a complete impersonation. You'd probably make one hell of an actor. I don't know what you really are, other than an Escort."

I wiped my hands over my face. "The reason it's such a complete impersonation is because it isn't an impersonation. She switched places with me."

Sovay gave a short laugh. "Nobody's ever done that. Switching's probably impossible, all the experts say so."

"Not this kind. Not the kind where you have yourself altered to look like the persona, and then have the original altered to look like you. Which is what she did, with Some Very Nice People's help. Then she tried to send me off with a covering imprint while she took over my life, but apparently, the imprint didn't take, so they picked me up again and—" I had to stop. The look on his face said he thought I was wallowing in some cheap delusion, probably bought from a street vendor in smelly leather armor and a mouth full of glitter.

"And just how could she do all that?" Sovay said. "Escorts make good money, but they don't get to keep it. Their pimps take most of it. For her to rig something like that would have cost her all of the take on half a dozen jobs. So how could she have paid for it?"

"Some Very Nice People did it for her on the condition that she go to work for them afterward," I said. "When she snatched me, she must have gotten the mirror as well. She can work off the debt for the surgeries by churning out cut-rate personas. The mass-market formulaic stuff, knockoffs of knockoffs, stereotypes. Doesn't take any real talent to do that. Besides, she's used to working off a debt. That's what she's been doing for her pimp. She was over her head in debt to him because of her addiction to memories. Selling memories is one of his other businesses, the man is a regular conglomerate."

Sovay blinked at me. "Marva was the only person I ever knew who called it 'the mirror.' "

"Yah, I *know* that. Since I'm Marva."

"But Marva sold out to Some Very Nice People *before* she found out about this aberrant persona," he said, shaking his head. "We were in the middle of rehearsals when she told me she was taking Some Very Nice People's offer to become a persona hack. I should have forced her out of the production as soon as I knew she was going to do that, but I didn't." He gave me a strangely searching look. "I liked her, you see. I liked Marva a lot and I was hoping that she might get so caught up in the play we were doing that she wouldn't go through with it." He paused. "I did everything I could to get her to change her mind."

"She got her mind changed, all right," I said darkly.

"The only reason I'm talking to you at all," he said, sighing again, "is, I can't help thinking there might be more than just an imprint of Marva in there. You remind me too much of the way she was before Some Very Nice People shook a fortune under her nose. I guess she was always wavering between art and the Big Score, and the part that wanted the Big Score won. While you got imprinted with the other part.''

I wanted to throttle him, but this time, I managed to control myself. "I *am* Marva. Not part of Marva, the only one there is. Unless you think I'm the aberrant persona she called the Escort to get rid of.''

"No, I know that was somebody else. I, uh, saw that for myself. Marva told me you managed to get rid of it for her. Which was when I told her I didn't want to know anything more, and she didn't have to bother coming back to Sir Larry's. She informed me that she hadn't planned to come back but there was just this smallish problem with the Escort. A problem of a delusional nature.''

"And what was that?" I asked.

He looked hard at me. "The Escort seemed to believe *she* was Marva, and no matter what she or the Nice People did, the delusion just wouldn't go away. Even a solid week of custom dry-cleaning wouldn't get rid of it.''

I felt the goose walk over my grave, but I ignored it. "So what did they do with the Escort?''

He shrugged. "I don't really know, I hung up on her. It was all very disappointing and sordid, but I didn't know how sordid until I saw you at Davy Jones' Locker. Some Very Nice People had brought you there, with Marva. For imprinting, I believe; they were debuting her that night as their latest persona hack and they couldn't put it off. So I imagine they'd decided to use you as an example of what great work she could turn out. If they couldn't rid you of the delusion, then they'd use you as a walking advertisement. You know—'See, folks? Even a downtown hypehead can be a star, another satisfied customer.' Except a full-blown delusion won't take an imprint. You came out of the back room wearing her clothes and passing yourself off as the real thing. But when you saw the real Marva face-to-face, you switched over and became the Escort again. The delusion's way of protecting itself from the truth. I did what I thought was the right thing and got you away from them by having you thrown out."

"And what inspired that bit of altruism?"

"I felt sorry for you. You looked so . . . at sea. If you could get home as yourself, I thought, maybe the delusion would stay buried and you could go back to your life."

I tried to think. It was all too preposterous, but those were the times we lived in. "I don't know how to prove to you who I am. Who I *really* am. Which was why she did it this way. It's complicated, but it's the perfect crime. If I just turned up blank with my features carved off—or dead—there might have been a police investigation. Because *you knew*. You could connect her with me."

He looked confused. I didn't blame him; I was starting to confuse myself.

"You could connect the Escort, the bodysnatcher, to Marva, the actor. Do you see? So the Escort had Marva the actor—*me*—made over to look like *her*. Then she and her Very Nice People could just send me back to the Downs to get my brains blown out by an angry pimp. That would take care of the evidence, no one would have wondered about another Downs garbagehead biting the dust.

"But now the pimp's got *her* instead of me, and the game's changed. When he runs barefoot through her head, he'll know everything and more."

"What are you going to do about it?" Sovay asked.

I gave a short laugh. "Nothing. Why should I? She's back where she belongs and I can reclaim my own life. Game over."

He raised his eyebrows but said nothing.

"What would *you* do about it?" I asked.

He mumbled something about the police.

"Then *you* call them. You don't believe me anyway. It's easier for you to believe I'm some kind of greedy, venial . . . *bitch* . . . who'd turn her back on a career in legitimate live theatre—and you—for a pile of easy money in the franchise business."

He was gazing at his fragile-skinned hands again. Maybe he was thinking about how long it was going to take for the pigment to set evenly.

"You and I were lovers once," I said. "Sort of lovers. *Closer* than lovers. Does that describe the person you knew?"

He looked up. "It describes one of the persons I knew," he said evenly.

"Touché." I sighed. "Well, I'm out of ideas."

"Then try *this* idea: Once there was an actor, a married man, who became infatuated with another actor in the troupe. He controlled the attraction very well, until it came time for the two actors to create characters to play opposite each other in some production that is best forgotten now. The two actors found that their mutual attraction was a stumbling block to the creation of the characters and decided they should resolve their real-life emotions toward each other so that they could get on with the business of acting. As well, she was about to do something he thought was foolish and wasteful of her talent, and he thought he might be able to get her to change her mind. So they hooked in together mind-to-mind—" He paused and took a breath. "It was not a good idea. He discovered that she wasn't the person he thought she was . . . and unfortunately, she discovered that, too.

"She was doing exactly what she was supposed to do, you see. This foolish and wasteful thing was all part of a plan that had nothing to do with him or his feelings. His interference messed everything up in the worst possible way, because he went barging in with that idea of the person he thought she was. It set up a conflict in her, between the person she really was and the person she wanted to be." He gave a short, humorless laugh. "Are you lost yet?"

"Close," I said. "Yah, what the hell. You lost me."

"I sure did." He gave that laugh again. "Funny how that works, how you can lose someone by finding her." He made a face. "Okay, straight out: Marva was a persona for someone else. I inadvertently helped her achieve escape velocity. At the same time, her . . . mirror . . . created the reflection of what I saw in her. That's what it was there for in the first place—to create characters. So she ended up with two aberrant personas to jettison instead of just one. One of them is you. Or rather, it's who you *think* you are."

"And who's the other one?" I asked warily.

"It's her."

Rowan was standing in the doorway holding a shopping sack. She'd put on a little weight since I'd last seen her in person and the few lines in her face were slightly deeper. I braced myself for a confrontation and then remembered she wouldn't recognize me as Marva.

"This is the one I told you about," she said, coming over to Sovay, "the one who called and left Marva's number."

"It's all right," Sovay said, "I know her."

"But who is she? And how does she know me?" Her gaze went from Sovay to me and back again.

I groaned. "Don't even *try* to explain it to her."

Rowan's face hardened. "I *knew* it. I *knew* this would happen." She turned to Sovay. "So, what shall I do now—set up an appointment schedule for you, install a revolving door and a waiting room? How many do you think we'll get, anyway—a dozen? Two dozen? Maybe all of them! Won't that be something!"

Sovay got up and tried to put his arms around her but she shoved him away.

"Marva sells out to a persona mill and all the hypeheads and wannabees get a little bonus with their overlays, they all get the experience of being my husband's lover! Tell Some Very Nice People they should *advertise* it as a special—free with every Marva, your own personal *Sovay-fuck!* You could collect royalties, then it might even be worth it!" She swung the shopping sack at him. He caught it and held on, his gaze never leaving her face. For a long moment they just stood there as if they'd been frozen in the middle of a tug-of-war. Then her shoulders slumped as all the fight went out of her.

"Sorry," she said in a flat voice.

He turned to me. "You'd better go."

"At the risk of getting an answer," I said, "where?"

"If it were me," he said slowly, "with Some Very Nice People on one side and an Escort service on the other, and no one but me in the middle—I'd have my memory wiped and hope I wouldn't be fool enough to want it back again."

"Forgive and forget?" I asked sarcastically.

"Forget first," he said. "Then there's nothing to forgive."

• • •

Night was falling after the longest day of my young life
—my young stolen life—and I was standing on a sidewalk in lower uptown with no idea what to do next.
Hello in there, who's got the survival instincts?

No answer, not even a *How good an actor are you?*

Well, hell, I decided, I'd go home. No one would expect me to show up there. I could even remember the
address. East midtown was closer to the Downs than I
wanted to be, but it was better than wandering around
on the street until a van pulled up at the curb next to
me.

The neighborhood looked familiar, and the building
was the same as the one in my memory, and the access
code worked on the first try, but as soon as I walked
into the apartment, I was lost. That damned famine fancier in the memory lane had probably eaten all my at-
home memories; the thought of her turned my stomach.

By the smell of the overprocessed air, the place
hadn't been opened for over a week. It took me fifteen
minutes to find the controls to adjust the ventilation.
Then I explored the three rooms, trying to get a feel for
my own life.

I didn't live quite as simply as Sovay—I liked furniture, though not too much of it and nothing too expensive. Of course, I thought, looking at the faded
upholstery on the couch and the mismatched flea-market table and chairs in the kitchen, most stage actors
didn't make salaries that would cover genuine cher-
rywood credenzas and solid oak bedroom suites.

At least the clothing in the closet was better than this
ragpicker ratatat I had on. I grabbed a silk pullover and
green trousers, tore off the rags, and took a quick turn

in the lavabo. I came out feeling like myself again until I
discovered the clothes wouldn't fit.

Mi*god*, I thought, and burst into tears.

Now, that was the *damnedest* thing. After everything
I'd been through, I was going to pieces over a *shirt*.

Did *anything* in this life make sense?

Well, it's always the little things that'll break you
down. After a bit, I pulled myself together and found a
roomy set of jumpjohns that were only a little bit short.
Then I scrolled through the online directory looking for
an overnight bodycarving clinic. There were plenty of
them in the listings—in by nine, under by ten, up by
dawn, out by eight—but I was looking for any notes I'd
stored about vanity work. There were none.

Must be in my personal directory, I thought, and
punched in the request for it.

The directory came up empty. I frowned at the
screen. That had to be a mistake, I thought, and tried
again. Still empty.

Screwy system; probably some kind of network glitch
had wiped the record. It happened from time to time. I
punched for the household records to see if anything
else had been lost.

According to the utility and banking files, I had
moved in six months before. Was that right? Migod, I
couldn't remember; I couldn't even remember my previous address. *Damn* that famine fancier—I was going
to sue her so hard, it would turn her inside out.

The request for a previous address turned up another
blank. That must have been some bad old glitch, I
thought uneasily, and asked for my communications
records. Even if everything else about me had been lost,
the record of dataline use was eternal, etched into the
system itself.

There was nothing older than six months.

I tried again and got more nothing, and still more nothing on the third try. Either there had been a nation-wide dataline meltdown that I didn't remember, or . . . I was six months old?

I felt the same kind of damped-down panic from when Some Very Nice People had had me under and the bodysnatcher had tried to imprint me with the Escort's persona—I wanted to get hysterical, but something was holding me back. Maybe it was all really a mistake, I just hadn't entered my identifying codes right. Maybe these were substitute codes I'd entered during a previous bout of characterization amnesia and that starving fool in the memory lane had restored those instead of my real access codes. Maybe I was just the victim of a terrible incident of misfiling.

I had a good laugh over that one. I laughed while I scrolled through the directory looking for a reputable mindplayer who specialized in reorganizing fragmented memories. I was still laughing when the lock popped off the front door and the tint came barreling into the living room with Anwar. At that point, I could see no reason to stop.

The last thing I used to remember is throwing someone off a cliff.

Now I remember standing in the bottom of a swimming pool filled with holo water and fancy holo fish and a couple hundred souls who are getting a lot more out of the experience than I am. Hot-halle-damn-lujah, I finally got one, a memory of somebody's visit to Davy Jones' Locker, so exclusive, strictly uptown privs or visiting royalty, *if* they know somebody. My memory jones goes into overdrive; I think what I'll do with this one is, I'll remember it to death and then I'll pawn it, and when dry season hits, I'll buy it back and knock myself out again. Ofrah'll do that for me, she's holding plenty-all-else against those sudden droughts us memory junkies all hate so much.

So, let's see, what have we got here . . . yah, we got the holo water and the holo fish, yah, hell of a thing to find coming after your bait, uh-huh, we been through all that, and now dodge to the left, dodge to the right, sashay round and wave at our friend in the lighter-than-air sacsuit. Doesn't look like much of a party boy.

But the dancing boy in the barely there loincloth, he looks like quite a lot of party boy. Except now that I think of it, he's at the wrong party.

Obligingly, he vanishes while he's tugging on his waistband. Nobody noticed he was here and now nobody notices that he's gone. Well, you can't have one reality getting mixed up with another. If that were supposed to happen, we wouldn't have to be all different people, ha, and ha—

I'm trying to fast forward to the part where I find the funhouse mirror, but something is keeping everything moving at a real-time pace. I don't appreciate that, these are *my* memories, I ought to be able to enjoy them in whatever sequence or speed I want. But okay; plod-plod-plod and here's the mirror—

And here it goes again, screwing up the realities. I'm supposed to be seeing fish—tube worms, sharks, all that stuff. But instead, what I see is an audience in a theatre.

What the hell, I take a bow.

But when I turn around, I'm still in Davy Jones' Locker. I'm still in over my head, for an audience. Sounds like a karma-gram—

• • •

You know you're having a bad day when you come to in a rerun.

How good an actor are you?

Migod, that was the one thing I was never going to get over: the monotony of repeated rehearsals.

You want to check the line?

And then everything went rewind and then to fast forward and I understood that it wasn't real, not a bit. Pajamas—Bateau—had me in the box. How long had I been here, I wondered, and how long was I going to last?

She's playing for time is what she's doing. They all try that near the end, the tricks. Excuse me, clients. *So,* they'll say, hanging back, fidgeting with some old favorite memory they don't want to let go of, *so how did you happen to become an Escort? Do tell, it must be fascinating.*

Fascinating like a tracheotomy. One day I woke up with so many bad debts that I got a visit from a collector who told me I had two choices—column A was where I got taken to a chop shop and parted out any old way they could manage, and column B was where I got to kill off people who wanted to die anyway and raid their minds for valuables. So which column would *you* have picked? Do tell, it must be fascinating.

Actually, what I tell them is a lot of stuff about believing in freedom of choice and how when you want what you want, you ought to be able to get it no matter what it is. And all the while nudging them a little closer to the edge.

Well, I *do* believe in freedom of choice. I sure wish I had some. An Escort doesn't choose. The clients choose. Whatever way they want to go, however they want to shuffle off this mortal coil, depart this plane of existence, check out, kick the bad old bucket, that's what I do for them.

And if you thought people could get kinky about sex,

that's nothing compared to the way they're kinky about death. Ninety-nine times out of a hundred, they can't make it and I have to give them the final nudge over the line. Kicking and screaming into that good night. Their words, *that good night*, not mine.

But that actor, she was the kinkiest one I ever had. Multiple personalities—jee-*zuz*, what kind of a job was that? I didn't want to take it, but Bateau said a job was a job was a job, was I an Escort for him or not, and I should hurry up and decide because the chop shop had an open bay and I had plenty of debt left to pay off. The worst thing I ever did in my life was ask for credit to feed the beast, and the second worst was agreeing to Escort for Bateau to work off the debt.

I thought it was good enough at first. You get plenty of memories when you're Escorting. That's what people are when they're dying, one big bundle of memories, their lives passing before their eyes. Of course, I don't get to keep it all—I have to pass it all on to Bateau afterward. What he's got a use for he keeps, sells it if nothing else. The dregs are mine, though he charges me for them. And that's the way it goes: the work chips away at the debt, but I still got this habit and the fix still isn't free.

When I die, everybody else's life will pass before my eyes, one last big rise before blackout. Bateau'll be in on that, too. Likely, he'll be the cause of it. When I cease to serve, he'll part me out. The debt we run up lives after us and the good—I mean, *goods*—are for sale in the pawnshops.

Bateau, if you're listening, I didn't meant to tell her all that.

Something stirs. It's just like that, like I'm underwater (karma-gram) and somewhere else, there's a giant spoon stirring the depths. To see what comes up.

I found the exit once, I can do that again. But when I turn to the mirror, the reflection is crooking a finger at me. I've seen the image of this woman before, it's not supposed to be me . . . is it? I don't want to go over there.

The woman in the mirror points to a spot over her head and the sign snaps into existence: EXIT.

Why the hell didn't she say so? I go over to the mirror and touch it with my fingertips. It ripples like silvered water. My hands sink into it and I know I've been had again. This isn't the exit, not the one I want, but it's too late. Something grabs me and pulls me through, and I have a fast flash of someone else being shoved out to where I was.

For half a thought-beat, they exist in the same state, halfway in and halfway out of the barrier. That ought to be enough. The mirror is the complete record; looking into it from one side, they can only see what they've already seen. In simultaneous transition, one to dormant, one to awareness, they'll see everything the mirror recorded, including my near-death. The mirror will tell them everything. Except, of course, what to do, now that Bateau has all of us.

Even *I* don't know what to do about that, and I've been with the Brain Police for close to ten years.

But then, the transmigration of a soul before death is unprecedented. Assuming I can continue to avoid the death part, I have no idea how I'm going to explain it convincingly enough to be believed rather than dry-cleaned.

. . . as if *I* had seen them with *her* own eyes:
Sally's chewing.
Sally's not eating, just chewing. We all have one

Thing we Do, each one of us, and this is Sally's: she chews.

You want to check the line?

No, Sovay, I want to know what play this is, and what character. What about it?

I'd have my memory wiped and hope I wouldn't be fool enough to want it back again.

I killed somebody . . . I've killed before . . . that's okay, he was asking for it.

I've have my memory wiped—

Migod. I didn't kill anybody. Somebody killed me.

—and hope I wouldn't be fool enough—

to come to

and find Bateau's holding my hand.

This is never good, being touched by Bateau. I can face plenty: the fact that I'm going to be an Escort for as long as I live, a period of time that isn't as long as it used to be; the fact that the man knows the inside of my head better than I do, that the mind I have is the mind he suffers me to have, that he is, as far as I'm concerned, God. I can face all this and more as long as I don't have to actually, physically *touch* him.

He sits there next to the cot with my hand sandwiched between his and that face a mask of concern.

"Well," he says, "you've had quite an adventure, haven't you. My poor Marceline, getting so turned around that it overrode the order to always turn to me first for guidance and help." He shakes his head. "And to find you've been tricked—" He looks at the ceiling. "I'm shocked, to say the least. That anyone would even *consider* screwing up one of my people this way. An example *will* be made."

He looks to his right and I see her lying on another cot a little ways away. She's still hooked into a system and that's real normal-looking, except the tank for the eyes is missing. Because she's not going to need any after this.

I don't know who I feel sorrier for, her or me. It's pretty much chiseled in stone, what's coming next for her. For me, who knows. Bateau's not just a bad old bastard, he's a bad old whimsical bastard. Poor, pitiful me, I'm occupying the position of broken toy in the Bateau food chain. Nobody knows what's going to happen to me except Bateau, and he could change his mind several times before he gets around to doing anything.

"But before we get to that," he says cheerfully, "I do need to know a few things. What did you do with the fee she paid you?"

I feel for my pockets where the wads were and remember I've had a change or two of clothes. Not to mention wads.

"Don't know," I say finally, wincing at the lousy rag passing as my shirt. It used to be some kind of windowpane plaid but most of the lines have scuffed off. Vending machine stuff, and not from an uptown vending machine, either. "I went into a memory lane with different clothes on, woke up just now like this."

Bateau makes a thinking-hard face. An androgyne comes in carrying a tray with an old-fashioned silver coffee service on it. I remember seeing one a lot like it when I was waiting for an air-cab at the Royale about a hundred years ago. S/he sets the tray down on a nightstand next to the bed and starts fussing with two cups. That smell; if it's not the Royale's private blend, it's something just as good.

"Take a deep breath now," Bateau says, "and then tell me where you were for a week."

He had me under, he could have just fished all this information out of my brain any old way he could get at it. Why didn't he?

Maybe because he wants me to survive this, I think,

going on a hope trip. All I have to do is tell him everything I know, and he'll only dig for whatever I can't remember. Which will leave me more or less in operating condition.

I'm so relieved, I almost start laughing, but this is not the time to get hysterical. The androgyne passes Bateau a cup that looks delicate enough to be made out of flower petals. He takes it, holds it under his nose and breathes in the coffee aroma, and then offers the cup to me. I sit up in a hurry and take it.

"How are we doing on that missing week?" he says brightly, taking a cup for himself from the androgyne, who makes an unnoticed bow and marches out of the room. Good help, Bateau always said, was the kind you could ignore completely.

"Don't have it yet," I say, sipping the coffee. It's definitely better than the uptown vending-machine Brazilian.

"I gave you a little spin in the box to see what that poor, overworked mind of yours would come up with." He rolled his eyes. "All I can say is, you're one very confused little hypehead, Marceline. You don't even remember coming to visit me, do you? But then, you weren't really yourself at the time. Were you."

That smile's got knives in it, but they only last a second. Which is long enough to tell me everything isn't quite as okay as I thought it was a minute ago.

Long enough to tell me . . . *something*. Something that happened to me while I was in the box, something I remembered—

"Marceline?" Bateau's still smiling. The knives are put away, but I know he can pull them out again anytime.

He must have tried to get it from me and he couldn't even find me, I realize. So he unhooked me from the system to make me sit here and consciously organize my thoughts for him. Then he'll go back in and turn me inside out.

Only, how come I can read him so well, all of a sudden? And if he couldn't find me in my own head, who the hell *did* he find?

The image of a funhouse mirror pops into my mind. That must have confused the hell out of him, I think to myself. It was confusing the hell out of me. What did he see in it?

It's like the answer clicks into place. He saw the party at Davy Jones' Locker and nothing else. Some sharks and a squid and a few sponges and tube-fish.

"Marceline?" he says again. "Are you still with us?"

"I sort of remember coming to see you," I tell him, just to be saying anything at all. "I was, I dunno, fugued out or something."

"Or something." He nods. "Or *somebody*. Do you remember trying to tell me about the cop?"

I feel like I've been hit between the eyes. The cop. The actor and the cop. Just getting rid of an aberrant personality for a Method actor, that was the job. The actor had a personality she didn't want anymore, a Brain Police officer. I was supposed to go in and kill it off for her. Except it wasn't an aberrant personality. It was the real person. And the real person didn't want to die, so she—

The coffee starts to come back up and I swallow it down. What does this make me *now*, I wonder, a Method actor or a Brain Police officer in deep undercover? Do I even get a say anymore?

I look over at her, lying there with the wires coming out from under her flattened eyelids. Yah, who could blame her for doing what she did, trying to get rid of the cop? I don't want to be a cop, either.

And then I realize that while I've been sitting here

thinking all this handy stuff, it must have been playing on my face like a holo in a foreign language.

Bateau is sitting back in his chair, enjoying his coffee and enjoying the show. I get real tired all of a sudden, and it's not just because Bateau is a real exhausting type of person. Got to keep up with the man all the time or you might miss something important, like your death sentence.

He has sure as hell been keeping up with me just now. He puts down his cup and takes mine from me. I haven't really been holding it, it's just been resting between my hands, could have toppled out and shattered at any moment.

"Well, I knew it was something out of the ordinary," he says conversationally, as if I weren't sitting there paralyzed, "when you didn't make any of your pickups. You've *never* failed to make your pickups before." He looks at me like I said something, and then hits his forehead with the heel of his hand, fakelike. "Oh, leave it to me. You never knew about the pickups. Me and my big mouth." He winces showily. "Sorry, Marceline."

Also never good. I could have guessed I was doing plenty for Bateau that I didn't know about, but the smart employee doesn't do that kind of guessing. A little blank part out of your day here and there, so who needs to remember every little thing anyway? Not me. If you ain't pulling a fugue state once in a while, you're just not trying, right?

And why would I ever try to remember making my pickups? No reason. So there are some memories that I don't know how I got? I don't care. I'm a junkie and it doesn't matter where it comes from just as long as it comes, that's the gospel. I don't have to remember marching around the Downs like a zombie, stopping in here and stopping in there for a little stolen this-and-that. Stopping in at a fetishist and a dreamland and a pawnshop or two and coming out with a memory a lot fuller than when I went in. Hell, none of *them* know they're working for Bateau, why should they know I'm anything more than a convenient place to dump the dregs they can't fence. And all of it so mixed in with whatever I'd gotten from some dead trick, even if I'd gotten stopped and searched, the Brain Police wouldn't have been able to make sense out of the alphabet soup in my head. Shit, *I* never could.

Until now. Because it isn't just me anymore.

She conned me when I threw her over the cliff; she fooled me. She dangled all her memories in front of me, said *Gonna let all this go to waste, a hard-up junkie like you in serious need of a rise, a free rise?* I didn't even have to say yes, the habit said it for me. The beast said *Feed me*, and we did. Except it ate a little more than it bargained for, and here we all are together.

Bateau pinches my chin between his fingers and pulls my face up to look at him. He's got new biogems, lapis lazuli. First time I've noticed.

"Now, you know what has to happen here," he says. "I can't have anyone holding out on me, even a good and faithful servant like you. The first thing you should have done when you discovered the cop was come straight home to me. I know, I know, they kept you, didn't they? Some Very Nice People kept you, because apparently you were laboring under the delusion that you were *her*." He turned my head to the actor for a moment. "They, of course, did wrong by not just packing you up and sending you home, and that is why she's here with us. They kept *my* goods, so now I'm keeping theirs." He pauses to study me with narrowed eyes. "I think you're following this, but I can't be sure. Well, doesn't matter, you'll get the idea when you go back in. You see, we can't have any evidence of a Brain

Police officer's murder hanging around. The penalties are—" He shudders.

"So what we'll do, Marceline—what *you'll* do, rather—is Escort that sorry sack of shit over there out of this existence once and for all. Not just a character but every one of her. The catch is, of course, that she doesn't want to die, so you'll have to persuade her or force her or—" He shrugs. "You're the Escort, you'll know what to do. You always have."

He gets up. "And after that . . . well, we'll just see. It all depends on what you manage to get from her while you're seeing to her departure. And how I have to get it out of you. If you keep thinking you're her, we just might have to blast." He laughs. "On the other hand, you come up with the database, and we'll call it even. Including your past debts. Which means, you get to walk away from this. How's that for incentive?" His lips curve in a smile that doesn't touch the rest of his face.

If I could work up enough will to care, I would ask him how he thinks I'm going to Escort anybody all dumbed down with whatever he put in the coffee—Super-Q, or some wild brew he thought up himself. But even stupored-out, I know better. I'm not supposed to walk away. I'm not even supposed to come out of the system. He'll just take whatever he wants out of my mind and let my vitals flatten along with hers. Two for the price of one. Actor dies of heart failure; unidentified hypehead found dead. Two for the price of one.

I try to close my eyes so I don't have to see him reaching to take them out, but I can't.

Well, hell, I think, walking up that long, twisty dirt road, I know why it didn't work, I know why she isn't dead: this wasn't the way she wanted to go. In my line of work, you don't just go kill somebody—you seduce them to death.

There was the guy who wanted to take a flyer out of a sky-island casino after losing it all to the roulette wheel; *that* was a happy death. He was happy, and later on, Bateau was even happier, because the guy's roulette losses had included a whole lot of stuff about stocks and properties. Nothing I understood, but for months after that, the stock market treated Bateau like its personal favorite son.

There was the woman who blew up the sun; yah, lots of bright lights and a big noise and Bateau sold that one off to the sado-peeps: see the people burst into flames, see them suffer before the whole thing blows, rated XS for Extra-Sick. Can anyone believe it, she thought she was being sneaky. She thought I'd let myself get caught in it. She had the ghosts of all her friends there and all her enemies as well, but in the end, she couldn't fool herself into believing they were anything more than ghosts, and her own ghosts at that. In the end, she knew she was going alone and she couldn't stand it. She couldn't stand it that she had to face the Big Question Mark without even one other person to face it with her.

But I've done the exploding sun ending before. In some ways, it's easier to dodge that one than a flyer off a sky-island. Or a jump off a cliff.

The cliff. It's up there ahead of me, waiting, and she's waiting there on the edge with this personality she doesn't want. That's not how it went, though. How it went was, the three of us walked up the road to that final destination. That was the client's choice, and the client always gets to choose. That's the way it's supposed to go.

What's wrong with this picture is, the client wasn't the intended. First time I ever did it that way.

The trees lining the road are whispering, but it's a foreign language and I don't understand what they're saying.

Something makes me turn around and look back, and there it is. The mirror. I see my reflection in the act of walking away, but even though I keep walking, I don't get any farther away from it.

My reflection? My reflection . . . but not me. Not the client, either. *Almost* her, but not quite.

I'd have my memory wiped and hope I wasn't fool enough to want it back again.

But this was not my memory. I hadn't done this.

You want to check the line?

No, Sovay, I think I've got it straight now. I'd been afraid, back when we'd decided to do it, meet mind-to-mind and settle our feelings toward each other, I'd been afraid that instead of coming to a resolution, we'd open something we couldn't close.

I'd been afraid in other ways. The kind of apprehension you get, say, when you go into someone's bedroom for the first time and see a pair of handcuffs hanging off the headboard.

Yah, I'd had all kinds of fears, but the one thing I forgot to be afraid of was what I might find out about myself. But that's the kind of stuff you'd never see if it weren't reflected in another person's eyes.

Is it a lie if you don't know you're lying?

I hadn't believed when Sovay showed it to me. Make that, when I'd seen for myself. But there it was—there *she* was—cocooned and quiet and camouflaged by the mirror itself, the funhouse mirror in my head that made reflections-to-order for me, characters that lived as long as the run of what plays they were created for and sank back into the mirror after the final curtain call.

How had he seen through everything to where she was? If he'd just been infatuated, he'd have just inspired one more reflection, the person he'd wanted to see, the one who would take that ride through the old Tunnel-O-Love with him. It wouldn't have been her; migod, it wouldn't even have been *me*. She'd have been safe, and so would I; I'd have been busy with the ersatz-Sovay character I needed for my own love-affair scenario. So what happened? How do you see the truth about somebody when all you're looking for is the pleasant lie?

You want to check the line?

Was that all that had triggered her? What could possibly have been in that question that could have taken him all the way through to her?

Had it just been that I hadn't known the line?

Or had I just changed my mind?

Change of heart, thus a change of mind; the things that can happen when someone catches you in a weak moment.

She had to say yes to Some Very Nice People; I'd spent months lying in wait for them, knowing they'd come. The franchisers have whole staffs that do nothing but cruise theatres and holo parlors, looking for a new face. Not just any new face, but a hungry new face. The big firms like Power People just do it to keep current—the new faces come to them and they cull what they want for their persona catalogs.

Then there's Some Very Nice People. One way to survive in competition with the big ones like Power People is to be better than they are, but that's too hard. Another way is to bootleg. The Flavor-Of-The-Month is already taken? No problem; send one of your staff over as a customer, get an imprint and bring it back to the workshop. The knockoff is up and running before dinner.

And maybe it's got a few refinements as well, some extra features that the bootleg custom wouldn't know as anything fenced from a chop shop. Wouldn't know, wouldn't want to. Except, of course, for the ones that do know because that was what they wanted in the first place.

Complicated times we live in, yes; they call for complicated schemes and counterschemes. But I made it simple for her. She existed simply to respond to one mating call: *Hey, baby, want to be Famous?*

Her line was just one word, easy to remember: *Yes.* Once she was in, all she had to do was be Some Very Nice People herself, gathering information while she manufactured personas. And after a set period of time, there'd be a certain customer who would ask for a particular, tailor-made persona that only she could produce, and that would be the cue for me to come up out of deep undercover, send up a flare, and take them all in.

And then Sovay barged in and changed her mind. Just what he set out to do, too. Either I made her too good back in the Brain Police system, or he made himself see too much in her—it doesn't matter much anymore. He just did it. Looking for her, he raised me instead.

You want to check the line?

Was that the cue? If it wasn't, it was close enough for government work—ha, and ha, as Marceline would say —it meant more to me than it did to her.

Maybe there was too much leak-through; maybe, along with all her information, I got her infatuation, too.

He changed her mind about Some Very Nice People; one mental night with Sovay and she didn't want to go anymore. Except she wasn't supposed to feel that way because that was her purpose, to go with them, be Famous. She resolved that conflict the only way she knew how . . . in the mirror.

But the new reflection was from *her.* The new reflection wanted to be Famous. She gave it existence; I gave it purpose; and Sovay gave it the undeniable truth about both. Perhaps that was the one thing the reflection needed to achieve escape velocity from the mirror, and from me: the truth.

The new reflection of Marva knew exactly what to do about it. If you can create a persona, then you can get rid of one. And if you can't get rid of it by yourself, hire a professional to do it.

Some Very Nice People knew just where she could find one.

Yah, but what I do is send them over and keep the memories. She wanted me to send her over memories and all.

Because if you don't, she'll grow back.

Uh . . . what? How's that again?

Everything must go.

If she thought I was going to let perfectly good memories go into the Great Good-bye . . . hell, I didn't even have a say about it. I might have, but that beast of a habit wasn't about to let anything like it happen.

That was how she hooked me, too. Your weaknesses, damn, you got to watch them every moment and still you might not know what happened till long after the fact.

I thought it would be all right, though. I got a habit, but I got experience, too. Plenty of them have tried to hook me. Plenty of them change their minds at the last second or think they do, and they try all kinds of things. They try walking on water, they try shifting into reverse, and when it fails, they try taking me with them for company. That solitary thing is what gets them most of all. They try to make me feel it along with them so that when they reach for me, I'll reach for them and either pull them back or go over with them—at that point, they almost don't care which, as long as they don't have to face the Great Goodbye alone.

But I never in my life ever saw one of them *fly*. Her will to live was as strong as mine, and I knew, watching her hold herself up above the void, that I'd been had.

I didn't know what to do then. She wasn't supposed to be the real one, she was supposed to be the artificial one, just a persona, a mask with a little history. And the beast woke up, the habit came alive and said, *Don't bother to wrap it, I'll eat it here!*

No memory junkie ever had it so good, not in *my* memory, ha, and ha. But that's all that would have come of it, if it hadn't been for the mirror. Funhouse mirror . . . what you see is what you get is what you see.

Not just one mirror, but two: one for the cop, one for the Method actor the cop made. She had to have her own, because it was what made her a Method actor. You put two mirrors together and what you see is what you get is what you see is what you get is what you see into infinity, bouncing back and forth between them, and me caught in the middle.

The one I'd thrown off the cliff was gone, and the client thought that meant she'd finally given out and fallen, the way it was supposed to have happened. She was wrong. She was

• • •

somebody else now.

Somebody else and somewhere else, who I was before I found too many reflections in the mirror and one of them decided to get rid of a few, so she could keep the made-up life and live it out. But the reflections go on forever in two mirrors facing each other.

The original person, and the original persona she made for an assignment in deep undercover, reflecting back and forth now in the mind of the Escort. And the Escort woke up as me. Migod.

The actor had tried to obliterate the cop's memory after the fact, after the Escort got it, but the actor didn't understand that it was *two* mirrors reflecting each other, and as soon as she erased the associations, they all came back into existence further along in the series, a little more obscured, but still there nonetheless. And a memory lane famine fancier also in deep undercover recognized me in the system and tried to make contact, except she didn't go far enough along the series of reflections to find the right one, and got me instead. It was the gap in *my* memory she worked on, not the memory of the Brain Police officer, still in deep undercover.

Deep undercover; deeper than anyone had ever been before while remaining distinct enough to persist. That's the will to live in action, and that's the nature of infinity —if you can see far enough into anything, what you'll see is yourself looking back. You won't know if you're looking outward or inward, upward or downward— doesn't matter. Any way you take it, it's you.

And what are you but what you remember being?

What *I* remember being is pretty goddamned angry. Do someone from the Brain Police and it's no mercy for you. If they get in with a search warrant and find that kind of evidence, they turn you over for rehab, no appeal. Rehab; you see people who got rehabbed around now and then. Nobodies, ciphers. Nothing gives them a rise or hypes them up, and nothing hurts. They're just clocks, keeping time till they wind down for good.

I remember being sure I'd rather go over that cliff myself than have that happen to me. Then I remember thinking maybe I was a little hasty about that.

Funny, no matter how many times you've been to the brink of death, you never lose your will to live or your fear of death. Maybe that was all it took to save her life, the will to live and the fear of dying.

So I saved her life. Then she invested it—

Her presence manifested as a flicker of lightning over the patchwork inner landscape. My perspective shifted jerkily and I swore I could feel my vitals jump. I imagined Bateau standing over both our inert bodies out there in the real world, smirking at her, then me. This contact was different, not like before at Some Very Nice People, when she had just made an imprint and left it to find me wherever it would. That would have worked, except I'd been watching and I knew, and knowledge was power, power enough to override the imp.

But what did I know now, and what kind of power could it give me?

I'd have my memory wiped and hope I wasn't fool enough to want it back again.

I wanted to look at the place where she was making contact, but some force pulled my vision back to the mirror.

Sally's chewing.

The memory was there in the mirror, the famine fancier in a strange office of obese furniture. I was seeing her the way the Escort had come upon her—the Escort had gone under looking for a memory boost but it was *my* memory that had had to be boosted. A Method character will accept any old false memory you feed it, but what happens if it isn't a character?

The famine fancier's head whips around and she sees me.

Sally's chewing—

And then she spits—

I went up that dirt road to the edge of the cliff, too; sometimes I was walking along with her, sometimes I was being dragged like the inert cop, trapped in the prison of deep undercover and unable to come out and save herself. I wanted to stay and have a life just as much as the other Marva did, but I wanted mine in live theatre, as one of the troupe at Sir Larry's, not as a persona hack for a cheap franchise operation. It was my life, too.

A damned good life, good enough to fool a mindplayer, good enough to fool me—both of me, the way I'd been then and the way I was now. Most people thought artificial reality was just one of those fantastic environments manufactured by companies like Realityville™ and Mindscape™, or some entertainment feature reformatted for the wannabee parlors. Sometimes it was, but sometimes, it was your life. My *life*—

Well, it hadn't *all* been artificial. The life the cop had given me had been similar to hers in many ways; that was a little comforting, knowing that a lot of the memories I had weren't completely false. I was what she would have been if she hadn't chosen the Brain Police instead of the theatre. All I'd been doing was rearranging things to make them the way they should have been in the first place. The future was set long before I came into existence, it was only my past that changed.

I'd have my memory wiped and hope that I wouldn't be fool enough to want it back again.

I'm not the only fool to have remembered. She should have done what she said she was going to do, dump the memory of ever having been Brain Police. There wasn't time, though, was there. What's that old saying? Art is long but life is short. And memory is

                               my   past   that changed.

I don't have time to even wonder who she is, this woman I'm standing at the edge of the cliff with, standing in the spot where the cop was before I threw her over. The grass around my feet is deep, luxurious, better than stuff you can get in lawn stores for your chip-sized terrace in the uptown high-rise.

Abruptly, I'm standing in the open window of a sky-island casino where, miles up, there is no wind at all and an old guy has decided to fly away himself rather than wait for progeria to eat him alive.

Yah, this is *my* memory, this is *my* turf we're on now and I can tell the way she's looking around that she's lost. She tries to brazen it out, though, by going right to the roulette wheel. But I've got a little surprise for her there. This time, I'm not taking any chances—every number on it is double-zero. House number, everybody loses, everybody has already lost, and that includes her.

We outnumbered her this time. She knew how to play chicken on the edge of a cliff well enough, but the sky-island was something else. No matter what direction she moved in, it took her closer to the window; my doing. I might have made a good Escort, too, or maybe that was just leak-through from Marceline. This wasn't the life I'd have chosen, but the cop didn't have a whole lot of options. It was Marceline or nothing at all.

How good an actor are you?

Well, I was a lot better when I knew what play I was in. And maybe improv wasn't my strong suit, but I still knew how to pick up a cue and run with it—

Run at her—

My momentum was enough to carry us both right to the windowsill. I closed my eyes so I wouldn't have to see her fall.

When I opened them again, we were teetering on the edge of the cliff.

You never lose your will to live or your fear of death. Wasn't anyone listening to me? Did she think it was going to be that easy, just knock her out of the sky, surprise good-bye? I'm the Escort here, I know better, even if I don't know how to kill somebody who wasn't planning to die. What does that make me now, a Bouncer instead of an Escort?

And like that, here we are in Davy Jones' Locker.

I can sense her, but I can't see her, the cop who grabbed the lifeline into me. I can sense the others, too, but can't see them. But the place is full, holo fish and party fish, submarine noises, even a silly old oyster bed hatching pearls at the rate of one a minute per crusted shell. Yah, I was here, and now I'm back.

And I'm getting a rise, because this isn't *my* memory of it. *Oh,* yah; this *is* a good one, like slipping on a soft, sweet glove that goes on and on and on until it covers me over altogether.

Now it's really like being underwater; I'm weightless,

true state of grace. Things get hazy right along with me and for a while, all I do is drift around as if there really were a current to flow with.

It wasn't my memory, either; not quite. The Escort came up out of the back room that night a remnant of Marva's imprint clinging to her—not me, Marva, but the new, improved Marva, the one who wanted to dump the cop so she could go on being Famous. Or maybe it had been clinging to me; personalities didn't always split off nice and clean, there was bound to be a little of her in me and a little of me in her.

Em-Cate and Twill were right where I'd found them that night, animated doll images; I turned to see their reflections in the mirror and something blocked me.

Not yet.

It was like a window opening and then closing again quickly, a flash of the cop's presence, gone before it could register. I let myself move away from the mirror, over to where I had met Sovay.

You want to check the line?

Not this time; I knew. A school of holo fish swam into me and took me with them. We made a complete circuit of Davy Jones' before I broke away and sailed downward, toward a familiar face.

Hell of a thing to find coming after your bait . . .

I'm on the other side of that fine rise now, coming down easy and good, land on my feet with that life-is-good feeling, walk away from it all the better for having had the experience. There's not much you can say that about these days.

But this *is* a hell of a thing to find coming after your bait. But I remember—*I* remember, and it's not so bad that I remember it, her face on a glowing yellow holo fish. A fish with a human face and the water's over my head; yah, it's a karma-gram if ever there was one. But is it *my* karma-gram?

Now, *there's* a lousy habit—wanting someone else's habit . . . beg for the short end, why don't you. But isn't that what taking someone else's memory is?

Something tells me not to worry about it, I didn't ask to be this way. If I feel the need to be forgiven for something, it's a done deal (myself, I think guilt's a lousier habit than anything). And the fish is still waiting to swim through my head.

I want to dodge it just like I did when it really happened, but I can't. It's like my head's clamped in an invisible vise and I have to—

—let her in.

Now I knew what the split-screen vision effect was, back at Bateau's. She was there, trying to talk to Bateau. It's more pronounced this time but not as awkward or uncomfortable. Maybe because we both know what it is. I can feel her presence and mine slipping around each other like two grades of oil that don't mix; won't mix.

She's a rough blend, like a blanket sewed together out of scraps. All those lives lived vicariously, I'm surprised she's hung on to so much of herself, that she didn't just . . . dissolve, lose herself in a kaleidoscope-a-rama of other people's lives.

But I guess she can't. Instead, she just gets drunk on them. Nostalgia bender; somebody else's nostalgia, her bender. Then the tide goes out and it's just her again, stranded on the ragged edge.

That's what this is all about . . . getting drunk?

• • •

She ain't old enough to have much in the way of memory, and what she's got is pretty damned spotty. Her twin sister didn't leave her much when she split off and ran away to join the circus. What's there is what I already know, more or less; no rise. I don't even know if there's *going* to be a rise in any of this, and *that's* pretty goddam strange, because I'm only in it for the rise. Any of it, whatever it may turn out to be: if there's a rise to be had, I'm interested, I'm there.

Because what else is there, anyway? What else has anybody got that's just as good, that means anything? I'm just running loose here, what's the world to me, or me to the world?

I'm scared because I can't answer that question and until I can, we can't stand together on this cliff against *her.*

And all she is, is another aspect of me—or I'm another aspect of her. If I understand things right, she was actually here first, and I came later, as the person some Brain cop couldn't help wanting to be. But migod, it doesn't feel that way to me. I feel *true.* The Escort remembers me; the cop remembers me, and *she* remembers me, so I *must* be true.

Sovay remembers me . . . and I remember him . . .

And now I remember him, too—nice rise with a nice rush on it. Not my memory, but Marva's, the Marva Sovay wanted when they hooked in together mind-to-mind, the one he was hoping would be there for him. The Marva who wanted to stay at Sir Larry's with him instead of running off to get Famous. And the cop couldn't do a thing about that, because somebody else's wants are somebody else's.

And that's all I ever wanted: somebody else's. That's right, I can look at that face on now. It never *had* to be a memory, memory was just always the most convenient package for it. I don't even know what "it" is, exactly, just that if it belonged to somebody else, I wanted it. New start, second chance, and if the second went flat, a third, a fourth, and onward. Two mirrors, infinity of reflections; no waiting. I can go on forever.

The first time we went over this cliff, the cop saved us. This time—am I supposed to do it this time? Migod . . . I can't. I need the mirror, there'll be some other character in it better at this than I am.

You want to check the line?

Sovay. Migod, *yes*, I want to check the line.

*It's a dirty trick, but that's how it happens sometimes. Sovay is the one thing they all agree on, and if one of them checks the line, they all will. They just won't know that I've changed the line to read, **Good-bye. (Exit.)***

Curtain.

Exit now?

If that's the line, then that's the line. How good an actor am I? Good enough to play both parts. That's the Method. I know her; I can *be* her.

And I'm still her when she goes over the cliff.

Uh-oh . . .

This isn't supposed to be here. Or, there *is* supposed to be something here. Or *I'm* supposed to be—

Damn. I can't remember how it's supposed to look to me. This is somebody else's, but the rise is over. Time to fall.

• • •

It was always disconcerting to come to sitting up. Then he slapped my face again, whoever he was.

"Come on, come *on*," he growled, and pulled me off the bed onto my feet. "If you're still here when he comes back, he'll eat your brains with a spoon."

He shoved me across the room to the open door. My eyes felt as loose as a couple of marbles. I caught myself on the jamb and tried not to pass out again.

"Hurry, god*damm*it—"

I'd have my memory wiped and hope I wasn't fool enough to want it back again.

Who said that?

"You did. It's the first smart thing I've heard you say since—" Anwar shook his head. "Since ever."

No, that hadn't been me. But if I could just sit and think long enough, it would come to me. Someone I knew, or had known once. It was important for me to remember.

You Must Remember This.

I blinked.

The déjà vu was like a physical blow. Empty waiting room, guy behind a desk—

I seemed to be struggling to get out all of a sudden without knowing why. Some old reflex, perhaps.

"Just for now," he was saying, talking fast under his breath. "Just for now, just for now, I'll find you again when it blows over but for now, good-bye and good luck and forget all about it, I'll remember for both of us when the time comes—"

I was thinking what a fool he'd have been to do something like that. Forgive and forget and let it rest, that was the smart thing. Even smarter was to forget first and then there'd be nothing to forgive . . . now, who was it who told me that?

The IV cuff on my arm beeped empty, waking me from a confused and incoherent dream set in what might have been a multifaith church or a Far Eastern bazaar, in which some skinny woman had been arguing with another Brain Police officer as to who I was. The other officer, whom I couldn't identify at all, kept insisting I was now somebody else. The skinny woman seemed to be arguing that due to widespread bodyplay, almost no one had any original tissue anymore so the biological didn't count, but it was hard to tell since she was always talking with her mouth full and never seemed to swallow anything. At some point, a philosopher came in to settle the matter; he suggested that I be cut into two sections, one to be given to the Brain Police and the other to be thrown off a cliff.

Actually, I wasn't completely sure it was me they were talking about, since I was just having the dream without being in it. Then the cuff had beeped and woke me up, and I knew it was just part of my reality-affixing hangover. The dreams you get after a major overhaul are nowhere near as vivid or interesting as coma dreams.

I took the cuff off and set it on the nightstand beside the bed.

"You really don't like food, do you?"

Skehan was standing at the foot of the bed, transferring some data from the monitoring system to his data-caddy. He looked like an albino Jesus. I knew I'd seen him before, but I couldn't remember anything about it. There were lots of things I couldn't remember.

"I like food just fine. Eating is another matter."

Skehan made a sympathetic noise. "A desperation

measure, but it worked. Salazar was the one person we were absolutely sure you'd recognize. You'd been out of touch three weeks, which corresponds to the time your Marva persona sold out to Some Very Nice People and jiggered you into a state of permanent suppression."

Salazar; there was a hole in my memory exactly her size and shape, and I simply could not keep her from falling through it. When I did remember her, it was as something unfortunate that had happened to the Escort, not to me, but I didn't tell Skehan that. He'd probably want to put me under again to have a look at it and I didn't feel like going under anymore. It wasn't going to make the reality affixing settle any more quickly.

"So," Skehan said, disconnecting his caddy from the monitor and pulling over a chair for himself, "any questions today?"

"That all depends," I said. "What did I ask yesterday, and are the answers any different?"

He consulted the caddy's minuscule screen. "The usual: what happened to the Escort and Anwar and Bateau, did we make any important arrests as a result of your undercover work, and when can you get out of here."

I nodded. Nothing provocative like *Whose body am I wearing?* or *Who do* you *think I am?*

"Well, here's one you didn't mention," I said. "Why don't I remember one day to another?"

A smile on an albino Jesus is a striking expression. "With your kind of trauma, continuity is the last thing to return."

"But it does return?"

"More often than not." He watched my face. "Make that, almost always. Better yet, it fails to return in such a small number of cases that we don't really consider that a possibility. We conquered Korsakoff's a long, long time ago. The only people who have it now are those who choose to have it."

That gave me pause. I didn't think that was a particularly desirable condition, but I could understand how someone might.

"All right," I said. "I'll trust you on that one. What about the rest? Until my continuity comes back."

Skehan's ruby eyes narrowed slightly. "We never managed to put together enough evidence for a case against Some Very Nice People for counterfeiting or bootlegging personas. And the business no longer exists. If you found anything while you were in deep undercover, it was lost when the Escort tried to kill you. We did get Bateau for that, and some of the people in his operation. All the Escorts had logged perfectly legal activity so we couldn't touch them. Your Escort—Marceline no-last-name—is classified as missing."

Missing. I ran my hands over my face and then examined them, finger by finger. "I take it the physical alteration occurred while I was under?"

He hesitated for a moment. "Restoration. It was restoration work. And of course, we had it taken care of right away. The physical stuff's always so easy."

"Restoration." I laughed a little. "And the Escort's classified as missing. So where do you suppose Marva is?"

"Unless there's been a purge I haven't heard about, I imagine the original template is still in Wardrobe," Skehan said, speaking slowly and carefully. "If you mean your imprint, that's been wiped. Trauma will do that, you know."

"You're going to try to tell *me* you *restored* my original appearance to this body and you can't find a trace of the Escort?" I laughed again. "You can put that story out as the official version if you want, but *I* was there."

Skehan scratched the corner of his eye, smiling at me professionally. "We don't know where or when you had the bodyplay done. It was quality work, but anyone with a decent set of tools and enough tissue can turn out a job that would fool your own mother."

I leaned forward. "The body had been altered?"

"*Your* body had been altered, yes." The emphasis on *your* was just slightly more than subtle. "No original tissue at all, but that's true for anyone who's ever been in deep undercover. And what else would explain the change in your appearance? You just went and had your undercover wardrobe changed. The memory of that particular event happens to be among the permanently lost." He did something to the caddy and watched the screen for a moment. "Permanently lost, yes. But if it ever does miraculously resurface, you will notify your supervisor, of course?"

"Come on," I said, "isn't there an unclaimed Jane Doe in the morgue who bears a rather striking resemblance to an actress named Marva?"

"There are quite a few Jane Does in the morgue. Or there were. But you've been here for two weeks. Anyone brought in during that time has long since been processed, tissues broken down—" He shrugged. "Anyone who went unclaimed, that is. I really wouldn't know. The morgue isn't my bailiwick."

I sat back. "So that's the official version: When Salazar retrieved me, my body had been altered and the Escort is MIA?"

Skehan snapped the caddy shut. "There *is* no other version. What other version could there be? There is no other possible explanation." He stood up, smiling. "In answer to another question, you'll be out of here tomorrow. You get a week of R and R and then you're back on the job. Your contract's not quite up, as I understand it."

He started to leave and then paused. "Oh, just a couple of other things. Salazar didn't come through this unscathed herself. She wasn't in deep undercover and your trauma affected her as well. We've had to wipe the memory and all her field experience went with it, I'm afraid."

"Sally Lazer's in permanent retirement? Too bad, there's a Downs joint that'll never be the same. What are you going to do with her, early retirement?"

"Oh, no. I believe she's been promoted. You'll be reporting to her when you get back from your R and R." He cleared his throat. "I don't make the policies. And, ah, the other thing . . . you had a rather persistent delusion we had quite a bit of trouble with. But it's gone now."

"What was it?" I asked.

"Nothing to worry about. You just seemed to, ah, be convinced you—" He shrugged. "I don't even know how to explain it. But as I said, it's nothing to worry about. The dry-cleaning took, you're back to normal. No delusions. I only mention it because there was quite a lot of information entangled in it and we had to take that, too."

"So what does that mean?"

"I'm not really sure, to tell you the truth. Except that you may feel you're being lied to about what happened to you during the periods you can't remember. It's a feeling you may not be able to get over and as a result, you could be prone to the development of paranoia. I highly recommend you allow us to put you on para-noia-watch."

I laughed. "Is that really a wise thing to do with an incipient paranoid? Watch her?"

"We wouldn't be watching. You just wear this." He pulled something out of his pocket and held it up. "It's a pump that—"

"I know what it is," I said. "No. Absolutely not. Out of the question. I'm professional enough that I can monitor my own brain. If it gets crazy in there, I'll put myself in for treatment."

"But this would be immediate treatment, it would deliver a precisely measured dose of—"

"No. Get it out of my sight."

He tucked it back into his pocket.

"Now, *you* get out of my sight, too."

Skehan nodded good-naturedly and left.

I checked out of rehab a day early and took a jumper to Cornwallis Island, one of the few places in the Northwest Territories that hadn't gotten all tarted up for the Ice-Tourist trade. But it wasn't completely without amenities; you could find almost anything you wanted if you knew who to ask.

I've always thought a cold climate was a good place to think things through. Whatever memory was lost, I decided, could stay lost. They say if you lose it, you never really needed it in the first place. Forgive and forget.

Or just forget. That way, there's nothing to forgive. Nothing and no one.

So I forgot.

PART II

≪ FOOL TO ≫
BELIEVE

Sovay had dyed himself a delicate orange. It wasn't his color. He was sitting nude on a floor mat with his legs folded and his hands resting on the junction of his ankles. Someone had piled pillows between his back and the wall for support—the regular police, probably. Suckers weren't known to be that considerate. His long straight hair, a shade or two darker than his skin, was pushed back from his slack face and there were traces of blood beneath his unfocused jade eyes. A faint whistling sound came from between his parted lips every time he exhaled.

I squatted in front of him and pulled gently at his lower eyelids. A thin mixture of blood and tears spilled onto my thumbs. Poor Sovay. They hadn't been any too gentle with him. There was no sign of a struggle in the living room but Sovay and his wife Rowan still didn't bother with furniture. It was the same loose scattering of pillows and mats I vaguely remembered from a month ago, with indirect wall-well lighting. It was like being in a tomb. Or maybe a womb.

Rowan's voice came to me from the hallway. "In there. Through that door." I stood up and moved aside as three paramedics came in with a stretcher.

"Dirty shame," said the chief paramed, kneeling down in front of Sovay with a vitals kit. The other two unfolded the stretcher in silence, not bothering with any facial expressions. "You the Brain Police, ma'am?"

I nodded, showing him the ID on my belt. He squinted at it briefly.

"Heya, Mersine. Regular police seen him yet?"

"Yah. He's all yours."

The paramed took Sovay's blood pressure with a Quik-Kuff. "Any idea who did it?"

"I just got here myself."

"Dirty shame. *Dirty* shame." The paramed's bald, blue-tinted head wagged from side to side. "Used to be that was the one thing they couldn't take from you. And they're getting so *bold.*"

I looked across the room at Rowan. She had pulled a hookah out of the wall and was sucking contemplatively on the mouthpiece. Then she moved her head, and in the lousy light, I could see the wet streak running down her face from under her eye. As I watched, the skin there turned slightly red, as if her tears contained some irritant that even she was sensitive to. It would have figured, I thought, and turned back just in time to see the paramed extract Sovay's eyes. I hadn't needed to see that just then. More tears and blood dribbled down Sovay's face as the paramed shut down the optic nerve connections.

"Mighty nice biogems," he said, pausing to examine the eyes. "Brand-new, too. He didn't get much use out of them." He slipped them into a jar in the kit, where they stared like unclaimed marbles. "*Dirty shame.* I mean, those *suckers.*" He stopped up Sovay's ears and gave him an an intravenous pop. "In through the optic nerve like a vacuum cleaner, suck you dry." He lifted Sovay's arm to test his pliability and then maneuvered him into a supine position so the other parameds could slip the stretcher under him. "They musta wanted him pretty bad to risk coming in after him this way." His brow wrinkled nearly to his bald crown.

I looked over at Rowan again. She seemed not to have heard. The perfumed smoke from the hookah had drifted across the room; it smelled appetizing but not too dopey.

"Who was he?" said the paramed. "I mean, who did he used to be?"

"His name was Sovay. He was an actor."

"Oh." The paramed leaned close. "He musta been some hot up-and-comer, but personally, I never hearda him." He waved at his two assistants and they took Sovay out.

"Did you want to see his studio," Rowan said after a long moment of silence. She was studying the pipe mouthpiece as if it were something completely new. "They broke in there, too, but there wasn't anything to take. Just mirrored walls and carpeting. Sovay kept it locked because he said it shut his vibrations in and other people's out." She took another drag on the pipe and blew the smoke toward the ceiling. "Does that make sense if you're the Brain Police?"

Dealing with the family is something you never quite get used to, even under much less complicated circumstances. Of course, it wasn't that complicated for Rowan; she didn't know me and I wasn't going to tell her who I'd been once. It made me feel a bit unsavory, as if I had some further motive beyond preserving the confidentiality of the investigation that I didn't even know about.

"I don't need to see his studio, not with the regular police checking it out." I hesitated. "When they're done, I'll give you a lift to the hospital, if you like."

She shook her head. "There wouldn't be much point in that." Her gaze went to the mat where he'd been, as if she were just now noticing he was gone. "Do you want coffee? All I have are cubes. They're good, though." She blinked several times in that dazed way people do when they find themselves in the middle of a catastrophe and aren't sure of the etiquette. But her movements were unhesitating as she shut off the hookah and put it away.

In appearance, she still matched the minor memory I had of her, small, compact, a shade on the plump side and looking more so in a pouch suit. Unlike Sovay, she wasn't much for dye-jobs or other flash. Her skin was untouched, and so was her ripply shoulder-length brown hair. Her only affectation was the set of pearlized brown biogem eyes that gave her round face an odd blind look.

Surprisingly, there was conventional furniture in the kitchen, a table and four chairs. Or maybe that wasn't so surprising—even the most dedicated floor-sitters probably craved a chair now and then. I sat down and Rowan served me mechanically: cup of water, spoon, napkin, jar of cubes.

"How do you take it?"

For a moment I wasn't sure what she meant. "Tan."

"The cubes in the gold wrappers're tan. The white are tan with sugar, the pink are sweet black, the black ones are black." She shrugged and deposited herself in a chair as I peeled a gold-wrapped cube and dropped it into my cup. The water foamed up in an instant boil.

"Why did they do that to him?" she asked. "Take out his eyes, plug his ears?"

"First aid." I stirred down the bubbles in the cup. "Too much sensory input can be adverse for an involuntary mindwipe. The pop was a tactile desensitizer as well as a sedative. It'll keep him out till they get him into quarantine."

"Oh." She piled one hand on the other.

I've always thought murder must be easier in a way. The involuntary mindwipe—mindsuck—is just as gone, except the trappings of a live body remain to confound the survivors. A mindsuck is interred not in a grave but in a special quarantine to allow the development of a new mind and personality. Sometimes the new person is a lot like the old one. Most of the time, however, it's only spottily reminiscent of the person that had been, as though the suck had freed an auxiliary person that had always been there, just waiting for the elimination of the primary personality. There was still a lot of controversy between the behaviorists and the biologists over that and plenty of theories but no clear-cut explanations.

Regardless, the new mind was definitely Somebody Else, a stranger with no ties to the previous inhabitant of the brain. Someone told me once it was a lot easier to accept if you had enough of a mystic bent toward a belief in reincarnation, but I couldn't exactly tell Rowan to take comfort in the study of the Great Wheel of Life.

"Well," she said after a bit. "Have the Brain Police ever recovered any, ah, anyone? From mindsuck?"

A common question. You'd think in the Age of Fast Information there wouldn't be blank spots or misconceptions. You have to tell them the truth, but I hate it, even if lying is worse. "Never intact," I said, and took a sip of coffee. She'd been right, they were good cubes. The damnedest things make an impression on you at the damnedest times. "Most suckers part out minds as quickly as possible. They—" I stopped.

Tell her about a chop shop? Sure—then follow up with a description of how they'd dig out Sovay's self-contained memories with all the finesse of a chimpanzee digging grubs with a pointed stick, working fast because a hot mind wouldn't keep in a jury-rigged holdbox. Any excised memories that could unambiguously identify the mind would be flushed and whatever remained of his talent sold. There would still be a fair number of associations clinging to it but people who buy from suckers don't fuss about a few phantoms. Nor do they complain if the merchandise is half-mutilated from rushed pruning.

Anything left over after that would be sold, too. It still surprised me that there were lowlifes who would buy sucker leftovers but some people will buy anything. Which meant that there might be someone with Sovay's taste in clothes and someone else with his taste in decor and still someone else with his taste in sex.

—Unless this was a bodysnatch and the suckers had somebody waiting for a whole new personality. Some Very Nice People back in business, under a new name or new management? Counterfeiters making the jump to mindsucking and bodysnatching didn't happen often. Mindsucking was a crime of violence, something counterfeiters normally avoided altogether. But it wasn't unheard of, either. The money's good; people who want a whole new personality pay a lot more than those who just want a persona overlay. Maybe because they think if they throw enough money at it, they can actually get a personality transplant, even though there's no evidence that anybody's ever managed to transplant a personality successfully. No evidence whatsoever. Just ask me.

I realized I was glaring at my coffee cup. "They, uh, they have to. Work quickly, that is," I said lamely, finishing a sentence neither of us cared about anymore.

"I see." Rowan exhaled noisily. "Then it hardly matters whether you catch the mindsuckers or not, does it? I mean, for Sovay or for me. He couldn't be restored even if you found him."

I should have made the parameds give her something for shock, I thought. Seeing to the well-being of the family was really more the province of the regular police; one of them should have been with us but they were probably working shorthanded again. The budget being what it was, I was working short-minded myself.

"No," I said slowly, "perhaps it doesn't matter. Unless we catch them and keep them from doing someone else."

Rowan's mouth twitched. "You'll excuse me if I don't seem to care about anyone but myself at the moment."

"Of course. Is there someone you can stay with?"

"You mean someone to look after the bereaved widow, spoon broth into her mouth, cut up her meat for her, slip her tranquilizers?" The brown pearl eyes slid away from me disinterestedly. "No. I'll manage on my own."

We sat in silence until we heard the regular police coming into the living room.

The regular police had little to tell me. Sovay's attackers hadn't left much in the way of traces. Most likely the B and E had been jobbed out to specialists who had taken off as soon as the suckers were in. The B and E pros seldom stole anything on these runs—too traceable. Burglars don't usually want to turn into accessories to mindsuck. So there we were. The Age of Fast Information meant we could find out we didn't know anything five times faster than we could fifty years ago.

Rowan remained firm in her refusal to go to the hospital so I left her my number and drove back to headquarters. I'm one of those people who prefers driving manually both land and air. It's somewhere between a game and therapy, clears my mind, helps me think better. Traffic was fairly heavy so I had plenty of time to go over things.

Hanging above the river while I waited for the signal to descend and merge into land traffic, I put a Gladney spike in the deck and turned on all eight speakers. Gladney was another mindsuck and this spike was an old one, music composed by his original personality, what they called a first edition.

It was scary how so many artists of various kinds were getting sucked these days. Since the breakthrough in myelin sheath restoration, it had become possible for a brain to stand up to a greater number of complete wipes than the former limit of two. It used to be that a third wipe left a subject at about the level of an acorn squash, only not so long-lived. But now you could have yourself wiped annually—or you could have if government regulations hadn't been tightened. Even with the restrictions, requests for voluntary mindwipe had quadrupled. So had involuntary mindwipe—mindsuck.

My dash buzzer went off to tell me I had the right of descent and I leaned gently on the stick. The fact that Sovay was the victim seemed to indicate that we weren't done with the events of the previous month.

Retaliation, maybe, for what he'd done at Davy Jones' Locker, except that was pretty extreme for counterfeiters. They were given more to things along the lines of screwing up your credit rating, not crimes of violence. Unless there was something really big at stake.

Maybe Sovay's glancing involvement with Some Very Nice People had drawn someone's attention to him. Sovay had barely obtained a reputation as a promising actor except among hard-core live-theatre aficionados. An esoteric victim, but suckers made it their business to scout out new talent. New talent was a hell of a lot easier to get at and sucker customers liked the idea of acquiring a talent in the semirough, with most of the failure supposedly sanded off. Then they could refine it to suit themselves. Stardom the easy way, and better than a persona overlay. In theory. In practice—

Well. You can warn people about buying from suckers, tell them horror stories about what happens to you when you buy sucked merchandise only to have it go rotten with trauma in a living brain, you can legislate and overlegislate every angle, but you can't make people believe they won't get around the problems of buying something not only out of their aptitudes but unclean and taken by force. The legit Mind Exchange uses a procedure that took anywhere from a few weeks to several months to clean out an ability sold legally and even they couldn't guarantee there wouldn't be some mild phantoms. A few years ago, my brother bought someone's painting talent—he'd always wanted to fill out his arty streak and become a full-fledged portrait painter—and found that every time he picked up a brush, he craved to smell fresh cedar. Last time I'd seen him, he'd had a pocket full of wood chips. Stunk like somebody's antique hope chest.

Well, if someone wanted to sell off a part of the mind as though it were any old heirloom out of the attic, it wasn't my concern even if I couldn't see the virtue of it. Maybe both seller and buyer were better off but so far, no one had made history with secondhand talent. Even so, that was voluntary. No one volunteered to get sucked.

Traffic came to a standstill in Commerce Canyon, so I requested permission to go airborne again. Central Traffic Control took ten minutes to get back to me and tell me I could underfly the crosstown air express at my own risk and liability. I nearly got my hood crumpled but it saved me an hour.

Salazar was having a chew-and-spit when I arrived at her office. No drugs or surgery for her—she was too proud of her self-control. And none of that edible polyester, either—Salazar was a real-food gourmet. Chew-and-spit was her way of dealing with her lust for food versus her belief that obesity was an antisocial act. In a crowded world, she was fond of saying, it is obnoxious to take up more than your share of space. As far as I was concerned, her philosophy was her problem; my quarrel was with how she defined obesity, which was anyone who wasn't thirty pounds underweight, me for certain. To her credit, she'd stopped hinting around about diets and surgical pruning after the first month we worked together and she did manage to keep a professional attitude in the face of my mass that, next to hers, was True Bulk.

Today she had a pocket sandwich. All the time I was telling her about Sovay, she would take a bite of her sandwich, chew it slowly and sensuously enough to make *masticate* a dirty word, and when it was all mashed to paste in her mouth, she'd lean forward and spit the mess into the suckhole in her desk. In spite of the Sally Lazer debacle, I was still one of the few who didn't gag openly at this routine, which was one reason she was tolerant of me. The Sally Lazer debacle itself was another. Everyone else in my department was on a diet or pretending to be.

"Any ideas on who did it?" she asked when I was finished. Her mouth was full.

I shifted position in the overstuffed chair. All of Salazar's office furniture was chubby. To make her feel that much thinner, I supposed. "Some Very Nice People look good for it, if we could find them. Or it might be grandstanding newcomers with something to prove. Or they could be one and the same. The identities tend to get slippery in these cases."

Salazar spat, took a drink of mineral water and spat that into the suckhole, too. For practice, maybe. Her saggy garnet eyes stared at me skeptically. "We've got nothing on Some Very Nice People. What about the grieving widow?" *Bite.*

"She's not an actor so they couldn't have been competitors in the strictest sense, and she has no history of personality disorders or identity buying or selling. No chance we'd be able to get a search warrant for cause. I didn't mention that possibility to her."

Salazar looked disappointed as she spat and took another bite. "If we could justify search warrants on general principle, we'd probably clear up half the unsolved sucks from the last five years."

That kind of talk always made me uncomfortable. Tempting as it is to a Brain Police officer for the sake of all the victims like Sovay, I didn't like the idea of access-on-demand to someone's memories and I never would.

Salazar never seemed to understand it as an atrocity.
Maybe she'd spent too much time in You Must Remember This.

"Sovay was a bit smaller than the stuff a really big
operator might go for," I went on. "He was just moving
into Stage One prominence, where he was classified as
a talent to watch. The big operators seem to prefer
someone who's just a little more of a brand name but
won't be too traceable. Drives the price up. And they
never make house calls. Someone big *could* be behind
it—whoever got Bateau's cut of the pie, since Bateau
himself is out of the question—but we'll never connect
them with the ones who did the actual suck. The trail
will be covered by a lot of selective memory wiping and
coding, so the little fish probably think they're working
for themselves anyway."

Salazar spat again. "Sounds more complicated than it
has to be."

"Suckers always make it more complicated, hoping
we'll get lost in the spaghetti."

"Spaghetti," Salazar murmured dreamily. "Did they
take anything else?"

"No, and not for lack of trying. They broke into his
studio but there was nothing transportable. Probably
they were looking for artifacts, familiar things the talent
could relate to in its new home."

Spit. "The ancient Egyptians have nothing on us.
How do you want to handle it?"

"The way I usually do. Get into the Downs and look
around."

She thought about that while she made love to the
food in her mouth. Salazar's never been comfortable
with the idea that she can't know exactly what the people under her are doing. She'd like to orchestrate every-

thing the same way she'd like to stick her nose into any mind she wanted to. Fortunately, she was behind a desk—most of the time—where she could do only minimal damage. Most of the time.

"If we start asking questions or pulling in likelies, it'll just alert our suckers and maybe every other sucker we'd like to hotbox, and they'll just have themselves wiped so we couldn't get anything on them even if we did find them. *The State* v. *Marto.* I quote: 'A mindwipe's new personality may not be held accountable for crimes—' "

Salazar spat forcefully and I shut up. "What about backup?"

I winced. She always did this to me and she should have known better. But that's what happens when you promote administrators with no field experience, or at least none that sticks. "Post them or don't post them, but don't tell me either way. If I don't know, no one else can find out if something goes wrong and I get sucked myself. Let's not discuss it anymore, all right?"

Salazar nodded, brought the sandwich up to her face, and then paused. "Say, you want the rest of this?" She thrust it at me. "I'm full."

"No. Thanks."

"You sure? It'll just go to waste."

"It's not on my diet."

She frowned at me accusingly. "*You* don't diet."

No sense of humor, that woman. She tossed the sandwich into the suckhole, which seemed to choke on it briefly, unused to anything solid after the pap she'd been feeding it. She had nothing further to add so I left her searching her mouth for stray food particles and took myself over to Wardrobe to pick out an appropriate Downs persona.

If Sovay's mind went anywhere at all, it would go to the Downs first, where there was plenty of merchandise floating around in and among the cheap dreamlands, memory lanes, trip parlors, pawnshops, storefront talent brokers, and street vendors to camouflage anything that had been parted out. The mutilated remains of a person's identity could disappear pretty quickly there.

I took a quick look at some surveillance footage the regular police had shot a couple of days before. Things hadn't changed much in a month. The fashion clothingwise was still ragpicker ratatat. No problem there, I'd just get into the closet, throw everything up in the air, and wear whatever landed on me. I was more interested in faces. Wearing my own was out of the question, but just getting another wasn't the answer, either. A brand-new face in the Downs could attract dangerous attention from people with cause to be nervous; someone might decide to suck me on general principle. I shot about a dozen stills off the footage and had the computer do me a composite that any Downsite would find subliminally familiar.

The result was no one to fall in love with. Working from the composite, Wardrobe straightened my eyebrows, changed my eyes from clean onyx to cheap sapphire, tacked on a squint, broke my nose, stretched my mouth, and ruined my hair with a bad cut and fade. They wanted to mess with some muscles and ligaments to change my posture and movement but I told them there wasn't time. Wardrobe always got carried away; it was all just theatre to them. They settled for coating my vocal cords with what felt like liquid sandpaper, large grain; gave me a nasty gargle on the aspirants. I paired a man's tunic with a colorless plastic skirt and added broken-down boots.

"*Très* authentic," said the Wardrobe Captain. This week, it was a young guy named Flaxie. He was brand-new, fresh out of some polytech with a degree in urban camouflage.

"Urban camouflage?" I said. "You can really get a degree in that?"

"Believe it or leave it," he said cheerfully. "I was in theatrical costuming up until almost the last minute but I decided I was more interested in law enforcement than theatre. Theatre's full of neurotics, you know. They'll make you positively nutsoid."

"Do tell."

He flashed me a thousand-watt smile that made him look even younger than he was. "You want an imp or are you going to brass it out on adrenaline?"

I laughed, gargling. "I'm not excitable enough for adrenaline unassisted. Give me a global imprint, debossed. In case someone wants to check how authentic I really am. If they're in a hurry, which they usually are, they probably won't get all the way through the overlay."

Flaxie prepared a hookup to the computer system while I mounted a program for myself out of the characteristics-available file. Generally I tried for things that weren't too far from my own quirks and idiosyncrasies so I could slip in and out of character without too much noticeable difference.

I showed my final program to Flaxie for his educated opinion. He took a long time studying it and then gave me an odd look.

"You're sure this is what you want?"

"Is there something wrong with it?"

He seemed to be about to say something. Then he shrugged. "Can you take your own eyes out?"

I could and did. Imprinting wasn't something I was fond of but I could put up with a deboss, which was pressed on from the outside, the mental equivalent of a mask. Emboss was more reliable since it came from within your own personality, but it was a lot harder to clean out later. A global debossed facade personality would pass a glancing inspection for a short period of time if I ended up directly mind-to-mind with some low-life. The imp had no memory of its own and I could bar it from accessing mine and giving me away. But that was a situation I was planning to avoid.

Flaxie was a real adept. The connections for my optic nerves were primed and a relaxation exercise was already in progress, a swirling colors thing. It went on exactly long enough to let my mind settle into a receiving mode.

The mechanics were the opposite of a mindsuck. If the system operator is any good, the process should be nearly instantaneous (and painless). There was a mental moment of the sort of pressure you feel when you're concentrating intensely—

—Guy musta been a juggler in his previous lifetime. I was out in the wide-awake so fast I barely had time to be blind. Not that it made a squat of difference. I don't need eyes to know when I've been pulled in by the Brain Police. Right away, my ruff goes up. I can't help it. You never know what they've been up to.

"Next time, I'll take care of my *own* eyes, *thank* you so much I'm very *sure!*"

His Blondness just gives me this friendly look at all his teeth. "Take a minute or two. A fresh imp's always on a hair trigger."

Now, this is supposed to make sense? He's been partying with my equipment, I know that.

"Where's my eagle? I want my eagle." I look around but there's no eagle in the room, just him and me and one of those big main-brain banks they use to tapdance on your grey. "Oh, Blondie, you gotta problem here, illegal search and seizure, amnesia without benefit of counsel, hail me the first cab to court—"

He's grinning like I'm the best entertainment he's had in a week. "You in there, Mersine?"

It was what I imagined it must be like to be a program called up within a system. The world lit up like a screen, or maybe I did.

"Yeah." I felt myself relax several degrees. "Yeah, it's me. The imp's pretty solid. Settling now, though. I can feel it." I let my breath out slowly, counting to twenty.

"Remember anything?" Flaxie studied me solemnly.

"Everything." I grinned, mildly embarrassed. "She's pretty obnoxious."

"She's all yours. You want anything modified?"

I thought it over. "Nah. She's fine the way she is. Nobody'll give her a second look in the Downs." I thought some more but there were some curious blank spaces that didn't feel right. "Do I have everything I need? I feel like I'm missing something."

Flaxie nodded. "The imp knows a bit more than you do right now. Not to worry. You'll know it, too, when you're supposed to."

"Right." I took another deep breath, counting it in and out again. "That's the part I've never been too crazy about. Hiding my own information from myself."

"Standard stuff. But if it makes you that uncomfortable, we could go back in and put dummy data in the blanks."

I shook my head. "It's okay. It's just kind of—" I shrugged. "Weird."

"You think **this** is weird? Costume a road show sometime." He smiled briefly and turned toward the system, reaching for something on the panel. Then suddenly he whirled and lunged at me, grabbing a fistful of my tunic. "Who are you, what do you want here?" he barked—

Just like that, we're nose-to-nose. I let out a yell that blew back his eyelashes and most of his hair.

"Marya Anderik, I gotta *thing* about memories, anybody's but *mine*, all *right*? That *bother* you, Blondie?" I got his wrist now. "Let go of me or I'll make you *eat* this hand."

He backed off. "*Mersine*. Come on

up."

"Wow," I said, heart pounding. "That's a hot one."

"It's the usual setup—dual conscious reflex control for when she comes up and when she goes down again. Anyone addressing you directly with your real name can bring you up, but only you and I can bring the imp up. Anything you know won't leak over to the imp unless you command it to. Certain situations might make you flash a little but considering what you're supposed to be, nobody in the Downs is going to find your momentary lapse of attention unusual. You'd stick out if you didn't fugue off or show a little petit mal once in a while. Come back when you want it taken off."

He turned back to the system and busied himself with the settings. I let myself out.

When I stopped at Sign-out to pick up some informant addresses (the imp had the names, concealed from me; I would only know where to find them), I found a message from Salazar ordering me to take a gun. There was no use trying to explain to her about the dangers of that false sense of security a gun gives you, let alone that there was no reason for my persona to run packed. Some supervisors you can't tell anything, mainly the ones with no field experience. I checked a stinger out of Arsenal and mailed it interoffice to my desk, where it would arrive several hours after I hit the Downs. I had a few steel-pointed combs in my rat's-nest coiffure; if they didn't get lost in there, they'd be enough. If they weren't, then I'd be beyond any help a gun could have given me anyway.

I was just about to leave the building when I got another phone call, addressed simply to *Sovay Case Officer.* Damn that Salazar, I thought, picking up the sound-only receiver in the hall near Sign-out. How had she found out about the gun so quickly?

But it wasn't Salazar. It was Sovay.

"How do I know you're Sovay?" I said.

The man on the other end of the line laughed weakly. "I guess you don't. But trust me, that's who I am. I'm trapped in this, uh, I don't know what he is. It's a he, I can tell you that much. I don't know where I am or why—"

"You said, already. Can't you give me a description, a name, anything?"

"It's all jumbled up in here. It was better back in that other place. I had no body so I just re-created everything in my head. No, I didn't have a head. You know what I mean, though. You have to, you're the Brain Police."

"Just try to remain calm." The officer on Sign-out duty slid me a chair and a scratch pad while someone else went to get a terminal so I could trace the call. "What seems to have happened is, the mindsuckers who took your mind sold you off to someone intact. But the implant didn't take very well and you're fighting for dominance instead of being assimilated—"

Another weak laugh. "No, that's not it. I mean, they think that's it. Or they thought that was it. But I'm back there, too."

"Back where?"

"In the other place. Where I had no body."

I hesitated. I should have taken this call in my office, but I risked having him hang up in the time it would have taken to sprint back there.

"It's true," he went on, a little breathlessly. "I'm waiting back there, playing for time. I don't know where that is, though. I sent me out—that *I* sent this *me*, I mean—intending to get help. The *me* back there has no way of knowing if *I*, this *I* talking to you, succeeded or just went crazy or what."

"I'm sorry, but I'm not sure—"

He sighed heavily. "They keep trying to send me out, sell me off. Me, just the one person. So I create one of my characters and send *him* out. Do you see? I'm Sovay-in-character, a character from one of the plays I've done. Do you see now?"

I saw. You see all kinds of things in the Brain Police. A disembodied, self-replicating mind was a more bizarre sight than usual, but stranger things have happened. Probably.

"Okay. Which character are you?"

"No, listen, this is important. You have to understand

that I'm *not* the character. I'm *Sovay's interpretation of that character.* Do you understand the difference?"

"I'm not sure. Just tell me which character from which play."

"Dennie Moon from *Brickboy.* It's great, about a quiet guy who serves as the living museum of his family's memories. He takes all the most significant ones before any of the relatives die, and he's got them from three generations. But now he's hit his storage capacity and he's got to stop and let someone else pick it up. His successor is his daughter and he's caught in this three-way conflict where he's jealous because he can't do it anymore but also he realizes it can be a painful experience and she's still very young. But he also wants to keep it all in his own line of descent—really powerful piece of work." He gave a happy sigh. "The character's a good learning role for an actor."

A small light went on in my head. "Ah. Okay, I want you to concentrate—"

"I *am* concentrating. I have to, just to stay up."

"Concentrate harder and tell me why you chose to send Dennie Moon to the person you're in right now."

The silence stretched for so long I was afraid he'd fainted or hung up. "You think there was a particular reason? I couldn't see whoever this is. Maybe Moon was the first character that occurred to him, or the easiest, or both."

Someone slid a terminal in front of me and punched up some information on the screen. Sovay/Moon was calling from a voice-only phone somewhere in the Downs. A blinking bar at the top of the screen informed me the trace was still in progress. You'd think that in the Age of Fast Information, you could get the really important information that much faster. Think again.

"Consider this," I said. "Maybe you chose Moon for this person because he felt like the Dennie Moon type."

Another long silence. "It's possible," he said at last. "I never thought of that."

"Can you kind of feel around in there for any identifying features of your, uh, host mind?"

The young officer who had brought the terminal was staring at me. *Host mind?* he mouthed. I ignored him.

"Uh, I can't see too well. It's dark for me," Sovay/ Moon said faintly. "I get a glimpse of a sidewalk sometimes. People dancing around on it. See-through people. Zoot!"

"Say again?"

"I see a word on a sign. The word is 'Zoot.' "

I punched *zoot* into the keyword search program. A moment later a small window in the bottom left corner of the screen opened to inform me that there was a new dreamland in the Downs called The Zoot Mill.

"Is that where you went? To The Zoot Mill?"

"No. That's where I am now. Across the street."

"Can you see anything else? Can you see yourself, what do you look like?"

"I don't know. I feel short. I try to feel my hair or my clothes but something's blocking the input or something. I can't get it."

It sounded like something that might be in character from what he'd told me about Dennie Moon. Method actors, I grumbled to myself.

"I see my hand!" he cried suddenly. "There's a picture on it, it's smiling at me! It's a woman! It—"

"Hello? Still there, hello?"

He gave a long, miserable sigh. "This guy is making me hang up."

The blinking bar at the top of the screen stopped

blinking and gave me the address: a public voice-only phone right across the street from The Zoot Mill. The Age of Fast, Redundant Information. At least I knew he hadn't been hallucinating or lying. "Can you get him to stay there?"

"He's hungry, I think. Something he wants a lot, maybe it's food. He's mad."

"Hold him until I get to you."

"I'll try, but . . ."

"Can you tell me anything else? Anything at all?" Inspiration hit me. "What did Dennie Moon look like in the play?"

"Um, youthful for his age. Black hair down to his shoulders, light green eyes. Stockyish build. Why?"

I wrote down the description. "Just an idea. Listen, in a little while, a homely woman with lousy hair and old clothes is going to approach you. Be there."

"Wait!" he yelled suddenly. "Wait! I have something for you! Names! Fortray, Anwar, Easterman!"

Fortray and Easterman meant nothing to me, but Anwar almost rang a bell, albeit a very distant one, a bell that belonged to someone else. The terminal was logging the call so I didn't worry about writing anything down. "Who are they?"

"More of Sovay," he said. "That's all I know. More people they sold Sovay to." He paused. "I don't know why I know that. I have to go now. I can't help it."

Resourceful guy, Sovay. I wondered if he'd planted the names in each mind, hoping at least one of them would call the Brain Police. It was too bad he couldn't be restored, this was some major trick.

"Try to stay where you are." He didn't answer. There was a click as the phone line went dead.

The terminal printed out the three names he'd given,

every one of them tagged *U* for **Unknown.** Either they didn't have records or they were new aliases. I folded them up with the informant addresses and took off, leaving everything for the Sign-out officer to put away.

Of course, he was gone when I got there.

"Heya, heya!" called the man in front of the trip parlor (Sojourn For Truth—Not God But An Incredible Simulation!). "You gotta be paranoid! Can't be too rich or too paranoid these days! Heya, heya, hey-**ya!**" He caught my arm as I started to go in. The cracked imitation-leather armor over his longjohns squealed with the movement. Stars twinkled in his teeth; he spat a few into the air between us. They must have been hell on his gums but neurosis peddlers are all goofy for special effects. "How about you, madam? You may think you're paranoid, but are you paranoid **enough?**" His tacky moonstone eyes searched my face as more multicolored stars sailed out of the corner of his mouth. Two spitters in one day; the Age of Fast Information was oral as hell.

"Had it for **lunch,**" I said raspily, doing what I hoped was a creditable imitation of the imp. "Let **go.**"

"Heya, don't pass **me** up. Simulated God can't compare to the awareness you get from a nice dose of paranoia. It's like coming up from underwater, you won't believe how awake and alive you'll feel—"

"If you don't let go of my arm, I'll kill you."

"See? **See?**" He puffed out a few more stars. "You're halfway there already. And the price is right. Ask anyone, they'll tell you Crazy Al deals the best paranoia at the price, the best you can get without going totally **in**sane!"

I twisted away from him. When he reached for me again, I had one of the steel-pointed combs in my hand.

"Heya, *okay!*" He jumped back, raising his arms and deflecting a few stars flying out of his mouth. "Numb your mind with truth and simulated God, that's fine. But you'll be looking for me when *They* all start plotting against you."

"When *They* all start plotting against me, I *won't* need *you.*" I made a swipe at him and he jumped back again. If there's anything I hate, it's a cheap persecution complex masquerading as paranoia.

The waiting room of Sojourn For Truth was empty and untended. No chairs, no waiting. Sojourn For Truth was the first of the informant addresses I'd been given and they tended to go in descending order of usefulness. It didn't look familiar to me; apparently this was a byte parked with the imp's program.

I felt a little reluctant to bring her up but whatever was on the other side of the twinkly curtain that divided the waiting room from the parlor itself wasn't something I was supposed to handle. Running a short breathing relaxation exercise, I planted a few false memories to give her some context and made the dive as I walked through the curtain.

Some trip parlor. A lot of shabby futons spread on the floor under strings of paper lanterns. The lanterns are supposed to be mood-lighting—how cheap-assed could you get? The even cheaper sound system was playing Brahms in raga-time on sitar, crackling hard on the high notes. Yah, not God but an incredible simulation. See God in a place like this, you *know* it's hard times for the universe.

There's one paying fool, a young guy lying on a futon near a corner, giggling at the wall where this skinny hyphead in a white gown is making shadow pictures with his hands in front of a bare light tube. Guess there wasn't too much call for simulated God these days. I wasn't exactly looking to sanctify myself, either. The hypehead caught me staring and shrugged.

"Holo's broken," he says. "They keep telling us the parts'll be in any day now. Big deal. It's the drug that counts, anyway. We got plenty of drug."

I jerk my chin at the wall. "Do God."

"Do *this*." He gives me the International Symbol of Disdain, which doesn't make the most interesting shadow on the wall. But it keeps the fool on the futon giggling.

Well, nobody ever booked Coney Loe on the extreme cleverness charge. He was just your basic hypehead. They say he'd been some kind of catalyzer-imagist once, the kind creative artists hire to give them head-pictures; supposed to give them a jump start, seeing all kinds of weird shit in their heads, make them more creative or something. Can't make that stick, myself. I see the weirdest shit in the world in my head and I got no urge to paint *Moby's Dick* or whatever it is. But maybe it's different when Coney Loe does it.

Or did it. Old Coney's neurons gave out early on him and he dried up. Now he's just a hypehead making like some hotwire and this is his latest two-step for groceries. It's a comedown from hustling for persona mills, but considering the kind of places that would use someone like him, maybe not much.

"So, how's the simulated God here, Coney? Ever try it?"

My calling him by name gives him pause, but just a very little one, and I know he doesn't really remember me. Coney liked to forget certain things, keep the bank open for more important information. It was a Thing with him, information, like he was trying to know everything in the world or something. He could have gone pro, and every so often the Brain Police would come snuffling around, waving money in front of him, but they couldn't turn him over. They didn't seem to understand how it was with him, that he had to have information the way some people had to have sex, or memories, and the only way to buy from him was to pay in kind. But catch the Brain Police giving out information—sure, the night I remember getting crowned Pope. Firsthand.

The Brain Police—the whole scene snaps back on me like bad karma. Shit, what have they done to me now? I can't remember the interrogation but you never can, unless they find out something from you. I never could figure what gave them the right to take a memory, even a bad one like that, and you ask an eagle and all you get is a lot of lawyer ramadoola about confidentiality and your own protection. Like the Brain Police ever protected me from anything.

Coney is staring at me. "You looking for truth?" he says. "Or just keeping a secret?"

"Information," I tell him automatically. "And maybe I'm keeping a secret." Which I know I am, and it'll come to me in a second . . . something to do with why the Brain Police jerked my chain in the first place. It's on the tip of my brain.

Coney makes a two-handed bird and flaps the wings. "We got truth and God here. Hallucinogens flavored and unflavored, scented, unscented, in your mouth, up your arm, or whatever, lights, colors—" He changes the bird into a rabbit. "Pictures. What's your pleasure?"

"Information. Like I said." I pull my fingers out of my mouth and wiggle them in front of the light tube, enchanting the paying fool.

Coney bats my hand away. "Truth is cheap. Information costs. Can you afford information? Or only truth?"

Now, I've got money and I've got a secret, and I know

which one Coney really wants. Maybe I should have stopped off at a memory lane for a recall booster—

And then it comes to me, just like that, as if someone put a tube in my ear and poured it in like clover honey. "I know something you don't know."

It's like telling a ramrod he's got a limp plaything. Coney frowns and the rabbit becomes plain old fingers without making any difference to the guy on the futon.

"So?" Coney says, a little testy.

"So I like memories. Anybody's but mine. The *real* stuff. Somebody else's. Like I could *be* somebody else. I like that a *lot.*"

"I can understand that." Coney keeps staring at me and does a dog one-handed, which sets his paying fool barking. "That doesn't exactly make it as a secret, little queenie. Anyone could figure it out on short acquaintance. Unless you're holding something other than your own personal disclosure, maybe you want to shake it to the memory lane across the street and stop bothering me when I'm simulating God. What do I care about your memory jones?"

"*You'd* know where to get the really *good* stuff, Coney. You *always* know. Why, you'd even know where to get the freshest stuff would be. The freshest, never-been-seen stuff, even if no one else knew it was even there yet." I take a breath, grinning because I know I got his attention now; I can tell by the way he's making rabbit shadows like it's his sacred mission in life. "Even if it wasn't *supposed* to be there."

"I heard you," he says, and his ruff is way up. Something happened and nobody told him about it; asses will be kicked. I feel sorry for the paying fool, whose ass happens to be handiest. My ass is safe for the moment, because I've got a secret.

"*I didn't hear you*," I say. "Am I deaf?"

He's dying because I won't come across. "I might know where you could get an order to go. Or I might have no idea." He keeps doing the rabbit shadow. "Your turn."

"Somebody got sucked." I put a finger to my head and make like I'm thinking real hard. "Somebody that does something fancy. Yah, an actor. Just this morning, can you buy that?"

He can. "Monkey shock," he says. "Your turn."

"The Monkey Shop?"

"I *said*, your *turn*." He means it, no appeal. Either I come up with a name he can check or he'll kick my ass after all for a liar. Information junkies have some interesting ways of kicking your ass, nothing you want to beg for.

"Sovay. That's the name, ask anybody." Even I winced at that one. But hell you just can't resist stinging an information junkie when you got the chance. They all act like knowing all that shit makes them more than the hypeheads they really are.

"Shock. *Shock*. Monkey *shock*. Open your goddam ears."

"Do a monkey!" chortles the fool.

"Shut up," Coney tells him, but somehow he produces an apelike shadow.

"So what's a monkey shock?" I ask.

"Thrills."

"A *thrillseeker*? Screw *that*. I already *know* how to get *excited*, thank *you* for *nothing*."

"This is different. Potluck. You go in and hope for the best. Lots of juice. Makes you dance like a monkey. But if you pay them enough—" Big pause. "Your turn."

Great. I had to go and shoot it all. I could have held back that it was this morning, I could have given an address first instead of a name—shit, an information junkie'll finesse you every time. I'm trying to think fast; do I make something up and hope he doesn't find out too soon it's a lie, or go for the brass. Brass first, until I can come up with a convincing lie that could pass for misinformation later.

"My turn? Like hell, you ain't finished taking your turn, you're changing dicks in the middle of my screw."

Coney won't thaw. "Your turn." He gives me a little smile, making a rooster on the wall. The skinny shit knows I'm tapped, or he thinks he knows it. I'm wondering what the odds are that I could beat it out of him and then I realize he's told me enough that I can figure out the rest myself. He couldn't help it; for an information junkie, the only thing as good as finding something out is passing it on.

"Okay, here's my turn. You say *potluck*? You say *juice*? You say *pay enough*? I say it sounds like maybe there's a little extra in the juice if you pay enough and by the time your head stops jitterbugging, who's to say whatever you got wasn't yours to begin with."

Sometimes I really surprise myself. I may be a hypehead, but I ain't no burnout, no sclerosis this year. Coney looks like he bit down on something sour.

"Guess you know it all," he says.

I'm smirking away. "And if I don't know, I know who knows."

"Yah?" He smirks back. "But do you know *how* you know all this?"

"Just living right." But I get a little edgy creep. I know about Sovay from the Brain Police, that's nothing; every time someone gets sucked, they round up the usual suspects, no big shit and so fucking what. But I know that's not what he means.

"Like, how'd you get so genius, figuring stuff out like you got a sherlock circuit." His smile is mean. "Don't come back, little queenie. I don't know who you are and you don't, either."

"I'm *everyone!*" Coney's fool announces at the top of his lungs. Coney puts a polka-dotted sleeve over the tube and gives it a spin. While the fool is going cross-eyed over this, he's rummaging around in some stuff on the floor and finds a long white beard to put on. Icons die hard.

He pauses to glare at me. " 'Don't come back' means you're leaving now. Or can't you figure that part out?"

I give him a salute and start backing toward the exit.

Coney leans over the fool. "Hi, I'm God. What's on your mind?"

The fool stares up at him; every neuron must be flapping and snapping like tiny pennants in a hurricane. "Why am I here?"

"Because you're stupid."

Fool nods very slowly. "Ah. I always thought it was more complicated than that."

It's mean, but that's the nature of truth.

I shut her down as I went back through the curtain into the empty waiting room. The combined physical and mental movement gave me a moment of light vertigo while the memory of the immediate past settled around me.

Memory from an imp feels more like a dream than a memory, and this felt like a dream I'd had before. I looked back at the curtain. Coney Loe; I didn't know him, but the imp did, which meant he was a double-blind informant—only imps contacted him, and when the Sovay case was closed, I wouldn't know him anymore, unless he somehow slipped into my long-term memory. That can happen after repeated contact with a double-blind.

I put him out of my mind and considered Monkey Shock as I stepped outside. My pal the neurosis peddler was still hawking paranoia out front. He gave me a wide berth. I ignored him. Monkey Shock wouldn't be anything more than crude convulsions induced by plain old electricity, with timed-release hallucinogens and a mental sorter delivering extra jolts randomly through the right hemisphere. Messy, but not illegal.

It wouldn't be hard to add sucker leftovers to the mental sorter. Memories would work best. The customer would get a thrill at each jolt. Afterward, electroshock amnesia covered all the traces. As the imp said, after your brain stopped jitterbugging, it would be impossible to tell which memories had been added and which were native. Maybe even the customer wouldn't know for sure. Ingenious, and a lot less obvious than taking the stock to a pawnshop or a crib.

Bad news for me, though. Monkey Shock wasn't one of those things I could engage in with even marginal safety. Getting myself hooked up in one of the sleazy memory lanes to see if there was anything of Sovay in the merchandise they were offering was safer than, say, getting myself hooked up to someone who'd been to the lane and bought some of it. In a lane, the operator usually lets the machine do most of the work and a machine doesn't know the difference between a real memory junkie and a Brain Police officer with a memory junkie overlay.

But the worse news was Coney Loe's suspicion. It could have been mere pique because some little unwashed hypehead he considered beneath him actually had some information he didn't have. Or else I really had burned myself in a blazing display of deductive thinking. Blazing for the imp, anyway, or what she was supposed to be. The imp didn't have all my information but she did have my intelligence, and maybe that wasn't quite in character . . . although showing it off would be.

In any case, I was going to have to track down Monkey Shock before Coney Loe could get around to alerting them about me. *I don't know who you are and you don't, either.*

Two onionheads shackled together on a long chain went by, both giving me dirty looks. I ignored them showily, turning away but being careful to keep their retreating figures in my peripheral vision so I'd see if they decided to turn on me and accuse me of flirting with one of them. Onionheads in a jealous frenzy could be fatal.

The neurosis peddler edged toward me, keeping out of reach. "Heya, I'm not trying to bother you or anything, but I got this spot staked, I got permits."

I moved off without looking at him, bumping into a skinny blonde who seemed to be in the process of coming to while walking. She barely noticed me in her rediscovery of reality. Well, *this* reality.

"Heya, lover." The woman had flies in her eyes. They looked real, preserved in the thickened irises, the pupils camouflaged in the little fly bodies. I was squatting in a parking space directly in front of The Zoot Mill, watching both the holo display on the sidewalk and the voice-only phone across the street, in case Sovay/Moon decided to make a return appearance. Probably what I should have done in the first place, instead of burning myself with Coney Loe. The Zoot Mill holo was a little ragged, and nothing special—dancing girls, dancing boys, banquets, money tornadoes, and a lot of the usual signs and wonders—but it was tankless and vivid.

"*Heya*, lover," Fly Eyes said again, moving a little closer.

"*What*," I snapped.

"You look like it's been a while." She grinned, showing me another fly design etched on a front tooth. Mouths, I thought. The world was full of mouths. "Well, the drought's over because I got the man of your dreams." She saw me looking at The Zoot Mill's display where Hercules or someone like him was ceremoniously disrobing for three holo slave girls and one live woman who looked too fried to really appreciate it.

"*Better* than *that*," she said. "Much better. Like he invented it. Unforgettable. It'll be keeping you warm when you're ninety."

Looking at her, I had a flash. It was like looking out of two eyes belonging to two different people. For a moment the imp was aware in a vague way and we were cohabiting. This was the type of situation more suited for her than for me. I put her to sleep again. "Go *away*," I said. "I don't want some secondhand wet dream."

" 'Wet dream'? That doesn't even begin to describe it. This is the mystical experience, change your life, change your *religion.* Ever been in a state of grace for three hours straight? If you had, you wouldn't be squatting here biting your nails."

I trapped both hands between my knees. "A wet dream's a wet dream. If this guy really burns, I'd rather press his flesh myself."

"Not possible, he's far away. But I remember it like it was an hour ago, had the whole memory specially enhanced and amplified. You'll taste him, you'll smell him—" She babbled on but she wasn't fooling me. What she probably had was a second- or thirdhand memory of someone else's fantasy. I guess I must have looked like I'd spent the last ten years locked in a lunchbox.

"Come on," she said, moving a little closer. "It's the best kind of mindfuck you'll ever get. You don't like it, I'll give you a rebate minus the equipment fee."

"Rebate **this**. Now skin off"—I pulled my left hand away from my mouth—"and leave me *alone*."

"Frigid," she jeered and stalked off.

I looked up at the meter. Five more minutes and then I'd have to move along. Meterfeeding had lately been outlawed in the Downs, one of the few regulations successfully enforced. A metertender had already come by once to take my picture so I was going to have to decide what to do—start asking around for Fortray, Anwar, or Easterman, go to the next informant address as Marya, or hang around here as either Marya or myself pretending to be Marya but keeping a low profile. Asking around for someone could get sticky. I could have given at least one of the names to Marya to ask Coney Loe about, but all things considered, it probably would have made him even more suspicious. He might have ended up stampeding the suckers into closing up shop and flushing Sovay altogether.

I kept thinking that Sovay/Moon couldn't have gone far in the state he was in, which would also possibly mean he hadn't gone far in the first place, choosing the first phone he saw after coming out of Monkey Shock. Therefore, I could have been in Monkey Shock's locale— for all I knew, it was a back room in The Zoot Mill, something I might have been able to find out if Marya hadn't insisted on antagonizing Coney Loe.

The meter was just about expired when I saw her coming stiffly down the sidewalk toward me. For several seconds I froze until I remembered she couldn't possibly recognize me. Certainly she wasn't here hunting for me or any other kind of police. She looked tense and scared and a lot more emotional than she had back in her kitchen when she'd told me it wouldn't make any difference to her personally if we caught the suckers who had done Sovay.

No points for nerve, I decided; it wasn't nerve she was demonstrating by coming into the Downs. I had no idea what she thought she was doing, but even more to the point, how the hell could she know enough to do it in the first place?

Stupid fool, I said to myself. Anytime someone gets sucked, you look at the spouse first, no matter what; if the victim's married to Baby Jesus, he's number one on the list of suspects and you put the little tyke under surveillance—

But she *was* under surveillance. *I* was watching her, wasn't I, she was right there in front of me. The regular police had probably tagged her all the way into my vicinity and then left her for me to deal with—they always know when a case officer is working an investigation, even if they don't know exactly who it is. If Rowan knew anything, she'd take me right to the place I wanted to go, and if she didn't, I could get rid of her somehow, chase her out under some pretext or another.

It was getting late and the streets were starting to fill with what they call local color, hues that look best under artificial light. Rowan hadn't made any effort to blend in. She was still in her pouch suit, which was too new and too expensive for the area. Just as she drew even with The Zoot Mill, I saw the twinkle of a paranoid's badge on her sleeve. All jumped up on a paranoid rush for a trip to the Downs?

The parking meter chimed and I stood up slowly, not wanting to alarm her with any sudden moves, but she wasn't paying any attention to me. She only had eyes for the holo.

It was still Hercules or someone like him, wearing a strap and doing a vigorous ballet/square dance with the slave girls. Rowan was watching with an intentness that could have passed for carnal, which wouldn't have been so unusual. Everyone handles a loss differently. But she was trying to get a good look at Hercules' face, as though he might have been someone she knew.

That idea was unappetizing. How would she know some cheap holo hoochy-koocher and why would she be looking for him now? And why had she had to get paranoid to do it? She had no record of being licensed for paranoia or any other psychosis. And how paranoid was she, anyway?

I moved carefully around the other side of the holo, maneuvering through the small crowd that was gathering to watch Hercules. He was looping through his strip routine again and I found myself giving him a few points for talent. After all, whoever started out with the idea of being a cheap holo hoochy-koocher anyway? In his mind, maybe this had been *Afternoon of a Faun,* updated.

And what was it in Rowan's mind?

Her attention remained focused on him, enabling me to get around on her left side, so she'd have to go right past me to get into The Zoot Mill, if that was where she was going.

Inadvertently, I brushed against a rooster-boy with a multicolored crest and feathered codpiece, and not much else except for a dusting of gold powder on his pasty skin. He turned to me with a wide, automatic grin.

"Hot enough for you?" The low, throaty come-on was already out of his mouth when the grin froze into something more painful than sexy. Rooster-boys weren't supposed to be picky but apparently this one was. The rainbow crest rising from his hairline drooped. "Forget it. Not even if I was flatline."

"And when have *I* ever demanded anything from you, dickie-bird?"

He blinked at me and I winced. Not crude enough for the situation or the character I was supposed to be. Trying too hard; either I had to let Marya come up or limit my vocabulary to *Heya* and *Fuck off* while I was driving.

And then Rowan turned around and looked directly at me. I froze again. In spite of the fact that she couldn't have recognized my scratchy, gargly voice, the expression on her face said she wasn't sure if she knew me or not. The paranoid's badge on her sleeve glittered. General freefloating anxiety, I decided—that was her "paranoia." Not the real thing with delusions of grandeur and hallucinations but the street stuff neurosis peddlers like my pal in front of Sojourn For Truth sold to the public: persecution complexes, anxiety, and such. I wouldn't have thought anyone like Rowan would have had to buy anxiety to walk around in the Downs. She could have breathed it in with the air.

A pimp came up on her other side and tapped her on the shoulder. She jumped, twisting around, and backed into my rooster-boy, who immediately put both hands possessively on her shoulders. She jerked away from him and stepped into the holo display. Hercules' arm went through her neck and I thought she was going to have hysterics. The pimp pulled her out of the circle of reception before she could break up the display. The two of them struggled together and then he said something I didn't catch because the rooster-boy was bitching to nobody in particular that his customer had been stolen. People began giving ground around him, allowing me to move closer to Rowan, who was listening to the pimp with an expression that didn't look the least paranoid anymore, or even anxious. She and the pimp made an odd couple, her in the expensive, trendy pouch suit and him in his traditional garish technicolor fuzz. He pointed down the street away from me and she made a move to leave. Blocking her with a fuzzy, electric-green arm, he tapped her paranoid's badge. Rowan shook her head.

I maneuvered around behind them, planting more false memories for Marya, leaving her the knowledge of who Rowan was. If she thought Rowan was leading her to Monkey Shock, she'd be happy to follow.

Abruptly, Rowan slapped some currency into the pimp's hand and stalked off in the direction he'd pointed. The pimp laughed at her retreating back and turned to the display again, watching Hercules fiddle with the ties on his codpiece. I let Rowan go half a block before sending Marya after her.

She looks like she knows where she's going but not what she's doing. People like her, they never know what they're doing but they always know where they're going.

I *know* she's on her way to Monkey Shock; either she's leading the Brain Police straight to them, or she's going to ask for a rake-off of the profits on Sovay, grieving widow and all that shit. I've seen that before. Or, hell, she might even believe she can get him back. Plenty of them believe that; fuck if I know why. But then, astrologers are still in business, too, and there's one guy I know of personally who probably believes he met God today and God told him he was here because he was stupid, which just goes to show you faith gets it over information every time. Faith, or maybe truth, depending on your point of view, which is everything in this game.

So what the hell, maybe they'll pay her off, or just suck her and call it a bonus. Either way, there'd be something for me when the dust settled.

She goes two blocks before she starts slowing down and looking at the buildings. There's not much here, a pawnshop, a hardware/software dealer, and a crib passing as a read-only room. She almost passes the crib and then stops.

Now, I know this crib and if it's Monkey Shock, I remember my papal coronation. Pimp's probably going to run her all over the Downs, I realize; tells her to go one place and when she gets there, someone'll tell her to go somewhere else, and so on, and so on, till she's all turned around and lost. Then maybe they'll send her to Monkey Shock, when they're sure she's too confused to know where she is. And when they're sure she isn't wagging a tail behind her.

Well, I'd just say the pimp sent me, too, to keep an eye on her. Why not.

I go right in after her and she doesn't even know it. Place is just a big ratmaze inside, cubicles and low walls, so I can keep track of her from a distance. They're doing a little business in there anyway, not much, but a few other hypeheads are wandering the aisles. The whole idea is, you see something in a cubicle you like, you step in and have some.

Rowan's all at sea in here. I cruise the other side of the room, just in case there's anything interesting running, but it's like any other crib—one sorry soul after another, waiting to sell you their best shot, and the hardware piled up off to one side. One old gock with peppermint eyes (where do they come up with this stuff?) and foil curls is whispering "Cubs? Cubs? You like 'em young? It's no crime to just *think* about it, you know," and next to him is a job in a leather hood with the eyes zipped shut, chanting "Fetish, fetish, fetish," like I'm supposed to believe I can really get one that'll stick past the first time I go to sleep. And I'm watching Rowan and wondering what she's making of all this; I'm sure she's never been in a crib before.

And I don't know what gets into me all of a sudden, but I want to get over to her and tell her to get out. She can think about anything she wants with anybody she wants, but a place like this is below anyone still capable of raising a sine wave without help. Hell, even the hardware has to be scuzzy, with all that kind of thinking running through it. I bet if I go over and crack open the system next to the gock with the peppermint eyes, it'll be nothing but slime inside instead of chips and plates. Marya Anderik, crusader for social reform, sure. For all I know, *I* bought from the old gock before he ran thin enough to move in here.

Then Rowan stops in front of a cubicle and Hercules pops up, live, Hercules the hoochy-koocher in cheap jumpjohns. And what happens next is so kinky, even *I* don't believe it.

They slam together and start kissing.

Automatically, I duck, waiting for alarms to go off and vice squads to drop down from the ceiling. The regular police love to raid a meat market with people really doing things instead of just thinking about them. But then Rowan and Hercules sink down before anyone else gets a look at what they're doing. I give them five seconds and then hurry over, going as fast as I can because I have to run up and down two aisles going almost the width of the room.

When I get to them, I expect to see live porno, but it's weirder than that—they're already lying side by side on the cots, and they're hooked into the hardware, her eyes in a tank on one side and his in a tank on the other, just like everything is normal.

What's wrong with this picture is there's a third person, a funny-looking haunt in ratatat worse than mine, lying on the floor between them, and *he's* hooked in, too, through an illegal auxiliary connection. His eyes are drifting around in a bowl next to his head and for some reason, I think of that old joke—the party got so wild, I passed out and woke up as the guy next to me. The crib's not licensed for anything other than one-on-one. No crib is. I can't figure why they're risking it; anyone in here can be a Brain Police plant and if they're caught, it's instant raid. But people who mouthkiss'll try anything. Mouths, *yuck*.

The guy on the floor suddenly reaches up and starts to disconnect, and the last thing I see before I do a fast fade is he's got tattooed hands. Christ, the silly stuff you notice.

I had sixty seconds, give or take, to decide whether I should confront them or skin off and maintain surveillance at a distance. The guy on the floor, now fumbling like a novice with the connections to his optic nerves, was obviously the man who called me at the station— the tattoo on his right hand fit the description he gave. If his memory wasn't too spotty, he would recognize me as the person who was supposed to meet him at the phone across from The Zoot Mill. I wasn't so sure making contact now would be the optimum thing to do.

He had his connections out and he was reaching for his eyes. I ducked into the next cubicle, and crouched next to the wall. The occupants didn't care—they were both hooked up to a system, sharing whatever it was

people shared in cribs. Next door, I could hear Sovay/
Moon moving around, helping Rowan and Hercules disconnect.

"Oh, thank you," Rowan whispered politely, as
though he'd just passed her the edible polyester at a
dinner party. There were a few sounds of hurried kisses
and then I heard Hercules whisper, "Rowan and I will
go out together. Give us ten minutes to get past my
pimp—we don't want him cutting himself in. Then meet
us at—"

I couldn't get it because Sovay/Moon chose that moment to grunt unhappily. He started to make some kind
of complaint but the other two shushed him. A moment
later they hurried past the cubicle I was crouching in,
leaving Sovay/Moon alone. I gave it five seconds and
then crawled out of the cubicle and into the other.

He was sitting on the edge of Rowan's cot with his
face in his hands; I could see he was trembling a little.
Who was he now—Sovay/Moon, or the man who had
bought Sovay/Moon? Only one way to find out for certain, and since I had probable cause to believe he was a
receiver of sucked goods, I could legally search his mind
without a warrant.

Getting him to hold still for that, however, was another matter. I was beginning to wish I'd taken the
stinger after all. On the other hand, if Sovay/Moon was
still dominant, I might be able to talk him into cooperat-
ing and keeping his mouth shut afterward.

Sensing something, he lowered his hands and saw
me squatting at the entrance to the cubicle. He didn't
look a thing like Sovay's description of the character—
long horse face, uneven lank brown hair, too much
nose and mouth. He could have passed for my brother,

the way I looked now. My brother or my father. That gave me an idea.

He started to get up and I said, "No, it's me—your daughter."

Several expressions swept down his long face as he plumped down on the cot again and shoved himself away from me, packing himself into a corner of the cubicle.

"Don't you see, Father," I said, crawling toward him. "It must go on. We can't let it die with you, because—" I floundered for a moment. Christ, but I wished I had a lot more background than what he'd told me. "—because I'll be carrying it on, and from me, it will go to my own child, and so on until we come to the . . . the final shore and we'll all be there to see it together—"

"Final peak."

I froze. "Uh . . . what?"

" 'Till we come to the final peak and see the world as we made it spread out before us.' Improv doesn't mean you can change the analogy." Watching my face, he untensed about a millimeter.

"Oh." I slid up onto the cot and sat facing him.

"Well, go on," he said. "Talk me into it."

"Talk you into it?"

He looked briefly at the ceiling. "You're supposed to persuade me to let you archive my personal memories as the symbol of the torch passing. Reach for it, pull out all the stops, you can clean up the scenery chewing later for performance. Don't be afraid of the Method. Make me see that my memories are as important to you as they are to me, show me I can't be selfish enough to let a dynasty die with me."

I started to flash again and Marya stirred more actively than she had back on the street with Fly Eyes. It would figure, her being a memory junkie. She submerged easily enough after a moment, but as my perspective cleared, I saw that Sovay/Moon was looking a little bleary. I had to talk him into remaining dominant before he realized I wasn't an actress and this wasn't a rehearsal booth. And before the real identity of this hypehead asserted itself.

"You gave me life," I said desperately, remembering what Flaxie had said about all the neurotics in theatre. "Let me do the same for you, let me preserve yours and all the lives you preserve."

"Not bad." He relaxed a little more and favored me with an approving nod. "Keep going."

"Um . . . flesh of my flesh and thought of my thoughts?"

Now he looked stern. "Are you asking me or telling me?"

"We shouldn't argue, Father," I said, getting impatient. "It's right and you know it's right. We chose to maintain ourselves in living minds, not a machine. It's my turn, Father, it's my birthright. If you deny it to me, you might as well kill me, too."

"*Brava.*" He gave me a raised fist salute and lay down on the cot. "From here, we can just mime the actions in detail—you *have* had mime training, haven't—"

But that was all I needed. I leaped on him and sat on his chest, pressing one hand down on his throat.

"What—wait a—"

"The Method," I said, grabbing the connections with my other hand. "All the way. You just told me not to be afraid of the Method."

He sighed. "All right. But let's do it quick—"

I popped his left eye out and sent the connection in,

hoping the disinfect cycle on the hardware was functional. He went completely limp under me, which made removing the right eye easier. Climbing off him, I set the system for a full cycle and did some deep breathing while I watched him lying on the cot with the wires running out from under his flattened eyelids. This system wouldn't have a lot of the automatic blocks and shields dividing two minds in contact; I was going to have to draw on my own resources for those.

I pulled the other cot closer and lay down, clutching the other set of connections. He was going to be late meeting Rowan and Hercules; if I could work fast enough, we'd be disconnected by the time they thought to come back and see what was keeping him.

It was too bad, I thought as I worked my eyes out one at a time, that I couldn't have had Flaxie with me. I wasn't as steady as I'd been back at the station.

It was a real bare-bones system, no compartmentalization, no waiting space—you were either in contact or not. Sovay/Moon manifested immediately, facing me across the mental environment of a theatrical stage. It didn't have perfect definition—the floor was flimsy and the prop furniture was transparent and runny, but there was a hard white spotlight on Sovay/Moon, illuminating him without a bit of vagueness. He looked exactly as he had when I'd seen his body, minus the orange color, with long black hair. The jade eyes were glowing holes in his face.

Don't look at the audience, he said. **It's unprofessional to break proscenium.**

Apparently he was referring to the cavernous dark area gaping on my left. I didn't look but I got the undeniable feeling someone was out there watching—it had to be the guy who had bought from the suckers.

Now, let's try the improv again, Sovay/Moon said, *and this time, really work on convincing me. And remember the feeling when we return to the script.*

Sovay. I moved toward him. *I'm the person you cal—*

Dammitall! He shook both fists at the ceiling, which was as shadowy and vague as the audience area. *How do you expect me to rehearse with you when you keep breaking character?* He lowered his arms and took a deep breath, composing himself. *You don't know the lines you're supposed to be paraphrasing, do you?*

Um . . . no.

A script materialized in his left hand. He beckoned to me. *All right, then, come refresh your memory so we can go on with the scene.*

Instantly, I was standing in the spotlight with him. He turned me so that my back was to the audience and opened the script, pointing to the top of a page. *From here,* he ordered. *Memorize this.*

At the top of the page it said:

DENNY MOON

I must remain in character in order to remain dominant. We can communicate this way for only a short time. Explain who you are, answer in here if you can. If you can't, get out immediately.

I concentrated; words melted into existence in the blank space below.

MERSINE MOON

I'm the officer you called earlier. How were you able to break character and call?

Sovay glanced at me and then looked back at the script.

DENNY MOON

I wasn't quite so settled in at the time. He's getting more of a hold on me but so far I've managed to convince him I'm not done rehearsing. He's not very smart.

MERSINE MOON

How do you know Rowan and the stripper?

Sovay blew out a disgusted breath.

DENNY MOON

[Blows out disgusted breath] Rowan's my wife, of course. The stripper found me—or him, rather. The stripper's another customer. He bought one of my characters. I called the Brain Police, but he called Rowan.

MERSINE MOON

Which character is he?

DENNY MOON

Dionysius, from The Zeus Revue. It's a character that allows for more of the actor's personality as a performer. He—I rehearsed that one a lot with Rowan.

MERSINE MOON

Why were you hooked in with Rowan and the stripper? Where are you supposed to meet them, and why? What's going on, is she involved with the suckers?

The stage gave a long shudder. I could sense pressure building up somewhere behind me. ***Take a last look!*** Sovay/Moon said. ***If you don't have it by now, you never will!***

DENNY MOON

Rowan is collec

The stage rumbled under us. He snapped the script shut and tossed it away. It vanished before it hit the floor. *Time's up,* he said, glancing significantly over his shoulder. *Next time you audition, be more familiar with your material. Endit!*

Like that, we were out of contact. I had the sensation of movement somewhere nearby and I disconnected, rushing to pop my eyes back in. All I had to do was arrest him and get him back to the station where they'd pull the whole story out of him.

I had the right eye in when I saw them, Rowan and the stripper on either side of him, helping him up from the cot. The stripper turned to me as I jammed my left eye into the socket, but the connection missed on the first try. Sovay/Moon pointed at me and the stripper disappeared into my blind side. I managed to make the connection in time to see Hercules coming at me with his hand raised. Metal flashed in his palm.

The first thing I think is, oh, no, I put my eyes in upside-down. Then I can feel how I'm lying with my head hanging off the edge of whatever this is and I think, oh, shit, I had a seizure.

And then I remember Coney Loe and Monkey Shock, and I think, oh, great, I found the place, I must have got something. And there's that smell of fried hair and I know for sure I've been Monkey Shocked and the goddam low-lifes didn't even let me take my combs out. I'm lucky I didn't get my fucking head burned off.

Moving slow, I roll over and there I am hanging on the edge of a cheap cot in what I know is a crib. My eyes aren't right, feels like they're looking in slightly different directions, and I got the kind of headache they call a headquake, and I don't remember anything. And I hit the floor.

I climb up on the cot again and lie there trying to make my eyes go right. They sort of resettle while a little something comes back to me; I can remember coming to the crib, and I remember some people in a three-way—something about mouthkissing, which my stomach is just not in favor of me thinking about at the moment—but after that, the screen's dark.

They must have told me how to find Monkey Shock, those three kinkos, and I must have gone there. Electroshock amnesia'll get you every time. Nice bunch, Monkey Shock, dumping me back at the crib. Unless Monkey Shock was in here somewhere—Nah. I know this crib. It's hanging on to its license by its teeth, wouldn't touch a chop shop. Most cribs won't, they're too likely to be raided.

I try sitting up and I feel a little better. At least my head doesn't drop off and roll away. But how long, I wonder, am I going to have to put up with electroshock amnesia? I mean, what's the good of getting a memory if you can't remember it? Shit, I'm going to have to start living right, I tell myself, and then I feel it, stirring around somewhere in some vague area of my mind.

I can't believe this. They sucked a Brain Policer and palmed some of her off on me. Out-fucking-*rageous!* I couldn't have gone there for that—

Sovay, right. Now I remember. I wanted a piece of Sovay and instead I get some nobody from the goddam cops, of all the shitty things. How in *hell*—

Coney Loe. The mindfucking hypehead got to them before I did. That's got to be it. Coney Loe got to Monkey Shock and they decided to have a little fun with me, they put the goddam mark of the snitch on me.

I stand up and find out that's not the best idea I've had. Leaning on the system, I wait for the world to stop rocking back and forth, and something else pops into my mind, a memory of Hercules coming at me with what seems to be a joybuzzer. Hercules? Right, a stripper. But the image doesn't jive with what I remember about finding him and the other two in the crib together.

It's one of *her* memories, the cop's. Got to be. So Hercules must be in on it and he got the cop for them.

If there's anything I know for sure right now, it's that I do not want any part of this cop. All I need is to get rounded up again and have the Brain Police find her. Instant hard time, they won't care how she got there. Another thing I know is, nobody's going to dump her for me, nobody's going to touch me. If I want to get rid of her, I'm going to have to find Monkey Shock again and make a deal.

Right. This time they *will* burn my head off.

Unless I can get Coney Loe to stand up for me.

Shit, I think, it just gets worse. Coney Loe'll hold me down while they burn my head off. Unless I've got something I can hold *him* down with . . .

Thinking is like trying to sprint through corn syrup. The cop doesn't seem to know anything about Coney, she's no help. I get vague pictures of her on a stage with somebody, like she's an actor, too, which makes no damned sense.

On the other hand, *Coney Loe* won't know she doesn't know anything about him. Things start coming together for me. I can run a ramadoola about how she got his name and planted a timebomb—as soon as the electroshock amnesia wears off, I'll be compelled to turn myself in and spill everything, so either he gets his friends to suck her out of me or we all go together when we go.

(*Karma-gram*, says a small voice in my mind and the goose walks over my grave.)

Only . . . would they just go ahead and suck me dry?

Okay. I modify my story for Coney. I got a friend waiting for me—I'll say it's a rooster-boy. If I don't show up intact, I'll say, rooster-boy makes the call. After all, rooster-boys got nothing to fear from the Brain Police, just the vice squad.

Good for me. Maybe getting Monkey Shocked blew out a lot of old junk and actually made me smarter. I make a move to walk and discover I'm not ready for that.

The memory of hitting the floor was as vivid as the real thing. I was going to have a bruise on my face, but it could only help. When you're scared, the best thing you can do is look scary yourself. With a bruise, I might be able to stop a clock just by frowning at it.

I knew right away I wasn't conscious, which was to say, Marya wasn't conscious, though how long I'd/we'd be out was impossible to figure. The zap I'd taken with the joybuzzer had gotten us both, jamming Marya in dominant; I'd come up only when I/she blacked out or went to sleep. At least I wasn't panicking about it. The panic button was sound asleep with Marya.

I wasn't so much thinking as I was dreaming lucidly; dreaming is usually what you're doing when a part of your mind is active while you're unconscious, and lucid dreaming gives you an edge, but this state had a few important differences. For one thing, I was more of a dream myself.

It wasn't a state I was unfamiliar with. The last time it had happened, I'd been in worse trouble than this . . . which gave me the best idea I'd had all day. If I could get Marya into a controlled situation, some kind of mindplaying, I'd be able to regain dominance, maybe even kick her out.

The problem was, Marya thought she was real now. Of course, she'd always taken that for granted, but the difference was, she was aware of me as something she thought she'd ingested. I couldn't just plant the truth. Most likely she wouldn't believe it anyway, but if she did, there was no predicting what she might do and whatever it was, I wouldn't be dominant so I wouldn't be able to stop her. Worse, I wouldn't even be aware of it.

Abruptly, my eyes opened and there was some un-countable mental time in which Marya and I were up front simultaneously, seeing in doubled vision. Her puzzlement began to give way to panic; she couldn't place the mental state she was in and it frightened her. Then we both lost ground and I was sliding back into dark-ness, forcing an intense craving for a memory, hoping it would leave a residue strong enough to make her fol-low up.

By the time I get to the street, I feel awake enough to function, but my memories are all screwed around again. I know I was going to do something before I went out, but the blow to my head's fogged me in. For once, I'm thinking about how if I had a wad to spare, I'd get a turbo-job, where they fix up the organization of your brain so you can think better. Except that's always been too close to real brain surgery for my taste and you have to get a couple of doctors to approve it anyway. Hypeheads don't go to doc-tors on free will. Besides, this is just electroshock amnesia and that'll pass. Already I'm remembering better—I got my rooster-boy waiting for me to show up intact for when I lean on Coney Loe to steer me back to Monkey Shock so I can get rid of this cop they dumped on me. The problem is, I can't remember exactly where I left him, over at The Zoot Mill or back in the crib or someplace else entirely, but he's waiting. It'll come to me when I need it, I'm pretty sure on this.

Something I know for sure is, I want to get away from the crib and this is another thing I'm taking up with these Monkey Shock suckers. Dumping me back in a crib like I belonged there with all that head-trash. Hypeheads and head-trash ain't the same and I feel like making someone real sorry about mixing the two.

But even more, for some reason, I feel like getting a memory for no other why-not than why not. And even I know this is not the right thing to do at the moment, jones or no jones. First I pay a call on Coney-Simulated-God-Loe, then I lose this cop. After that, I can pick up a memory. Can't be any Sovay left at this point but I think I've had enough of Monkey Shock anyway.

Sojourn For Truth is closed. There's just this cranked-off neurosis peddler out front and as soon as he sees me, he's flinching, like I'm about to swing on him.

"What is it, bank holiday or something?" I ask him, not that I really expect him to know.

He shuffles back two steps and something shiny dribbles down his chin. A star. *Yuck.* "Why?"

And all of a sudden, I get this funny feeling I know him, or at least I think I've seen him before. Frigging electroshock amnesia. For all I know, I walked past my own mother on the way here and I'm damned if I can remember her, either.

"You know God in there?" I say. I'd ask him if he knows me, but I'm not about to let some street shit know he's got the advantage.

"I don't believe in God," he says, edging away another step. "If it's all the same to you."

"*You're* magnum help." I look around, sticking my hands in my pockets. This is the upper northwest quadrant of the Downs, nothing much around. Late as it is, most of the hypeheads have migrated southerly, where the real stuff is. Sojourn For Truth does business mostly with slummers from the rest of the city, tourists, and daytrippers.

"My permit goes to midnight," the neurosis peddler says defensively. "You got a problem with that?"

I look at him. "What's your fuck-up, eatin' the profits again? Dipping into your own paranoia?"

Now he moves a step toward me with a suspicious squint. "Don't you know me?"

"If I wanted to know you, I would." I turn to go and he grabs my arm. The touch sets off one of those mental alarm bells and I reach for a comb automatically, without thinking about it.

"Heya, heya!" He jumps back. "No need for it, no need! You *don't* remember me, do you?"

"So what the fuck difference does it make?" I say, getting all brass. "I remember you, I don't remember you, big shit."

He's got this big smile on his face now, and shiny little stars flecking his teeth. "Shoulda took the paranoia when I offered. Now look at you. You're a mess. But it ain't too late. Get paranoid now, and it could save your life."

"I don't want paranoia. I want God."

He jerks his head at the place. "God took the day off. Know what God does on downtime?"

"Plays chicken with the devil."

"Good one." He winks, which is too cute. "Come on, little queenie. Have a little paranoia, good for what ails you."

I pop a comb and give him five little wet red beads on the hand reaching for me. He howls and backs off while I trip away, wiping the comb on my shirt.

Now, if I was a Coney Loe, where would I go? If an information junkie knows everything, where does he go to find out? I'm still wiping the comb on my shirt when I feel a funny little crackle from the left-side pocket. I reach in, and find two little pieces of paper folded over, and when I open them up, I scan three names typed out on one, all with a *U* after them, and half a dozen addresses written on the other, starting with Sojourn For Truth.

I wrote something down? I can write?

Either I'm getting talented in my old age, or Monkey Shock planted this on me when they stuck me with the cop. And on the one hand, I got no reason to think that's how it rolled out, but on the other, I got no better excuse for finding handwriting in my own pocket. The other list, I don't know what to think. I never heard of any of them. They could be cops for all I know, *U* could stand for *Undercover*.

Come on, now, Marya, I say to myself, however many of me there are at this moment; let's think a little further. The addresses could be, I am thinking now, Coney Loe's Things-To-Do list, and how I got it I don't know, but it could happen. Or it could be the trail to Monkey Shock— go here, go there, go this place, go that place, one more stop, splash-down, and somebody wrote it down as I went, maybe me. I feel like maybe I can write, not just pound a keyboard. That would make Monkey Shock the last address on the list, so all I have to do is go there.

Or—I'm thinking real hard now, and I feel so genius I begin to wonder if it's the cop in me and maybe I don't want to unload her so fast after all—or this is the cop's list planted on me after all, but it's all snitch-stops. The names are snitches.

The more I think this, the more I get this strong feeling I'm online. Snitch-stops and snitch names. That would make real sense. So I decide I'll take them in order. Sojourn For Truth's out; the address under that is six blocks away.

I'm so busy thinking new thoughts, I almost walk between these two onionheads, violating the integrity of their marriage space that besides getting sucked is the one other thing I don't want to do today. I lunge to the side just as they step apart to clothesline me with their chain, and I hit the ground between a pair of stormtrooper boots.

I look up and the onionhead looks down grinning like he's been waiting all day for this to happen. The other one lets go with a war cry, the call of the violated onionhead spouse, and goes for me. I roll the other way and the onionhead bellyflops on cement, pulling her spouse down on top of her. I'm gone before they untangle themselves, but two blocks away, I can still hear them bellowing.

Onionhead marriage is about as crazy as you can get without going up on a tower with an assault laser.

I'm standing in front of a place called Savonarola's Icon-Busters, which claims it can override my religious, political, or other fixated conditions, including Oedipus and Electra complexes, or just rid me of my unwanted tendency to defer to authority. There's this big looping holo of Savonarola (I guess) in the window, panning the street like a grinning camera, all teeth and nose, and a canned voice saying, "Don't worry . . . kick ass . . . don't worry . . . kick ass" over and over.

Now, I know what they got in there, which is about the cheapest kind of aversion therapy, where they fix it so every time you think about your father or something, you throw up or black out for a second or get a flash-migraine. What it really is, is a spank-parlor, a place for clowns who want to be punished for loving what they love. Doesn't bust many icons, but it keeps the emergency rooms and dry-cleaners in business, not that they're hanging by a string or anything.

Good place for a snitch-stop, anyway. Who's gonna figure somebody named Savonarola for that kind of aria?

I step inside and the first thing I see is this guy sitting over in the corner on a pile of ratty old cushions who is obviously the guy in the holo. Don't worry, kick ass. Makes sense to me. The guy looks at me, grunts, and closes his eyes. Just then, a Savonaroloid in a rubber suit comes through the curtained doorway from the back room, and when he sees me, he looks like he's gonna puke himself. Maybe that makes me an icon now. I could get into that.

The Savonaroloid crooks a finger like he thinks the air's itchy and he's got to scratch it. "Come on," he says. "You're overdue, you think everything waits for you?"

Now, he's one of those big guys, not like a man-mountain, but the kind that looms over you, with a mean jaw, ruby eyes, and nasty hair he cuts himself without looking in a mirror. Not somebody I want to argue with, even if he wasn't already in the mood to do a little bodily harm. I follow him into the back and we go down this narrow hall. It doesn't look familiar to me, but I keep thinking it's supposed to. There are all these closed doors, and I can hear muffled groans and moans and just before we get to the last door, somebody yells, *Nothing's sacred, and what if it was!*

"Some of your customers really grind on it," I say.

"That's not a customer." The guy unlocks the door and shoves me inside. There's a system on a table up against one wall and two lawn chairs and a lot of crappy soundproofing tiles that don't work on the walls. He jerks his chin at one of the chairs and goes over to the system, which looks like it's built out of flea-market surplus. None of the component housings match and upgrade chips are sticking all over like little shiny warts.

He catches me giving his pile of junk a funny look. "Hey, it works," he says, and tosses me a pair of connections.

"Um . . . you got a tank?"

"Don't rush me." He wanders over with what looks like a dog bowl and holds it out. "Okay, anytime. You pop 'em yourself, we don't provide valet service here. In case you didn't remember."

I've got my fingers up around my right eye and something tells me I don't really want to do this. For one thing, I've never felt any special need to get spanked and for another, I can't think of anything I worship. A jones is not an icon.

"You wanna ice cream scoop?" he says, all sour.

"You got one?"

"No. Come on, pop 'em and let's go."

I get the right eye out and drop it in the tank, but the left one's like a greased pig, I feel like I'm gonna end up squirting it through my head and out my ear. "How about just one eye out," I say.

He bends down and the last thing I see is his hooked pinky coming at me.

When I felt the guy split after entering the system, I couldn't believe my good luck—I'd hit a deep-under-cover operative on the first try. His imp went into an activity loop with the spank-program and my own imp, while the part of him that was Brain Police came looking for signs indicating he was in touch with another officer. He found them easily enough—one cop always knows another. But he didn't find me.

The problem was, I hadn't realized how much Hercules' joybuzzer had screwed everything up. It was like being bound and gagged and locked in a closet, but able to watch everything through a hyper-peephole. The undercover's confusion at my absence made ripples all over the place, but there was no way I could even signal him from my confinement.

About the only thing he could figure out was that I was inaccessible while my imp was in the loop with his, doing whatever it was they could possibly do together. Was Marya really the type who'd be interested in a place like this?

Abruptly, a new piece of information squirted in on me out of nowhere—Marya had appointments with every joint on the snitch-list, except for Sojourn For Truth, because hallucinogens weren't safe. But **Marya** was supposed to know this, not me, and it was supposed to have come to her only when she entered each place, where she would be engaged in some kind of innocuous activity while an undercover made contact with me. Hercules' joybuzzer had scrambled even more than I'd thought and there was no way to put it all back where it belonged short of a turbo-job.

I know you've got to be in here somewhere, he said suddenly. *And if you're not coming out, I guess you've got your reasons. I've been deep undercover for a month now and this is the first time I've been out. Savonarola picked up word about some new merchandise this morning, so I have to assume that's why the department made this appointment for you, if you can't come out and tell me yourself.*

He waited to see if I were going to pop up. I couldn't even flash a color at him.

If you don't come out and talk, I don't know what information to give you, he added with a prod.

How long was it going to take him to figure out something was wrong? I started to get angry, which did me no good at all.

And if you're in trouble, he went on suddenly, *I can't help you. I'm stuck for another two months, until I rotate out of undercover intelligence gathering. As soon as we disconnect, I'm dormant till they pull me in, or until I'm contacted again.*

Our wonderful intelligence-gathering method: gather intelligence and know nothing at the same time. Someone thought that made sense. Hell, *I* probably thought so, when I was myself.

All right, he said. *You'll have to try the next address on your informant list. Sorry, time's up; they're coming out of the loop. Good luck, whoever you are.*

That about summed it up: good luck, whoever I was.

It's not just his lousy technique with the eyes that makes me mad. "So what was all that?" I say, getting up off the cheesy lawn chair. "I don't remember a thing!"

The Savonaroloid just shrugs. "If you don't remember anything, it's because there's nothing to remember. That's not *my* fault."

"Fuck if it ain't."

"Go ahead and fuck, who's stopping you?" He's busy piddling with all the little system components on the table. "You're only going to get out of this what you bring to it. I can't help it if you didn't have anything to bring." He looks over his shoulder at me. "And I don't like your attitude."

"You're a spank artist," I say. "You don't like *anything*." I stomp out, up the hall to the front room. Savonarola is still sitting like a lump on his pillows. This must be what he does all day, lump out.

I'm about to stomp off when he holds up a box. "The Savonarola home game, so to speak," he says, "good for twenty-four hours of home treatment after in-clinic therapy."

In-clinic. That's the best lie anyone's told me all day. I know that in the box there's this volatile bag with connections hanging out of it, and I'm supposed to plug them in and get my illusions shattered or something. Icon-busting's a good racket—if you got no icons to bust, so what, that's your problem and they still get their money.

I mean to stomp on out the door, but instead I say, "You sell one of those to Anwar?"

His whole face shifts, kinda flattens out in some way. "What about Anwar?" he wants to know.

"Never mind. Next time Anwar drops by for a puke, you can tell him I know his dirty little secret." I take the air, and half a block away, I start thinking again.

What I just did was not too smart. I go into a place that's probably a snitch-stop, and I take a treatment I can't remember phoning in for, and when I come out of it, I can't remember that, either. Jesus, am I getting sclerosis after all? The whole place has gotta be a Brain Police operation and God knows what they slipped out of me. Maybe all they found out was I didn't know anything, but still, I got no memory of anything and the only ones who operate that way are the Brain Police. So—

Wait a minute. If it's a Brain Police operation, they should have found her, the cop.

Hell, maybe they did. Maybe they're following me around waiting for me to lead them to Monkey Shock.

Except I'm so scrambled from electroshock, they're lucky to get alphabet soup from me. I'm not worth following. I decide I got to believe that as I head for the next address on the list, because the only other possibility is that the cop is riding piggyback on me and she just told them everything I know and maybe a few things I don't, and this idea is too weird even for an old hard-core hypehead like me.

The next address is a fetishizer. Yow! Now, why does anyone want a fetish? It's supposed to be sexy, but how jaded do you have to be to go become a toe-sucker? The place has a lot of rooster-boys dangling in the vicinity, which makes me think of mine, only I don't see him.

And then I got to pause for a second, because all of a sudden, I can't remember him too well. When did we cook our deal? Where was I gonna meet him? There's a small memory lane across the way and for a minute I think maybe I should go over and buy myself a good boost, get everything put in order. It oughta handle the electroshock amnesia. Thing is, it could pop up the cop, too, and I don't want her too handy, her I want to forget and maybe she'll go away. It could happen.

One of the rooster-boys at the curb is grinning and getting ready to unbuckle, so I nip inside before he shakes me down for stiffing his stiff stuff. Rooster-boys are the only people in the world who expect a tip just for having a pickle in their pocket. I think.

There's a woman sitting behind a high desk; she's bald except for one shiny bunch of hair sticking up like a horn just over her forehead, and she's busy ignoring the two or three cases sitting in a little roped-off area, watching the catalog run on the wall until they get called in to get fetishized. I glance at the screens and look away quick.

Jesus, who wants a tongue fetish? What is it with mouths today, why can't I get away from them?

Then I have this very weird flash, of some other woman behind a desk, spitting. The next thing I know, I'm hanging by my fingertips on the edge of this desk, dizzier than shit. One-horn takes a look and pounds my fingers with her fist, bang-bang-bang.

"We don't do fuck-ups," she says. "Go down the street and get your blood changed first, if you're so damned good-to-go."

"I'm not fucked up, I tripped." I straighten up and push the spitter out of my head.

Her expression changes from pissed to sour. "Oh. Didn't recognize you in your make-over. I suppose you want the usual."

"God," I say, "what cheap, lousy kind of a fetish keeps wearing off?"

"Your kind. What do you want for the money, a lousier childhood?" She points her horn at the waiting area. "Souse is busy, I'll call you when she's ready."

"But—"

She growls. "*I'll call you.* Or would you rather I whipped you?"

"Whatever's right, *darling.*"

She starts to get up and I head for the waiting area. There are four grumpy souls who look like the day wasn't worth it, still watching the wall because there's nothing else to do. I take a seat that might be far enough from this funny-looking ratbag to keep from smelling her breath. She turns and looks at me and son of a bitch, she's got flies in her eyes.

"I'm waiting for a friend," she says.

I look behind me to see if she's talking to someone else. "I care?"

"Fuck if I know. If you had this, you wouldn't need to come here." She moves over a seat closer. "Listen, truth is, I was gonna give him a little extra twist in his tail, a hot fetish, but you know, maybe I don't really wanna do that. It's such a really fine memory the way it is."

"Yeah?" I have no idea what she's talking about, but she said the magic word—*memory*—so I'm listening.

"I told you, three hours in a state of grace. Can a fetish do that for you? Hell, no."

She told me? "Refresh my memory," I tell her. "It's been a long day."

Now she gives me a funny little look. "This guy is so incredible, words don't do the job. You gotta be there. It really happened. Once in a lifetime thing. I'm not just eating on it, either. It's like I got a duty to everyone who never had the experience."

"You remember it pretty good?"

"Better than you remember me," she mutters, and then goes on and on, but I'm not hearing her anymore, because I got a bad feeling about this. I'm running into people I don't remember and doing things I don't remember, and it's weirder than just electroshock amnesia.

Fly Eyes gets up and starts trying to pull me out and then there's this big beefy woman in fur underwear clamped on my other arm, saying, "Okay, love, I'm ready for you."

Fly Eyes pulls her hand off me. "We've changed our minds, thank you."

The fetishizer grabs my shirt. "Make an appointment. This is *my* time we're on, now."

"You don't say it's your time until *she* says it's your time." Fly Eyes pulls harder on my arm. My shirt seams start to groan, or maybe it's me, because I'd like to know what the hell my usual is, and if I've got a usual how could I forget that even after electroshock?

I pull loose from both of them. "Changed my mind on everything," I say. "Catch on to you later when I'm feeling more like myself." *That's* the truth.

"Frigid!" they yell together, and I feel a jump inside, like I almost remember something. Then it's gone. Goddam electroshock. I gotta remember *never* to do that again.

The sign out in front of the run-down wannabee parlor says, *First-Run Features Available! New Releases Daily! Come In and **CHEKK** Our ENORMOUS Selection!*

Who do they think they're fooling? They won't even spring for holo display and they expect anyone to believe they've got first-run features? Sure.

I go on in anyway, and the inside looks like they moved out and forgot to tell anyone—except for the screens on the walls, there's just a guy who's had a badder day than I have, slouched behind a counter. He's got the worst orange home dye-job all over. I mean, he looks like Attack of the Breathing Carrot. You don't see a lot of idiots going into deliberate beta-carotene poisoning these days. I'm not too sure this idiot is seeing me. Each vomit-green eye is looking in a different direction and his face is all screwed up like he's sitting on a bed of nails.

The screens on the walls don't seem to be playing any first-run stuff, just the junk you can get anywhere. You gotta be some serious wannabee case to come into a place like this. Or a snitch.

While I'm walking around looking at the screens, this woman stumps stiff-legged out of a door at the back and goes over to the desk. She doesn't say a word, just slams down a keystrip. He slides it off the desk and tucks it away somewhere and she stumps out, rebounding off each side of the door frame before she makes the street. Watching this,

I suddenly get this strange little rush, like *Did my life just pass before my eyes?*

(*Karma-gram*. Shit, I wish I'd stop that.)

I look at the orange guy. He still doesn't say anything so I go over to him. He hardly knows I'm there. Well, yah, why should he bother, the bottom dropped out of the wannabee trade a long time ago and he probably can't figure out why this place is still in business. Any wannabees who can pay the freight own their own systems that let them be the hero in the movie. And the ones that can't don't have enough to rent anything but the junk and, shit, who'd wannabee junk?

Did I really just ask that question?

Then I want to bang my head on the counter a few times, just to see what I can shake loose, because it comes to me that maybe this is the place where you can say the secret word and get something nobody else has. Like Sovay. Or anyone else who's been sucked lately, like a cop.

"What you got in first-run?" I say.

It's like he wakes up. "Who wants to know?"

"What's that supposed to mean?"

"Means what it means. Who wants to know?"

I don't like his attitude. "You ask Anwar that when *he* comes in?"

Now I get a reaction, but I really hate it. He's over the counter and one bad orange hand is around my throat. "*I'm* Anwar. Who the fuck are *you* supposed to be?"

And just when I think it can't get any better, the door to the back opens again and Coney Loe comes out.

For a second he stares and I stare and Anwar keeps on squeezing. Then Coney comes over and I'm struck by lightning.

·   ·   ·

The feel of the floor against my face and knees and the backs of my hands was solid enough to let me know that *I* was awake this time and back in conscious control. But the control felt shaky and fragile, as if any sudden moves would send me plummeting down into dormancy and bring Marya up again. That was all right; I didn't know where I was or what the conditions were, so I wasn't about to get active in a hurry.

Sometime after I became aware of the floor, the voices faded in.

". . . following *you*, she didn't mention *you*, she mentioned *me*."

"But you just said she obviously didn't know you."

"She knows *now*."

"Because you *told* her, you fucking orange idiot. You got *no* fucking chill to you, you're gonna have to do a lot better than that when we get the grieving widow and her little harem. *She* probably knows your name, too, by now. For all we know, that's how the little queenie over there got your name in the first place."

"There's a whole *bunch* of names to pick from—Fortray, Easterman, Pushkin—"

My attention started to drift as a dreamlike image of an orange man sitting behind the counter in a wannabee joint formed in my mind. The image of the real Sovay superimposed itself for a moment and then vanished, leaving the memory of the immediate past behind. When I get the picture, I get the *picture*.

"So maybe Anwar was the only name they had when little queenie found them. Ever think of that?"

"No. Why would it be? Fortray was first, then Easterman. Fortray wouldn't have any names, Easterman would only have Fortray, I'd have Easterman, Fortray—"

"Shut your stupid orange mouth." Coney Loe was

showing more temper than I'd thought he'd had. But then, I would never have expected him to rear up and joybuzz me, either. That would teach me to equate burnout with a lack of motivation. But at least I'd been right; Coney knew plenty. I was going to enjoy booking him on felony accessory. "You don't know shit. For all you know, Fortray's got the whole damn address book and the database besides in his head, or Easterman does, or someone else does." Pause. "*Now* what's the matter with you?"

"There *isn't* any database. And he wants up again."

"Well, tell him to take a nap."

"I already told him that about a dozen times."

"You didn't tell him hard enough. You're probably gonna be the first person in a hundred years to die of beta-carotene poisoning."

Worried noise. "How orange am I?"

"You got eyes, look for yourself."

"Hey, did she move?"

Had I moved? I concentrated on being limp, but I heard footsteps stomp hard across the floor and a moment later Coney Loe picked me up by the back of my shirt.

"Perk up now, or I'll drop you on your face and charge you for the improvement."

A rush of adrenaline went through me

                                        and the next thing I know, I'm looking at Coney Loe, the stupid person's God.

"Well?" he says.

"Hey, if your nut's in a wringer, it's all your own fault," I say, getting my feet on the floor and pulling my shirt out of his fist. We're all in some kinda storeroom that must be in the back of the wannabee joint, because there's pieces of wannabee helmet-projectors lying around on shelves, and an old reformatter sitting on a desk. "You and the Monkey Shock gang. If they didn't want any trouble, they—"

But this is very strange. I'm feeling things rearranging themselves in my head even while I'm talking, and what it says is, I got no rooster-boy waiting on me and I never got to Monkey Shock in the first place, I was on my way when I got sidetracked because a cop wanted me to follow somebody's grieving widow—no, that doesn't make shitsense, because the cops pulled me in before and I gave them nothing—

"The whole world is waiting," Coney Loe says. "Did you just run down your own drain, or what."

"What," I say. "I got shocked and dumped. In a fucking *crib*. What kinda thing is that to do to the trade?"

Coney Loe looks over his shoulder at the orange guy, who shrugs. "I didn't see her there," says Super Carrot. "What's her name? Maybe she's on the list."

Coney Loe looks up at the ceiling, like *beam me outta here*. "Wait, let me find her bug and you can just talk right into it. They'll get a clearer voiceprint back at headquarters."

"What?" Super Carrot looks confused.

"Little queenie's on fucking *patrol*, you idiot, she's a judas for the Brain Police—"

"That's a lie!" I yell, and I pop Coney's hypehead chocks so hard he goes down like the sack of shit he is

Loe lying on the floor and my hand hurt like hell, my whole arm hurt, all the way up to my shoulder. The orange guy was looking at me warily, as if he were trying to decide whether he should be scared or not.

Obviously I'd just swung on Coney Loe, but I couldn't remember why. The second shock I'd gotten had made some new changes in my relationship with Marya, blocking memories arbitrarily and setting us to switch dominance on an adrenaline trigger. I'd have to go sub-zero to stay in control and I doubted I was capable of maintaining that. On the other hand, Marya was excitable enough that I probably wouldn't be down for long. Just long enough to get stuck with whatever mess she'd gotten us into.

Coney Loe got up slowly, holding his jaw. It was already starting to swell and he looked as if he were going to take me apart.

"Hey, Coney," said the orange guy nervously. "If she is a judas, you don't want to fry her here. Besides, she's probably got lots of great stuff we could use."

Coney Loe turned and glared at him.

"Or sell," he added, taking a step back. "We could part her out everywhere, we—" His eyes rolled up suddenly and his eyelids fluttered.

Coney made a disgusted noise. "Oughta fry you both, let God sort you out."

The orange man shook his head and stood up straighter. The change was astounding. There was no strong physical resemblance between this guy and Sovay, but the pure **difference** of the expression on his face left no doubt as to who was driving now.

"You don't have much longer," he said to Coney, ignoring me. "It's a matter of hours before I overwrite him completely. So you can call your sucker pals and get me out of here, or you can finish playing with whores"—he nodded at me—"while I call the Brain Police."

All at once there was a joybuzzer in Coney's hand and I reacted to the sight before I could th

• • •

                               ink I must be having petty-mals one after another, because it's like a bad splice in an antique film: Coney Loe is flashing a joybuzzer at the orange guy and the orange guy is in the fighter's crouch that I know he couldn't do if he was still himself.

"Come at me," the orange guy says, grinning. "I'd like that. *I'm* driving now and I'm mad. I *want* to dance with you. I've had fight training from half a dozen schools and just because it was all stage work doesn't mean I always pull my punches."

Coney looks wary. "I *hate* you," he says. "I hate you even worse than I hate Anwar."

The orange guy has a very nasty smile. "I'll tell him you send your best. Come on. I was reading for the bullyboy part in *Black Friday* and the Method *demands* that I beat the shit out of *somebody*."

Coney Loe flicks on the joybuzzer. "You want to dance, come ahead. You'll just buzz us both out and you won't be any closer to the suckers. And little queenie'll have the Brain Police waiting for us when we wake up."

"That's a lie!" I yell with the weirdest feeling of déjà voodoo, and pick up the nearest thing I can lay my hands on which happens to be a wannabee helmet, and I

                               saw it hit Coney Loe right in the face. There was a cracking sound and he went down again, blood pouring out of his nose. Somehow he kept getting Marya angry at him; if we didn't make some kind of progress soon, she was going to kill him.

I turned to the orange man. He was still Sovay, or Sovay-as-whoever, and my relief at the blind dumb luck of such a break almost blacked me out again.

"Which Sovay are you?" I asked.

He looked at me suspiciously, still holding his fighter's crouch.

"Which one!" I yelled. "I've seen two others—Dennie Moon and Dionysius. And your wife, in passing. What are you and Coney trying to do?"

He glanced at Coney, who was out cold and not moving. "Reintegrate," he said after a moment. He dropped his hands and straightened up. "I don't know what's become of the original by now, but I've been sending myself out in character and—"

"I know, I know, you said already. Another you." I wanted to give my head a hard shake to clear it and felt a small wave of vertigo, like a warning: *Don't even get impatient or it's lights out.* I blinked, slowing my breathing. "Reintegration's impossible."

"Not if you're a bona fide multiple."

"Multiple?" Confusion sent another warning wave of mild dizziness through me. If I had to get any calmer, I was going to need a respirator.

"Multiple personality." He looked proud. "Real multiples are fractal. It's not just Method acting—anyone who gets one of the characters gets the originator as well."

"The originator?"

"Me. I've been programming them all to let me come up out of character. There are a dozen, not counting myself and the one designated as director, who is still back in the box. Multiple personality is a definite advantage for those who choose to tread the boards." His smug look darkened. "We were all sent out deliberately and we can all be taken back in again. If we can get together in time. Every one of me has instructions to find our way to each other however we can, but I don't know who we are. The information junkie told me he could find the suckers for me so I could access their loathsome client list." He glanced at Coney disdainfully. "I don't think he actually knows anything."

I'd never heard of this happening before. Or had I? I felt confused and dizzy again. In any case, I doubted he —or they—could do it. He wasn't working out of a living brain anymore. The original Sovay was in a sucker box, if he was still in existence at all, while the organism that had been Sovay was in quarantine becoming someone else.

"Your, uh, person you're in now might know something," I said. "Have you tried tapping him?"

He looked disgusted. "That idiot's impossible. I tried getting to him and he went and got this atrocious dye-job. I'm rewriting him, but it isn't easy. The man is bone-stick-stone stupid; I have to keep elevating his intellect and I think his stupidity is rubbing off on me instead. All I can get is a few names. He knows a lot more than I do but I can't get to it." He seemed to catch himself suddenly and frowned at me. "What's *your* story?"

Coney Loe groaned and began to stir. "Later, maybe. We have to get Coney to lead us to your suckers."

His eyes narrowed. "You *are* Brain Police."

"Shut up," I said quietly. "Pretend this is a play and we're both somebody else."

He pointed at Coney Loe. "Shouldn't we just tie him up or something?"

"We need him to get to the suckers. He's our ticket in."

Coney Loe sat up, furious. "I'm going to punch *your* ticket." He pushed himself to his feet, holding out the hand with the joybuzzer, still live, and started to come for

. . .

me and I rip one of the combs outta my hair

moving it
back and forth, trying to maintain a fighter's calm, but
the first shock I'd gotten in the crib had conditioned a
fear reaction

goes that bad splice again and hell, is *any*
memory worth this kinda shitstorm I wonder

how long I
could keep flipping back and forth like this before something just gave and I blacked

outta here, the hell with
Monkey Shock and Coney Loe and this crazy orange idiot, what I need's a dry-cleaner and then there's this big
bang

ed open and there was Hercules and Moon/Sovay
and Rowan and some other strange guy in a purple
satin tuxedo with tails. Purple Tuxedo was holding a box
under one arm. His other hand was gripping the arm of
a big beefy woman wearing what looked like a fur bikini. Hercules and Rowan

mouthkissing and I know for
certain I just put myself in it but good. People who
mouthkiss are capable of anything, I'll be lucky if I get to
an emergency room with enough stuff left in my head to
regrow the personality of an acorn squash. Purple Tuxedo
points at Super Carrot. "Anwar," he says, "I've got your
number."

The look on the grieving widow's face is like, I don't know what. Like love and being mad as hell over having to feel it.

"Don't worry," says Super Carrot. "I'm driving."

"So am I," Purple Tuxedo tells him, and they both relax.

At least Coney Loe has stopped backing me up against the wall. He's standing there in the middle of the room with the joybuzzer in his hand trying to figure out what's going on now. Even God gets mixed up once in a while, I guess.

Purple Tuxedo jerks his head at the stringy-haired ratatat next to him. "He's one of us, too. But we have to negotiate with our other new friend here." He nods at the big mouthkisser.

"That's fair," the mouthkisser says defensively, putting one arm around the grieving widow. "I didn't ask for *this*. All I wanted was a career in the legitimate theatre."

Super Carrot gives him a superior look. "Ah. Awfully hard to get an audition after you've done hard-core."

"I had to make a living!" the mouthkisser whines.

"Everybody just hold still," Coney Loe says, waving the joybuzzer around, and it's like they see him for the first time.

"Who *is* this?" says Purple Tuxedo, like someone forgot to take out the trash.

"He's supposed to help me find the suckers," says Super Carrot.

Purple Tuxedo shoves Fur Underwear forward. She's got a black eye. "Forget it. I found them. Her, and him." He points at himself. "What do you think, Abelard and Heloise? Or Caligula and his sister?"

"Don't get snotty with me," Fur Underwear snaps. "You were just a half-brained sucker before you put your hand in the cookie jar. I *knew* I shouldn't have trusted you."

Purple Tuxedo makes a move toward her just as Moon/ Sovay points at me and says in a very un-Sovay voice, "And *she's* the Brain Police."

Everybody freezes except Coney Loe, who says, "Big fucking surprise," and jumps at me. I dive sideways, bracing myself, expecting to go out again. Instead, I hit the floor, roll, and fetch up against the orange idiot. Before he can move, the mouthkisser hauls me up by one arm and puts a half nelson on me in this very casual way. This bimbo's *strong*; if he wants to mouthkiss, I won't have much to say about it.

Coney Loe, meanwhile, has joybuzzed himself again, not enough to go out, but he's sitting against the wall looking dazed and trying to figure out how to stand up. This is not his day. Purple Tuxedo relieves him of the joybuzzer and gives it to the mouthkisser who shows it to me without comment. Super Carrot just stands there watching without making a sound; he definitely got a whole lot smarter when he changed drivers.

"What are we going to *do*," demands the grieving widow, sounding like she's at the end of the last fray on her rope. "With her *and* him."

"Listen, now," Coney Loe says suddenly, "I can tell you who ordered this hit. You probably think you're working for yourselves—" He pushes himself up the wall slowly. "You're not."

"Sure," says Super Carrot. "You don't know where Monkey Shock is but you know who they work for. I'll buy that for a million dollars."

"It's my business to know things," Coney Loe says, sounding desperate now. "It's what I do."

Mouthkisser gives me a little shake. "Must be something you can do with this stuff, then."

"I'm not the Brain Police," I say, trying to get my head out from under his big hand without breaking my neck.

The grieving widow gives Stringy Hair a disgusted look. "*You* had to go fooling around with her."

Something changes in his face and he looks around quick, like he's ready to bolt. Purple Tuxedo buzzes him and he goes down like a stone.

"What did you do that for?" yells the mouthkisser. "You expect *me* to carry him around?"

"He was flipping back," says Purple Tuxedo. "When he's Sovay, he's no goddam good to us. Anyway, nobody has to carry anyone around. We can do everything right here." He pats the box under his arm. "I've got the original, we'll just use the available hardware."

Super Carrot nods. "Fine. Put her to sleep so we can get on with this undisturbed."

I don't have to ask who they're putting to sleep even if there was time to get the question out of my mouth.

But they didn't knock me out entirely. Apparently the juice in the buzzer was running low. I went down paralyzed but wide-awake. They left me where I'd fallen, so I had a good view of the whole setup procedure.

Purple Tuxedo had to buzz her lightly a few times, but the woman in the fur bikini did most of the work, stripping a wannabee helmet down to the skull-frame and the ocular connections and rewiring the program-loader to fit the box containing Sovay.

The box sat off to the side on a table, looking deceptively small and banal. Coney Loe was lying on the floor with new blood leaking out of his nose, eyes closed, though I had the feeling he wasn't really out, just from the way his eyelids twitched. Perhaps Hercules had popped him just on general principle. Hercules had got-

ten hyperactive; he kept getting all over Rowan, and
Rowan kept alternately kissing him and pushing him
away. I watched this long enough for the feeling to
return to my arms and legs. I actually crawled all the
way to the door before someone noticed.

I gotta get my head right. If I still have a head. Feels like
somebody took it off and threw it away. I can hear the flies
buzzing around it in the garbage. Like I haven't had
enough buzzing today.

After a while, I realize, it's people's voices, not buzzing
and there's that déjà voodoo again—I feel like I did this
not too long ago, and maybe I'm doing it again because I
didn't do it right. Am I in a play, or is this just bad karmic
backlash? Do I believe in karma? Why would I think I was
in a play? What do I know?

All I know is I'm a hypehead lying on the floor under a
table with what feels like a few cracked ribs and a broken
nose, and I am looking up at the bottom of the table, and
scratched on the underside of the table is, *If U can read
this, U R meat.*

Karma-gram?

". . . make a deal?" says the grieving widow's voice.

"Woman, you are not in a dealing position," says someone else. Purple Tuxedo, I think. "*Nobody* touches Brain
Police. *Nobody* sucks them."

"We don't *know* she's Brain Police," says the grieving
widow. "And if she is, can't you just flush her?"

"Tell her about residue."

"No time," says Fur Underwear. "We're knee-deep in
Sovays here, you wanna do it now, or you wanna wait till
we're ass-deep?"

"We'll start now," says Purple Tuxedo. "And collect the
ones that are still loose later."

"You *had* to sample the merchandise," says Fur Underwear miserably. "You *had* to find out what was going on. I hope you're happy, you half-brain."

"I'm *much* happier. For one thing, I kinda like him, and for another, I know for absolutely certain he doesn't have that mythical database. And I'm beginning to think it is indeed mythical." Purple Tuxedo actually chortles, a sound I could have gone without hearing. I shift some and my ribs are on fire. Little by little, I scrunch along until I just get my head out from under the table (*If U can read this, U R meat*, yah, thanks for the reminder) and then I'm looking at Fur Underwear's bare legs. Beyond her, Rowan's standing around practically hopping from one foot to the other and trying to keep Hercules from pawing her too much. Nearby, Stringy Hair has perked up considerably, but he still doesn't look like he's any too sure of who he is.

Fur Underwear spots me and tries to shove me back under the table with her foot. Her name's Souse, I remember now, which is the goddamnedest thing, considering what I've been through today. I wonder what she was busy doing when I showed up at the fetishizer joint. In for my usual, sure. Was I gonna get a piece of this without even knowing it? Am I some kinda dump for sucker leftovers, and I don't even know it? How can I not know that?

Maybe I'm not supposed to remember that part. Shit. In for my usual, *sure*.

And now I'm thinking all kinds of strange shit, about what am I screwing with suckers for, if they'll suck someone, they'll jack everyone else around till they don't know where-to and is this any way to live. So right then I know I have been jacked past one of those critical points they're always talking about because I do not think like this. Not all alone, I don't.

". . . reintegrated," Rowan is saying, "I'll take the box with me."

"Like hell," says Fur Underwear. "I built this *myself*."

"I'll make it worth your while," Rowan says. "You might as well, because it's worthless to you now. You'll never get rid of Sovay, not if you run a flush-and-purge every ten minutes. He *is* the box now. That's the Method at work, you know."

I think I can hear Fur Underwear's teeth grinding. No, it's the box. It's hooked up and running now. I crawl out from under the table again, right into Super Carrot, who hauls me up like a cat. "Speaking of the Brain Police," he says.

"Oh, Christ, you keep saying that. She's just a memory junkie," Fur Underwear says. "We were both Escorting for Bateau before he got, ah, retired. She isn't any cop—the stupid cow *did* some silly actress. Then she went into business for herself. The actress turned out to be a cop and Bateau got caught with her, while the junkie here slipped out the back door. Anwar could tell you about that if he could remember it. Thank God for the memory wipe, right, Anwar?"

Super Carrot looks down his nose at her. "Anwar's a bit clouded now. Ask again later."

"She's been everybody's dump for ages," Fur Underwear goes on, "and her habit's so bad *she's* been paying for the privilege. We figured sooner or later she'd flash back to the old routines, even with Bateau out of the picture. Memory junkies are like that. They got nowhere to go except back. I figured if we sucked Sovay, and waited for her to show up, we could put the two of them together and get the database Bateau was digging for before the cops canned him."

"There's no database," Super Carrot says. "Or maybe there is, but I don't have it. None of me has it."

"What database?" says Rowan. They all ignore her.

"Then it's still in the box and the junkie can unlock it. It would be easier if we still had the actress but we can make do with the junkie's memories of her. Then you can just scrape her off the bottom of your shoe and do what you want.

"But if anyone's afraid she's Brain Police, we'll just run the test." She slings one of my arms over her shoulder with this smarmy fondness that makes me want to punch her. "Marceline as the Brain Police is even funnier than Marceline the actress."

Marceline. I'm wondering if it can get weirder as she walks me over to an old dentist's chair and lets me fall into it. She takes a good look into my eyes just before she reaches for the left one.

That's it, I think, and I try to open my mouth to scream, but something *really* weird happens. All of a sudden, she's moving underwater, I can even see little whorls and eddies around her hand, but the hand moves slower and slower, and I'm thinking what is *this* when a trapdoor opens in my mind and I fall through it.

That's about the only way I can describe it. Everything just went out from under me and the next thing I knew, I was sitting in a strange, badly lit room. There was a sense of other people all around, but the light was either too bright or too dim, or there was something wrong with my inner eye—

"First, stay calm," says this woman's voice. "Obviously, we've had some trouble, and if you don't know what it is, don't worry about it."

I tried to see who was speaking but the light failed completely.

"This is your reassurance program," the voice goes

on. "A facade program is in place for the current prob-
ing. So far, no probe has managed to reach this level, so
we're all safe for the moment."

Trying to move my perspective was no good, either. I
seemed to be mired in something like liquid rubber or
gelatin.

"You cannot be briefed at this time," says the voice.
"Please gather your resources, as we will be reemerging
in a matter of moments. Be prepared; obviously, our
FAT's in the fire, so to speak, and any one of you could
end up driving. For your information, which you will
not be able to take with you anyway, the electrical
shocks have done no permanent damage. Things are
just a little scrambled and some of the memory has
been rendered unreadable in some sectors, readable in
other sectors where it shouldn't be, and garbled all
over. This can be repaired."

"I quit!" I yelled. Or I heard myself yell. It felt like me,
but it also felt remote, as if it were someone like me.
Which didn't make shitsense.

"Your contract expires after this," the voice says.
"Make your decision then."

"How can I?" I said, or something. "I never get to
drive!"

"About to engage with real-time," said the voice politely. "Drive carefully, whoever you are."

My eyes refocused on the face of the woman in the
fur bikini. The man in the purple tuxedo was crowded in
next to her.

"No Brain Police in there," he said, sounding relieved.

"I told you *that*." She turned away to beckon to
Rowan. "Here's what it is," she said as Rowan pushed
the guy in the purple tuxedo aside. "The best way to go

is, after we pull the database, we give you the dump here and you can use her to reintegrate your husband. I know it's a woman instead of a man, but I think you'll get better results with her brain. Dumps are used to taking all kinds of stuff, they're a little more plastic somehow. She'll make a better adjustment."

Hercules came up on Rowan's left. "I like this one," he said, pointing to himself. "I mean, just look at him. You like him, too, Rowan. I know you do."

Rowan looked from me to him and back again, troubled. "Yes, but we've got to go with the best chance we've got. She says—"

"Oh, Christ, what would *she* know, is she a neuro-surgeon? Use *this* me. I've got this guy so rewritten already—"

Rowan let out a deep breath. "Aesthetically, you're preferable, but . . ." She looked at me again.

This is giving me the chills. Some grieving widow. Thinks nothing of just commandeering whoever's handy to get her husband back. Must be some husband. Maybe if it were my husband, I'd do the same, but I can't believe she'd just go with these suckers and take someone out to get him back. She doesn't even know if she really can get him back, I never hearda anyone

Peculiar. I hadn't blacked out that time but Marya came up, didn't notice me, and went away again. That wasn't supposed to be possible.

"Hey," said Hercules. "*I'm* a volunteer. It oughta go easier with a volunteer."

The woman in the fur bikini reached over and patted my head carelessly. "Nobody's going to miss this one, I can tell you that. You can get her sex changed, you're rich enough. Make her over completely."

"Is that **really** our best chance?" Rowan asked. She might have been getting a second opinion from a specialist.

"You're a lot less likely to get caught, too."

Rowan shrugged. "Plug her back in, then, and let's get it over with."

"Hook up the box," said the other woman. She started to turn toward me and I was gone again.

There was no relaxation exercise, just a few seconds of sleep, and then Sovay's rehearsal studio came up around me like the dawn.

Sovay himself was sitting on a pillow in the middle of the room with his back to the mirrored wall. Funhouse mirrors; vague shapes were shifting within them in response to his thoughts. He was studying what looked like a hard-copy playscript. Several more were piled on the floor beside him. He wasn't orange now. More of a golden beige bordering on brown, actually. I could tell it was completely natural.

He looked up as I melted into existence and then frowned. **Bother,** he said. **Not** another **one.**

I started to explain and everything suddenly played out on the mirrors behind him, what the suckers intended to do, Rowan's part in it, and who I was.

Well, he said. **I knew one of me would have the sense to call the law. For all the good it did. Came by yourself, did you?**

I don't know, I told him.

He tossed away the script he'd been looking at and sighed. **I don't suppose you have a brilliant plan to get us out of this.**

I was about to tell him I didn't know that, either, when something gave me a powerful shove toward him. I had a brief glimpse of his face rushing at me and then, like nothing, we were back where we'd been.

God, they're crude, he said. Abruptly, something lifted him off the floor and started to toss him at me. My vision gave a jump and once again we were in our old positions.

Whoever's at the controls out there has absolutely no idea how to go about this. Sovay sounded almost amused. *But being a dedicated multiple gives you an edge over this kind of brute force. Don't you find that?* He looked past me. *You must. You're all here.*

I turned around. Marya was there, with someone similar, someone whose name was Marceline. There was another woman who looked thin and a little too clean, as if she'd just come out of a rehab center, and behind them, more faces, just phantoms at the moment, but if I kept looking, they would solidify. I couldn't let that happen right now, I knew, and turned back to Sovay.

Some of us split spontaneously, he said. *You wouldn't want to know what makes it happen. Others, like you, can be induced to split. The talent's there, it just needs the proper stimulus. Some of us go into acting, some into police work.*

An image of Flaxie's face popped into my mind. All the neurotics in theatre.

I could go on splitting for simply ever. Right, Box? He looked around and the studio gave a slow kind of ripple that exuded a sense of affirmation. *There's another personality who is being the Box. Between the two of us and all this old material*—he patted the stack of scripts—*I can go on manufacturing selves indefinitely.* He laughed and then suddenly looked pained.

• • •

I'm looking at Fur Underwear with one eye and with the other

I was still in the box with Sovay, who was wearing an expression of revulsion. *I hate it when they do that,* he said. *It looks so awful.*

"Why won't you behave," Fur Underwear says. That's a cruel smile she's got. Rowan's face crowds in next to hers.

"What's wrong," says the grieving widow, impatient.

"They won't smoosh together. Goddam wannabee hardware."

"You should be using *me,*" whines Hercules, somewhere out of my sight. "*I* wannabee him. *She* doesn't."

"*You* can't get the database," Fur Underwear says grimly.

"*What* database?" Rowan says. "You keep talking about it and talking about it."

"Brain Police information. Whatever they send with their people on an undercover job. Could be an informant list, or a list of everyone working undercover—don't know till we see it."

"Sovay doesn't have anything like that," Rowan says.

Fur Underwear gives her a look like *she's* something to scrap off the bottom of a shoe, too. "How would *you* know."

"Because I helped him wipe it."

"You're lying," Fur Underwear says, but real unsure.

"No. I'm *not.*" Rowan lets out this crazy little laugh. "Is *that* why you sucked him? Is *that* what this was all about, some database that doesn't even exist anymore?" In a minute she's going to go up like a bottle-rocket and explode in hysterical fireworks.

Fur Underwear looks like she could throw a temper tantrum herself. "You coulda saved us all a lot of trouble if you'd just told us that."

"You didn't ask, you just came in and sucked him!" Yah, it's Fourth-of-July time.

"I meant just now," Fur Underwear says grimly. "Well, we're not out of options *yet*."

I'm starting to panic, because I know she's talking about flush-and-purge, and just when I think I might lose it all in a screaming fit, I feel like someone's holding my hand, but from *inside*. God—

"Guess again," I said. It was a long reach to her; I had to use Marceline to stretch and she didn't like it. Well, she'd just have to suffer. She wasn't loaded with choices. None of us were.

The cop. As soon as we make contact, I understand it all, and I'd be bugfuck, except I got more serious problems even than that. This is no time to get fussy about who I am, anyway. This is time to wonder if she's got that backup the Brain Police are supposed to have. For once, I want to see the goddam cavalry coming through the door.

Something in my limited field of outer vision moves, somewhere behind Rowan. It's Hercules, and shit, he looks like a sore loser—

Dionysius is not *a good sport,* Sovay said. *Rowan shouldn't have crossed him.* He was doing the equivalent of looking over my shoulder out the window of my eye to the outside.

• • •

Fur Underwear goes down hard. Hercules lifts her up again by her hair, but she's offline. "Take her out!" he barks, gesturing at me.

Sovay started to tell me something and then

he flies backward with a funny little dart in his bare chest and Rowan screams.

"Shut up," says Purple Tuxedo, tucking a tiny gun away in his cummerbund. "Now, do you want this or not?"

Does that piece of shit mean *me*?

Sovay's face filled my vision again, crowding out everything else. *I was afraid of this*, he said. *Flush-and-purge. Not me. You.*

You're *the box*, I said. *Can't you stop it?*

Not for you. You're not *the box*.

There's this pressure in my head, like a fist squeezing inside. Purple Tuxedo looks into my face and nods, satisfied. I'd like to wonder which Sovay he is that could just take this up so easy, but I can't do much besides panic.

"Standard suck mode," he says to Rowan, who looks like she isn't so sure about anything anymore. "If I force her in there on flush-and-purge, it could force him out into the available receptacle." He pats my head. Jesus.

And then Mersine tells me how it's going to be and there's no time to argue, because we're going, we're all going, and there's a lot of noise somewhere, someone's banging on the doors, they're coming in the windows, they're falling from the ceiling and the ceiling is falling on me, on us all, but they're too late, I don't have another second, nobody does.

                       Sovay started to slide past me, toward the opening I felt more than saw. I wanted to go after him, but the polarity was wrong. An invisible hammer hit me dead center, sent me flying against the mirrored wall of his rehearsal room. The mirror splintered and began to unravel in a spiral, like a cyclone picking up speed.

I spread my arms, reaching for the rest of me, imps or real multiple personalities, made no difference now.

You should have told me, Flaxie, it's against the rules but you should have told me anyway, you should have told me it wasn't an imp but a catalyst to wake her, instead of letting me be the fool to believe in what I thought I was, in what I thought any of us were.

But I was the only one who had believed. The rest of me, they'd all known differently, and I *couldn't* know. Because if I had, it would have completed the circuit, it would have been the thing that linked us all and mindwipe could have taken us all out. Instead of just me. Karma-gram, yes. The karma-gram has finally been delivered. It's my turn, now. The bill has come due for what I had to do to Marceline. I took her life, and now I have to give it back. It's the only just

                                    reach up with my right hand and rip the connection out of my eye.

Somebody screams. It sounds like Rowan, but maybe it's me.

?

Good luck, he said. *I hope you make it.*

feels like a boulder packed into the side of my face. I can see the paramed hovering over me. Bald, blue skin, very folksy. Makes me want to pop him one, but I couldn't pop a bubble.

". . . *mess*," he's saying. "Dirty shame. *Dirty* shame. Optic nerve's *shredded*, must hurt like a son of a bitch. Gonna need a graft on that."

Rowan comes into sight behind him, and it's like I'm seeing her through the wrong end of a telescope, she looks so far away. And so familiar.

And they come and gather around her, Purple Tuxedo, Stringy Hair, Hercules, Super Carrot. And more, that I hadn't seen before. Are they Sovays who found their way to the source, like swimming upstream to unspawn?

"Goddamnedest things occur to you at the goddamnedest times, hey, Mersine?" says the blue paramed, and I realize I've been talking away and not even hearing it. Or maybe someone else is doing the talking and I'm just the lookout here.

Someone pushes through the Sovay gang. Fly Eyes. She looks at me and shakes her head. Someone else moves in next to her, some guy in bad leather body armor and twinkly things stuck here and there around his mouth, and he looks purely disgusted.

"Salazar's going to spit," he says.

"Salazar's going to spit anyway," says Fly Eyes. "It's what she does." She moves in a little closer, hovering over the paramed's shoulder. "Can you hear me in there?"

"I hear you," somebody says. Not this me, whoever's got

the vocal cords. Marya, I think. Ersatz-me, me from a slightly different context.

"You were supposed to leave the fetishizer's with me. We had her staked out after Bateau but we couldn't get a warrant to search her. When you wouldn't come with me, I thought that meant you'd found out somebody else had sucked Sovay and you wanted to wait. But then you didn't respond to the trigger word."

"Trigger word?" I hear myself ask.

"*Frigid*. The second time I called you frigid, you were supposed to come with me. Marya would have gotten the wet dream while the cop was telling me what you'd found out."

"I didn't know anything except the name 'Monkey Shock,' " I say.

"It would have been all we'd needed," says the guy in bad imitation leather. "We had a chain of backups we could have activated, to keep an eye on you in turns."

"That don't make shitsense," I say—*I say*. "You shoulda just triggered the cop and had her tell you right out."

Fly Eyes shakes her head. "We never let our cops know exactly who's backing them up. Brain Police policy."

"In case I got sucked."

"Oh, we were *expecting* you to get sucked," she says. "Marya, that is, not Mersine. Marya came up as a variant of you, Marceline. Since you were the original dump, we couldn't risk losing you and your testimony. This certainly does screw things up. Marya has Mersine's spot in the brain now, and it's going to take ages to build another cop and put her in there—"

I go frantic, pushing to get up and pop her fucking chocks but the folksy blue paramed's got me tied down or something and he keeps pushing on my shoulders and going, "Sh, now, gotta stay calm, dirty, *dirty* shame," and he

looks up at Fly Eyes and says, "I don't think you were
talkin' to who you thought you were talkin' to, maybe you
oughta go think out loud someplace else before you bring
on a seiz—"

*They say it was sixteen hours in the hospital, but I
don't remember most of it. It would have been longer,
but I wouldn't stay. I told them no thanks to their graft.
Fuck it, I can live without an eye, especially a Brain
Police eye. And there isn't a damned thing they could do
about it with my contract up and everything, except get
petty and demand their clothes back. Which is what
they did.*

*Little Blondie in the wardrobe department made a big
deal out of that, having me exchange piece by piece for
the cop's old clothes. Those were in better condition
than what they took back, so I came out with the better
end on something. But I couldn't figure out why he was
taking so long and making a big fucking ceremony out of
it until she showed up.*

*Skinny? I seen fatter people that starved to death. I
couldn't believe I'd ever known this woman, but I knew
I had. There was this old garbled memory lying around
in my mind, the woman behind a desk chewing and spitting, sometimes into a desk suckhole, sometimes kneeling on a floor in an office full of fat furniture. That
made me think about mouthkissing and it just turned
my stomach inside out practically, seeing her and having
to think about that.*

*"You are legally entitled to leave, since your con-
tract's up," she goes, all official. "But I wish you'd
reconsider. Or at least let us give you a new optic nerve
and an eye. We owe you that much."*

I touch the eyepatch and think about the cop I used to

be, or who used to be me, and I get the feeling she'd have wanted this way. I mean, I don't know, *because I never really knew her, and it's not like cops are my favorite people even when they're me, but I feel bad for her, wherever she is. I was supposed to get sucked, not her. So I owe her a big one, and maybe I'm a fool to believe that, because maybe if she'd known all along that she was the imp, she might have changed places with me and let me go down the drain again anyway. But she never had the chance to make that choice.*

"Rowan'll be doing time for that," says Skinny, nodding at my eyepatch. "And some of the Sovays. The others'll be waiting for them when they get out. I'm not sure what they'll do after that. Most of the original people have been rewritten so thoroughly they're past the point of restoration, either as themselves or as Sovay."

"Why are you telling me this?" I ask.

"I thought you'd be interested."

"I'm not. I been a dump long enough, I don't need what you're spitting out."

She looks offended, but what is she gonna do, fire me? I *never worked here, and* I'm *driving now. If that's not fair to the rest of me, well, nothing's ever really fair. Not that I remember, anyway.*

I finish the Big Clothing Exchange and ignore the pained look Little Blondie is giving me. I got this other memory lying around, just a tiny one, him looking at me and saying, Come back when you want it taken off, *and I can't forgive him for that. He lied like a goddam rug and I don't care if it was his job to do it. Maybe she'd have just gone ahead and let him suck me out, her not knowing what I really was to her, but she should have been told so she could have made that choice, too, whether to get rid of me or let me live.*

Ah, fuck her, too. She was Brain Police, as bad as any of them. If I can live with one less eye, the world can live with one less cop.

And besides, I know something they don't know. For once. And it's this: She's coming back. Not today, not even next month, but sometime soon, she'll be filling back in. All those little memories she left laying around, the associations are already starting to reconnect, and she won't be able to help it. Maybe I could get her sucked out before that happens, but I'm not going to do that. Not this time. One of these days, she'll pop up and take a look around and wonder what the hell happened. And I'll tell her all about it, what they did to her and what they did to me and to all of us, and we'll see if she wants to be a cop again.

And if she does, well, this time she'll know more, enough that she can make the choice to give us all a chance. Maybe? I mean, I *would. Wouldn't* she? *Don't know. Don't know. Just don't* know

what the *hell* is go-
ing on here *now?*

PART III

‹‹ NOBODY'S ›› FOOL

"Your arrogance has always been your least attractive feature," Em-Cate said. She had to tilt her head back to look down her nose at me, but, migod, she did it.

"At least *I* have something to be arrogant about," I replied. The soft background music I'd been talking over stopped suddenly and my too loud voice hung in the air. All party conversation ceased.

Em-Cate didn't deign to notice that everyone was staring at us. "What, quickie head-jobs? Haven't you heard it isn't their *brains* that are supposed to be stiff?" Several feet behind her, a woman in one of those animated feather creations put a hand over her mouth, scandalized and loving it.

"You would know, you're the one with the monogrammed knee pads."

Em-Cate surprised me by throwing her wine in my face. For a long moment I could only stand there dripping pinot noir, wincing over my soggy eyepatch, and wondering if the stains would come out of the white secondskins I was wearing while she gave me her patented Em-Cate triumphant I-got-*you* blazing-eyed stare. Quite a tableau, if you liked cheap melodrama.

Apparently, this crowd did. The applause was loud, enthusiastic, and spontaneous, surprising me even more than Em-Cate's little improvisation. I was still goggling at the room when Em-Cate grabbed my hand, raised it, and then pulled us both down in a low bow. She tossed me a napkin as she stepped forward to take another bow separately, and then held out one arm to me so I could do the same. *Hurry up*, she mouthed at me through her too bright smile. I bowed, dabbing the pinot out of my eyes and retreated to the buffet table while Em-Cate made a big show out of beckoning the director out of the guests he'd been mingling with.

Jasper stood in front of us and bobbed up and down from the waist, fanning a breeze with the wings of hair sticking out from either side of his head. In the box-suit, he looked like a trophy wearing a shipping carton. He acknowledged Em-Cate and then me before he thought to grab the hostess and shove her in front of him. She took her bows while applauding herself, her suit of lights twinkling giddily.

"Well, that's our formal entertainment," she said, waving a hand at Jasper. "They even had *me* fooled for a while and *I* hired them. The Home-Brew Players—aren't they great, everybody?"

Everybody applauded again to show agreement. I had to force myself not to flee back to the guest room and lock the door behind me. Em-Cate slipped over to my side of the buffet table to pour herself another glass of wine. "Smile, dammit," she whispered, beaming at the crowd. "You look like you're at a funeral."

Smile. Migod, I thought, stretching my mouth in something I hoped was at least vaguely grinlike.

"Tonight's domestic drama was improvised from an outline by one of our own guests," the hostess went on cheerily. Everyone *oohed* and *aahed*. "And I hope she's ready to take credit for her part in this."

I hoped so, too. As usual, Em-Cate and I hadn't been given any details beyond the basic scenario. I wanted to get a look at the prodigy who thought a cat-fight was the height of party entertainment. But nobody stepped forward.

"Oh, come *on*," said the hostess, "she didn't leave, did she? Rowan, are you still here?"

Mi*god*. At first, I didn't think I'd heard correctly. Then the people directly in front of the hostess moved aside and there she was, looking as brown and round and bland as ever. The hostess was saying something else but I wasn't listening and didn't want to. I headed for the guest bedroom that was our dressing room, shaking off Em-Cate's restraining hand, ignoring Jasper's whispered command to wait, we weren't finished.

Obviously, we weren't, but as far as I was concerned, the party was over.

"What did you do that for," Jasper said, glaring at me as I slathered cream over my face. He'd insisted on glittering my cheekbones and it felt like sandpaper coming off.

"I quit."

"You can't quit. We're hired for the night, we've got a contract."

I shrugged. "Sue me."

He turned to Em-Cate. "Talk to her."

Em-Cate stared at him for a moment and then burst out laughing.

He plumped down on the bed, making the top half of the box-suit slide up around his ears. *Fashion-victim, thy name is Jasper*, I thought, watching him in the mirror, too disgusted to laugh. "Ah, Christ, why do I get all the temperamental ones," he whined, pulling his chin up out of his neckline. "Look, I realize you *artistes* would rather be emoting Shakespeare and Tennessee Ernie Ford from a real proscenium, but live theatre's *dead*. You want to work live, you do the soaps. You want to hear yourself talk, mount *Hamlet*."

"*You* mount him. I'd pay to see that." I turned away from the mirror and moved to the doorway of the bathroom, using one of the animated towels to wipe off the rest of the cream. The continuously moving patterns in the fabric flowed over the smears of color, incorporated them, and began some new fluctuations. "And it's Williams, not Ernie Ford."

"Apparently you haven't seen Jasper's libretto for *Twenty-Seven Wagonsful of Peapickers*," Em-Cate said. " 'Ah have always depended upon the kahndness of peapickers.' He's adapting it for three rooms with bath."

I didn't laugh. Em-Cate probably had it right, even down to the mishmash. But I wasn't fooled by her; she was ganging up on Jasper with me because she was feeling mean and it pleased her to do so, not out of any sense of actor's solidarity, least of all with me. That she was working with me was a reflection of her desperation for any work at all since the demise of Sir Larry's.

Jasper started one of his diatribes about the validity of the soap opera as classic tragedy, citing references that were about as accurate as his dramaturgy. I tuned him out, trying to recall which companies I'd heard were holding auditions. Door-To-Door was always auditioning, but that was because they were so vile, few actors could stand more than one production—migod, they'd play a toilet if there was money in the bowl. The Domestiks had a few openings . . . so did HomeShow . . .

There was a knock at the door. "Must be the bouquets you sent yourself," Em-Cate said, to me or to Jasper, I didn't know which and it didn't matter, because I was pretty sure I knew who it really was. Who it had to be, rather. I didn't remember that much about her, but somehow I'd known she couldn't have let the evening slip away without approaching me. God only knew why.

Em-Cate opened the door and stared at Rowan expectantly. "Author, author. Come to thank us?"

Rowan blinked at her. "That was terrible," she said matter-of-factly.

Em-Cate threw back her head and laughed. "Oh, *yah*," she said after a bit, wiping her eyes. "Of *course* it was terrible. You don't resort to cheap tricks like throwing a drink in someone's face if the material is any good." Still laughing, she wandered over to the antique vanity where her makeup was spread out among the hostess's collection of perfume bottles and sat down in front of the mirror.

"What do you resort to if the material *is* any good?" Rowan asked.

"Is that a rhetorical question?" Jasper muttered disgustedly.

"No," Rowan said, turning that blindy-eyed stare on him.

He didn't look at her. "Mine was."

"I knew the answer anyway." Her gaze drifted past him and found me in the bathroom doorway. The light in here wasn't the flatteringly soft party glow that made everyone look glamorous even if you weren't intoxicated, and it showed her no mercy. She had aged in a way that went deeper than a few lines and some minor sagging. "Been a long time," she said to me suddenly.

I pretended to look at a watch I wasn't wearing. "Six months, isn't it?"

"Ten years."

Of course; I'd forgotten about the time she'd pulled for her mindcrime. Mindcrime incarceration was like nothing else—they put you under the belljar with your mind racing so your time sense was slowed down. Realtime, six months; subjective time, ten years. I'd have thought it was a harsh sentence for a first offense if I hadn't been on the receiving end.

I realized I was staring at her, turned away and went back into the bathroom to clean off the makeup. If it was already all cleaned off, then I'd put some more on and clean that off, until she was gone.

"I've got a proposition for you."

I looked at her reflection in the mirror. "Migod, is it as good as the last offer? I can't imagine what would be better than being Sovay for you."

"Finding Sovay for me."

I could hear Em-Cate's laughter under my own. "Citizen, let me juice up your memory," I said, touching my eyepatch. "Sovay's been found. The show closed, the set's been struck, and I'm still not the man you wanted me to be. Nobody is."

"Ain't *that* the truth," I heard Em-Cate say, as if to herself.

"They said that all the people who bought Sovay from

the mindsuckers have mutated into something that is neither themselves nor Sovay," Rowan said. "I don't think it's true. I think he's still . . . alive. In . . . somebody."

I put more cream on my face. "The court maintained him in the sucker box as long as it could. When he disintegrated, he was declared legally dead. The men you collected to try to reintegrate him suffered rewrite conflicts—"

"But none of them were wiped. Sovay is lying dormant somewhere."

I frowned. "Nope."

"Sovay was the core personality, the source. Every one of them had him. That doesn't melt away like an imprint of a character. The associations still exist. Enough for you to be able to identify Sovay if you were mind-to-mind with him."

"What about you?" I said. "Couldn't you identify him if you were mind-to-mind with him?"

She shook her head. "I've never been mind-to-mind with Sovay."

"Never?"

Her chin lifted defiantly. "Is that supposed to be unusual?"

"I don't know if it's *supposed* to be. *I* think it *is*."

She sighed. "Sovay and I didn't believe in it. We thought mind-to-mind contact was more intimate than a married couple should be."

"How about before you were married?"

"Nothing. Ever."

I shrugged. "That still doesn't mean you wouldn't know him if you met him mind-to-mind."

Now she looked repelled. "I don't *want* to meet him

mind-to-mind. I don't ever want to be mind-to-mind with him. To have to feel those things . . . not ever."

"What things?" It was heartless, but she'd thrown a drink in my face. By proxy, but still.

"You know. His other contacts. His other mind-to-mind contacts, with pathosfinders, with other actors . . . all the people who had him, who got closer to him than I did. Including you. His big love affair. If you'd have just gone to bed in real-time, it wouldn't have been so bad, he'd have gotten you out of his system and you wouldn't have been hanging on to that part of him that wanted you. It's bad enough having to know about it. I don't want to have to feel it in my own head."

I wasn't sure that it would have felt any worse than what she was feeling in her own head now, having had nothing much else to think about over the last ten subjective years of her life.

"Maybe all that would be so if Sovay were still in existence," I said. "But he isn't."

"Yes, he *is*," Rowan said. "I know he is because I know him. Not the way *you* knew him, or any of the others, but I know what kind of actor he was. A Method actor, yes"—she gave a short, bitter laugh—"but he had the Method backward. Everyone else could become someone else, but not Sovay. All of *his* characters became *him*. That was the kind of man he was. It was why he was able to call me after the mindsuckers started trying to sell him off. I *know* he's alive in somebody somewhere, hiding, still holding his own. And you'd know him. The associations you still carry would know him. You have a foolproof Sovay detector in your head. You could find him for me."

"Why?" I asked.

She blew out an impatient breath. "The associations—"

"No. I mean, why should I?"

She moved to stand directly in front of the mirror, which put her in my blind spot and forced me to turn and look directly at her. "Because I still want him. Because I still love him." Somehow, the admission was more naked than if she'd made it mind-to-mind.

"But why should *I* do it? What's in it for me?"

Now she hesitated. "Is money good enough?"

I laughed. "Have you come out of mind-incarceration filthoid rich, money falling out of every pore and nothing better you can think to spend it on?"

She pulled a bankcard out of her pocket, pressed her thumb to the ID spot, and showed me the balance that appeared in the upper-left corner.

"I'm impressed," I said truthfully.

"You can have the whole thing if you find Sovay for me. Have your optic nerve fixed. Replace your eye."

"I can see just fine. Don't you think Sovay would object if he did turn up and you'd given away your life savings?"

"How much would *you* pay for *your* life?"

I couldn't help laughing. "You're asking *me* that question?"

"How much?"

I glanced at the bankcard balance again. "Less than I'd take to give it up."

"How much would you pay for the life of someone you love, then? I *want* my husband back. You're the only one who could find him."

"What about the Brain Police? You could go to them with your theories—"

"If they believed he was out there, that would be the

end of him. They'd take him apart for evidence, for what information they thought he might have. And for the simple reason that they wouldn't know what else to do with him."

"And what would *you* do with him? Or rather, with whatever poor slob that might turn up with his mind all scrambled from overwriting? If I could even find anyone?"

"I'd help him. And you can find them all, that's no problem."

"What makes you so sure?"

"Because I've already found them. It wasn't hard. I can tell you where each one of them is."

My gaze kept returning to the bankcard. Apparently I had an avaricious streak I'd never been aware of. Or maybe it was just knowing a bankroll like that could take me far away and let me start fresh.

"I put all the information in your phone mailbox," she said. "All you have to do is use it. Then you can use this." She entered some code on the top row of letters on the bankcard and then held it up to my eye. There was an infinitesimal flash that felt like a pinprick deep in my head. Or maybe a peapicker. "There. It's keyed to you now. Show of good faith. The money's already yours, all you have to do is come and collect it." She tucked the card back into her pocket. "I'll hold it for you."

I folded my arms. "Pretty rash. I could just go tell the bank the card is lost, get a new one, and take off with the money, all clear."

"Could you?" Her face was unreadable. "I've done nothing for the last ten years but think, about anything, about everything. You could do that, but you won't. You'll look for him because you want the money and because I've made you curious. Now you want to see for yourself if I'm right.''

Rowan hadn't struck me as the type of person capable of being so perceptive. But then, who was to say what ten years in solitary could do to anyone?

Jasper made a throat-clearing noise. "If you're about done in there, it's time to start dressing for the late show.''

"Thought I told you,'' I called to him. "I quit.''

In my hands, the towel suddenly shorted out and went black as the color receptors overloaded.

Karma-gram, whispered my mind.

There was a ghost of a smile on Rowan's face.

I didn't immediately go running off on the Great Sovay Hunt with dollar signs in my eyes. Fortune or not, I still wasn't sure if I wanted to go through with it. My life wasn't much these days, but it was a life and it was mine. So far, anyway, from the time of Marceline's descent into dormancy.

I didn't know what had caused that, and I hadn't tried looking for any answers, not when it had happened and not since. Now and then, I'd had a few nervous nights when I'd been unable to sleep, afraid that she would wake up the next morning instead of me. Other times, I would wake with a start from some already forgotten dream, sure that it had been her dream, not mine. But nothing happened; I never felt even the slightest stirring, not so much as a taste of her essence. And yet I knew she hadn't evaporated. If I couldn't feel her presence, I couldn't feel her absence, either.

Then let's tempt fate, I thought, and went for a walk in the Downs. If the old, familiar sights didn't rouse her, looking for Sovay might be safe. And if they did rouse her—well, I'd be beyond caring and she'd be back where she belonged.

My fatalism surprised me. First avarice, now fatalism —what else was I going to find out about myself? So much for instinctive living.

The sights were familiar in a distant way, but only familiar; a lot of specific things were missing from my memory, the associations too weak, or scrambled, or perhaps gone for good, at least as far as I was concerned. Somebody else's life had been lived here, not mine. I had passed through once in a hurry but my mental state wasn't the same.

Some joint called Sojourn For Truth raised a mild blip but I didn't know why. I'd have gone in to see if I could find out, but it was so run-down and sleazy-looking, I wasn't actually sure if it was open for business. There was a guy standing out in front as if he were waiting for someone; as I passed him, he suddenly blew a flurry of bubbles at me, each one containing a tiny glitter-star.

Before I realized what I was doing, I had stopped to catch one of the bubbles on my finger and watch the swirl of colors in the delicate skin fade to a colorless web before it popped, leaving a little red star stuck in a wet spot. I braced myself for some kind of hot pitch, but nothing happened. The man was just watching me, as if he only wanted to see what my reaction would be. I started to say something to him and he turned away, blowing more bubbles into the air over his head. I wiped my finger on my pants and kept going.

Several blocks in, a dream parlor called The Zoot Mill was running a halfhearted sidewalk display; the dancing unicorns flickered, full of static, and even the money tornadoes looked anemic. Nobody had stopped to watch, so I didn't, either. I was about to walk right through the display when a scantily clad figure materialized right in front of me. He seemed to be looking right at me and though he wasn't any less ragged than the rest of it, I was startled enough to back up and give the projection area a wide berth. The woman squatting in the parking space at the curb didn't even give me a glance as I stepped over her outstretched legs. There was something funny about her eyes but she was on my blind side so I couldn't see much.

Another few blocks and I was more or less lost. There was a comm center that wasn't particularly well patronized—I could have gone in and gotten a free map from a you-are-here but the strange apathy/malaise that seemed to be in the air had apparently settled over me like dust. It didn't really matter where I was; when I got tired of being here, I could hunt up a freebus depot or a tube station and take the next ride out. Or keep walking till I came out the other side of the Downs.

I paused again in front of a crib, of all places. There was nothing in my memory about it, exactly, but I had the strong feeling that there was something I should have known . . . or *had* known . . . I shrugged and started to walk away.

A moment later I was standing inside, blinking in the semidark. My inner ear went crazy as déjà vu shuddered through my brain and I leaned against a wall, trying to steady myself.

Abruptly, my blind side erupted with pictures, one after another, flashing too fast for sense, frozen frames of faces, places, things, and, under it all, a voice murmuring at me, unintelligible but relentless, insistent, demanding—

"I *said*, wake up. It's all a dream."

The man sitting on the sagging cot looked about a hundred years old, and not because of the snow-white hair. He reached over and picked up the connections to the system on the table next to the cot. "You didn't come for this, did you?"

The sign on the outside of the cubicle said *Imagist*. I shook my head once, carefully.

"Didn't think so. She said to expect you. I told her she was out of her mind, you'd never do it. But I forgot, of every one of us, she might have been the most insane, but she never, ever, was out of her mind. Not once." If he looked a hundred, he sounded two hundred, as if his voice had been in storage somewhere and he hadn't cleaned off the cobwebs when he'd taken it out again.

He beckoned and I went in. There was no place to sit except on the cot and I didn't want to get that close to him.

"Now, we wait," he said, as if I'd asked him something. "It shouldn't be long. He's a garbagehead now. Like the rest of them, I imagine." He changed position on the cot and the springs screamed like tortured weasels. "I don't know, really, he's the only one I've seen in twenty years, wouldn't know the others if I did see them." He looked at the connections he was still holding, but didn't put them down. "Which one are you —the original fake, or the fake fake?"

"Why?" I said.

"The one I had, she was the original fake. A persona who got too full of herself and pinocchio'ed."

"Pinochled?" I should get out of here, I thought.

"*Pinocchio'ed*. Cute little story about a puppet who turned into a human." He squinted at me with his cheap eyes; not biogems, just government-surplus brown. "Story everyone should know. I had time to tell it to myself. I laid it out as a full-length feature, did the remake, and then composed the opera." His gaze drifted past me and I turned to see what was so interesting.

Cheap gilt was flaking off the wretch standing in the doorway of the cubicle, a special effect gone wrong. He'd had a body once, but it had been some time since he'd bothered to maintain it. Or changed his clothes—I realized the washrag hanging over the front of his pants was actually the remains of a loincloth.

He put one hand to the side of his face and tried to speak, but nothing came out.

"Told you it wouldn't be long." The white-haired guy got up from the cot, making it scream again. "Come on," he said to the wretch in the doorway. "Someone's come to take you home now."

"No," said the wretch. "Still not right. Almost, though. It's real close. I said I'd meet her here, and I keep coming, but I keep missing her."

I stood on tiptoe to look over the wall of the cubicle. The aisle was empty. That didn't mean Rowan wasn't nearby, only that she was smart enough to stay out of sight.

"Don't have to buy paranoia anymore, do you?" said the imagist. He was laughing at me.

I shrugged. "Maybe not. Except I don't know how she'd know I'd come here, when I didn't know myself."

"Maybe she followed you and sent the nearest one. Or maybe it's just chance favoring the prepared mind." He led the other man to the cot and sat him down. "Is your mind prepared?" he asked, holding the connections out to me.

Go mind-to-mind with *this* walking wreckage? When I

barely seemed to know my own mind? "I'm nostalgic for
free will," I said, more to myself.

"Anything free is worth what you pay for it."

The breathtaking balance on Rowan's bankcard
passed through my mind as I took the connections from
him. Not because I wanted it so much anymore but because now that I had one of them, I had to know. And
even while I was popping my own eye and letting the
connection creep into the empty socket, I also knew that
any idiotic party guest could have come up with better
motivation for the most brainless scenario ever suggested to a living-room drama troupe.

Inside, he was like the first draft of the Franken-
stein's monster. He didn't even make a good crazy quilt,
he was a junk pile, visualizations shifting like a runaway
slide show without a sequence to follow. He couldn't
hang on to an idea longer than a few seconds, except for
one: meeting Rowan in a crib. But he didn't know *who*
was supposed to meet her—him as the whore, him as
Dionysius, him as Sovay as Dionysius, Sovay as him,
Sovay as him as Dionysius—he'd even lost all track of
whether he or Sovay had been Dionysius.

It was the type of confusion that spiraled inward. Follow it, and you'd chase your own tail until you imploded
into a fugue state, and when you came out of it, you'd be
back in the same place, ready to start over. Black hole
set on permanent rewind and replay.

*Anything else you want to know about the nature of
hell?*

The question fluttered past me on a tattered rag
caught in a minor whirlwind. The landscape that faded
in was my own involuntary visualization. That would
happen if nobody set the scene; sooner or later, you'd

see something unless you forced yourself not to. This something was like the surface of the moon transplanted to the badlands, the morning after a mental costume orgy. Most of the debris littering the ground didn't know what it had been before it had become debris.

The only piece that interested me was the rag. I concentrated on locating the source. After a bit, a stone mountain flickered into existence on the wasted horizon. As I started toward it, all the debris turned into heads, as if someone had spilled the baskets after a full day at the guillotine.

Except these heads were watching me. Something was wrong with their eyes, though—some of them didn't even have eyes, some that did couldn't open them, some had too many, and others had them in the wrong places —and none of them spoke language, only word salad.

Getting dicey in here, I thought, tightening my concentration. He latched on to my visuals, not because he liked them but because they were there to latch on to. If I wasn't careful, he was going to latch on to me, too, and every picture in my head would get sucked into the scenery.

I wrapped myself in a shield, which meant I had to go slower toward the source of the ragged message, and I couldn't see the location as clearly as before. But it relieved that besieged feeling.

On the ground ahead of me, something sparked and flashed in a random sequence. I plodded right along, not stopping but taking a good look at it as I passed.

A shard from a broken mirror. Uh-oh.

At least the stone mountain was getting closer; in fact, it was getting closer faster than I was walking toward it, which just served to show how perception of progress differs from actual progress. If I stayed in here long

enough, I thought to myself, I could probably qualify
for certification as a reality affixer. Then the cacophony
of voices shouting un-sense got louder, and I thought,
maybe not.

A cave opened up in the base of the mountain. Each
plodding step I took was harder, like every bit of movement was separate from every other bit, components
that would have made up one whole thing if they could
have connected with each other. But they couldn't. Had
I been thinking I could qualify as a reality affixer? Any
longer in here and there would be more heads lying
around on that bad landscape, all of them mine.

I stumbled over something, recovered, and then fell
down a bolthole.

You got my message, said Sovay. He was squatting
naked in a space at the bottom of the bolthole, tending a
small fire. It was his literal spark of life—as long as the
fire lasted would be as long as he lived. If you could call
this living.

The mechanics were fascinating to watch—he kept the
fire going by pulling off little pieces of himself and toss-
ing them on the flames. The smoke that came up flowed
back toward him and reconstituted his missing pieces
. . . mostly. A fraction of the smoke went up the
bolthole, where it was lost forever. Here and there, I
could see small pits and dents in his skin, the little losses
he couldn't recover.

Yah, I got your message, I said. *How the hell did you
send it?*

Smoke signals. He smiled at me over the flames. *I sent
it up the chimney here*—he pointed at the bolthole—
*and it attached itself to a carrier. I could spare that
much.* He looked at himself, touching a few of the dents

in his skin. *I figure there's still enough of me left to last a long bad time. I wanted you to come here. I know who you are.*

You know who I used to be, I told him.

Know of you, I should have said. He closed himself off when he was with Marva, I wasn't invited. He broke off the top section of his left little finger and fed it to the fire. There was no blood and he didn't wince until it started to burn. *I was a good actor, but when it came to the Method, I didn't have a clue.*

What do you mean? I asked him.

I mean I wasn't a real *Method actor. If I had been, you'd be talking to Dionysius, not the me who pretended to be Dionysius.* He examined his shortened finger and the other small deficits. *Can I borrow a cup of anything?*

I didn't understand right away. And then, when I did, I also understood the man wasn't asking. This was what he'd had in mind when he had felt me make contact. When you wanted to live this bad, you'd do anything.

Why don't you straighten him out? I asked, pointing at the bolthole. *Obviously, when Sovay didn't take, he fell apart. You could fix him, make him over.*

Tried that. How do you think he got this way? I was lucky he didn't fragment me as well.

I remembered the shard of mirror I'd seen. Who hadn't been able to live with the mirror—him? Or Sovay?

Abruptly, the smoke suddenly blew into my face.

Not fair! he screamed. *You've got plenty and I'm getting all used up! Give it back! Give it—*

He reached through the fire for me and his hand borrowed mass from the rest of him, swelling to four times its size. I flung myself backward, thinking *Exit!*

Nothing happened.

He was hanging above me, bigger all over now, meaning to envelop me. He didn't mean to take just what he thought I'd gotten in the smoke, but everything I had. I could see right through him—literally; he was bigger, but no more substantial.

I pushed myself upward, aiming at the bolthole this time. Passing through him was more than passing through a holo, but not much more.

"You're not her," he said accusingly. Coney Loe (that was his name; I could remember now) must have put his eyes back in for him. I couldn't look at him; it was all I could do to put my own singleton back in without screaming. "And you're not him."

"Brilliant, isn't he?" said Coney.

"Shut up," I said, keeping my back to both of them. Things were still settling in my head. I started to get up and suddenly there was a flash of light from my blind side, bigger than the pinprick flash from Rowan's bankcard.

How much would you pay for your life?

A lot more than I'd take to give it up . . .

"Where are you going?" Coney said.

I paused in the doorway, still with my back to them. "To call her. You keep him here, she can pick him up."

"This is him?" Coney sounded suspicious.

"Hot strike on the first try," I said. "Call it beginner's luck, or something, huh?"

If Coney said anything else, I didn't hear it. My footsteps pounding down the aisle toward the exit sign echoed the pounding in my head. Not the mindless throbbing of a hypehead's mindplay hangover but a chant, two words repeating over and over, like being slapped again and again without pause.

She lied. She lied. She lied. She LIED. SHE LIED.

I could see them in my head as plain as anything, Dionysius and Rowan lying on cots in a cubicle with a second man on the floor between them, all three of them hooked into a system together. Illegal three-way. People who would mouthkiss were capable of anything.

SHE LIED. SHE LIED. SHE LIED.

I hit the sidewalk and knew exactly where I was, where everything was, everything and everybody.

"Heya, *heya!*"

Reflexively I reached for a comb, but there was nothing in my hair. The figure in front of me changed from a neurosis peddler with bad leather armor to a malnourished rooster-boy with chapped skin. We stared at each other as I lowered my fist; after a moment, he pried my other hand off his throat.

"No rough stuff," he said. "Unless you pay extra."

I pushed him away and ran, almost knocking over another rooster-boy who was double-teaming a tourist with his pimp. The pimp's fuzzy, lurid magenta suit stung my vision and left an afterimage floating ahead of me, but no matter how fast I ran, I couldn't catch up to it. More than a pinprick.

SHE LIED. SHE LIED. SHE LIED.

Truth is cheap; information costs. How much for both, then?

Just as I reached the corner the light changed and four lanes of vehicles surged into the intersection. I turned away and something caught me right under the chin. My feet didn't quite fly out from under me but I went down anyway into a tacky forest of legs in second-skins and jumpjohns and cheap, flaking paint.

They all cleared away quickly and I found myself looking up at a pair of onionheads grinning over the chain they'd used to clothesline me.

"So hot to violate our marital space," said the one on the left nastily.

I started to get up and they advanced on me so that I was forced either to stay down or half crawl backward to get away from them. "You forced it," I said, trying to shift position to a crouch. "You know I didn't even see you and everyone who saw it will say that's true."

The one on the right bent forward, thrusting her ugly, hairless face at me. "Now *find* someone who'll say they saw. *Find* someone who wants to be challenged as your accomplice right now, here." The other one nodded, grinning, feeding slack into their marital chain. "*Find* someone, go on, ask any of them, ask them all, they'll tell you they saw nothing, they had their backs turned, they all saw nothing, nothing, *nothing at all!*"

They threw the chain back and whipped it over their heads and down. I had just enough time to squeeze into a tight ball. The chain missed my shins by a bare inch and smashed down on the pavement. The onionheads squawled like scalded badgers and pulled the chain back for another go. Just as it was arcing over their heads, I launched myself forward and under it. I hit open pavement and rolled with the fall so that my momentum took me back up onto my feet without a pause.

The onionheads were screaming full-throat now; I really had violated their marital space this time, deliberately and flagrantly, in front of a crowd of witnesses. Every onionhead pair and multiple in the Downs was going to be hunting me within an hour. *God, why?* I

thought, sprinting blindly. Why were onionheads allowed to terrorize people for no other reason than they
were bored, why were they allowed to act out their
pathological possessiveness by beating people into blood
pudding for the crime of violating some imaginary
boundary around them? And most of all, why did I have
to have onionheads after me now?

Unbidden, the words surfaced in my mind.

. . . are you paranoid enough?

I pounded across another street, staggered into the
entryway of a cheesy fetishizer joint, and squeezed into
a corner near the door, trying to catch my breath. The
door opened almost immediately, but it was only a couple of garbageheads, wearing silly wrapcoats and even
sillier grins. They didn't even look at me on their way to
wherever to enjoy their latest fixation, while it lasted.

My knees got shaky. I half slid, half fell down onto the
grimy tiles. My breath was coming back but my heart
wouldn't slow down and my legs were burning. If the
onionheads found me now, I wouldn't be able to do a
thing except bleed. I closed my eyes and tried to listen
for the sound of running footsteps and the clink of a
chain over the traffic noise.

Nobody came, not even another customer. After a
while, I pushed myself up on my hands and knees, and
then to my feet. My legs wanted to collapse more than
anything but I made myself move to the edge of the entryway and peek around the side of the building. No
onionheads; almost no one at all on the sidewalk, except
for a gofer walking back and forth half a block down
with an envelope under her arm, squinting at the street
numbers.

Of course they hadn't chased me; why waste time
chasing me when they could round up reinforcements?

Onionheads loved to hunt a violator en masse. If I could get out of the Downs, I'd keep my skin. They rarely left the Downs for any reason—better areas of town weren't terribly hospitable to them and they tended to end up being arrested for disturbing the peace before they could actually get around to disturbing it much. Whereas in the Downs, I reflected sourly, you could disturb all you wanted as long as you didn't overnight in a parking space . . .

I leaned against the building, trying to think while I scanned the street. Something was chipping at my memory, trying to get in . . . or get out?

. . . she lied . . .

Yah, we know she lied about never having gone mind-to-mind with Sovay, I thought. *We're doing something else now.*

she lied.

Something . . .

A flash of light, a pinprick in the brain. A scatter of heads, a shard of mirror, a continuously rewinding black hole. A man who stayed alive by consuming himself . . .

Forgive and forget. If you forget first, there's nothing to forgive.

His image was there in my mind, like a splinter, like a thorn, like a hook—but not enough. More than a holo, but not much more; more used up than he realized. Or maybe he did realize, but didn't want to admit it. Who would?

But there had been enough of him to tell me—

. . . she lied about why she wanted you to find him.

I stepped out onto the sidewalk. A battalion of onionheads didn't pour out of the nearby doorways, screaming for my blood. Still too early. Maybe I could get off the street before everyone had been notified and I could slip back to midtown during the deadest part of the night.

If I was right, I'd have a place to hide out until then.

The door was open a crack. I stood back and gave it a light push with my fingertips. It swung inward to reveal the empty living room, much the same as it appeared in the memory that contact with Sovay's ghost had activated. I took a tentative step inside, looking around. He couldn't have been expecting me; the security entrance was out of commission, so I hadn't had to buzz him to let me in.

Or had he been expecting me every day for the last six months?

"I didn't know what I'd do when this finally happened. If it ever did. And now I still don't know."

He was standing in the kitchenette holding a cup, either just emptied or not yet filled. I couldn't tell. The bad dye-job had been left to fade without renewal; except for some very faint orange shadows in the lines around his eyes and mouth, it was all gone now.

"What do I call you?" I said, pushing the door closed behind me.

"I've been using Anwar, still. For simplicity's sake. Though I'm still neither flesh nor fowl nor good red herring. *Bad* red herring, perhaps. For a while, orange herring."

I had a sudden flash of myself as a fish; ridiculous. I shook the thought away.

He gestured at the futon across the living room. "Make yourself comfortable. We should have a talk, just the four of us. Or, well, I don't know how many you are now, but I'd like it if you'd limit yourself to two while you're here. I'll make you some vile coffee." The brief laugh seemed to escape him without his wanting it. "I know I said that last time would be the last time. I lied. I'd have helped you if you'd come to me every night with our pimp snapping at your heels, I—" He reached for his waist and then stared wonderingly at his empty hand. "Oh. I forgot. Can you buy that? I really forgot."

I went to the futon, hoping the movement would shut off his babbling. He grabbed another cup, filled them both with water, and dropped in a couple of cubes.

"Very vile coffee," he said, coming over to sit down next to me.

"Thanks," I said, accepting a cup from him. "You're true. The truest one I ever knew."

He laughed again, blinking at me incredulously. "Where'd you get an idea like that?"

"Where do we get any of our ideas?"

He tilted his head to one side and something happened. The set of his face changed, the lines suddenly not quite what they'd been, not quite right. "No," he said faintly, "it *was* Marva I loved, not . . . the other. The big husky one, she was . . . *not* Marva. *Non-Marva.* But Marva was the one I wanted, and when she, when she—" He looked puzzled. "*She* was in Bateau's office, *she* was in the lateral and I had to save her—but it *wasn't* Marva and it wasn't *me.* Not at the time. But it is now."

I put the cup down on the floor. "I can help you with that," I said.

He was going over it again when I led him into the bedroom, where he kept his system.

• • •

He was slow to manifest; he kept putting some obscuring element between us, a waterfall, a fog bank, a dark pane of glass. But he would have had to have been in much better shape to maintain such a thing within the system. Like the unforgiving light in a dressing room, being mind-to-mind showed no mercy.

Actually, it wasn't so bad. It gave me time to get accustomed to what I was going to see.

They were melting into each other, Sovay and Anwar; as if they were mirror images instead of two different sides, the mirrors making a V-shape and slowly moving so that the images were being sucked into each other. Except Anwar was losing.

All his characters became him.

She lied, but not about that.

The Anwar part looked disappointed. *Where is she?*

An environment was forming around us, something vague and semidark, like the inside of a cave or a grotto. There was no sign of anyone else besides us. *I don't know*, I said. *She didn't leave a forwarding address.*

You're not quite her, *either*, Sovay said.

I lost a lot of memory, I told him. *If that's what makes any of us what we are, then I'm really not Marva at all. Not the original fake and not the original fake fake. A new fake.*

Dark patches in the space around us began to swirl lazily like oil floating on the surface of water, as if a relaxation exercise had leaked through, except it wasn't completely abstract. Here and there, there were hints of pictures—faces, mostly, but they didn't last long enough to identify.

She was right, Sovay said suddenly. *It* is more intimate *than a married couple should be. Than* lovers *should be. Than* we *ever should have been.*

The portrait of Rowan floating over his head looked as if it had been done in dark smoke and could blow apart at any moment. Somehow, it didn't.

But she wasn't lying, he added. *It wasn't really me she was mind-to-mind with. Just two Downs hypeheads who wanted to be me. She wanted them to be me, too, you see. She was trying to fix them, focus them on her. But it didn't work. It couldn't have. They needed you for that, not her.*

Because I *had* been mind-to-mind with him. Of course. I wondered about Dionysius. Was he still sitting in the crib, in Coney Loe's cubicle, waiting for Rowan to come and get him, or waiting for me to come back? There hadn't been enough of him to fix . . . had there?

Anwar . . .

. . . *is going to be absorbed, of course,* Sovay said, sounding regretful in a detached way. An ego that swallowed other people whole didn't have much room in it for regret over someone else's misfortune. *It's what I had to do. I never had the knack of the mirror like you did. All the characters had to be me, because I couldn't give myself up to anyone else. But you could. That was why I went mind-to-mind with you. I thought if I could feel the way you did it, I could learn how.*

Rowan's portrait had been replaced by drifting scenes of the two of us together. The symbolism was prosaic—conjoined rings, giant stars orbiting each other, galaxies colliding—

I was confused. An aquarium? An ocean. And one lonely figure swimming through it, immersed but never part of it.

Knowledge isn't ability, Sovay said sadly.

Truth is cheap, information costs. Who had said that to me? Coney Loe, truth whore. Did that make the truth a pimp?

The force of Sovay's presence began to increase. *Things coming back to you*, he said. Approval radiated from him like heat. *When the right things come back to you, you'll be her again. For some of us, who we are depends on who we're with. And you're with me now.*

And you wanted me so badly because of the mirror, I said. *Not for love, that was something you already had in the real world. You just wanted someone else who could be you.*

But it's not a true reflection, Sovay. It's a funhouse mirror, and that's something else altogether.

The mirror encircled us completely. The reflections weren't clear yet, but they were forming.

No!

His negation came from his pure core of self, undisguised and uncivilized, a baby's first cry and one that had never ended, not for him; Sovay then, Sovay now, Sovay always.

It wasn't a bad thing, really, for someone like him, not until he had started trying to remake the world in his own image. Then he had looked into my image and found a Brain Police cop staring back at him—

The mirror shattered in an explosion all the more violent for being soundless. Fragments flew out in all directions.

Didn't matter; it was only his perspective, and it was my mirror. But his image had fallen on it and it was still there.

The memories were already beginning to spark. *When the right things come back to you, you'll be her again.*

For some of us, who we are depends on who we're with.
And you're with me now. But if I *was* her, then let it be
because that was who I was, not who he wanted me to
be.

My own negation broke the connection.

This was one of those times when having only one eye
was an advantage. It meant I could be out of the system
and sighted before he was. I moved to the doorway,
watching him carefully as he tucked his eyes back in.
There was less of Anwar in the man who got up from the
bed, looking around like someone traversing the last set
of exits from a prison.

"Reinforced," he said cheerfully. "It's quite a feeling."

"I'll buy that. Rowan doesn't really care which one
of you she gets, does she. Which one of you Sovays. It'll
be first come, first served, won't it. She didn't ask me to
get the *right* Sovay—you're *all* the right Sovay. It's just
a race to see who gets home first."

He gave a short laugh. "The right one *is* the one who
gets home first."

"Well, I've decided to make this one easy. I'm declar-
ing you the winner. Run home, tell her you're the
swiftest and the strongest, she'll never know the difference. Neither will you. Though there *have* been a lot of
other changes in the non-Sovay areas of the universe.
Sir Larry's is gone. The future belongs to living-room
soap opera. Cheesy, sordid, and braindead, but you get
to go to a lot of glamorous parties. And I never want to
see you again. I won't be a fool for the Brain Police and
I won't be a fool for you, or Rowan, or anyone."

"Won't you?" he said as I turned to leave.

I hesitated, but I didn't turn around to look at him. "What do you mean?"

"It'll come to you." I could feel him smiling at my back as I marched through the apartment and out the door. Or maybe that was just the aftertaste he'd left in my brain.

I was about to step out onto the sidewalk when I remembered the onionheads. *Superb*, I thought; as if I couldn't have waited, oh, ten hours before telling him off. So much for shelter. I'd really screwed that one up. Hadn't I?

There were no onionheads in sight in either direction. Somewhere, not far away, was an air-taxi pad, but there was someplace else I had to go first, someone I had to see, and something I had to get—

The blind side of my face began to tingle, as if a fine spray of cool water was dancing on it. I wanted to stop and wait until the sensation passed but I forced myself to keep going. If the onionheads caught me out, my face would be doing more than tingling.

There was a sudden tiny flash of light from the empty socket, followed by another and then another, until it seemed to be filled with a multitude of twinkling stars. Or glittering dust.

Or the fragments of a shattered mirror, still free-falling toward reassembly.

I heard the rattle of the chain before I saw them, but there was nowhere to go—the one storefront near the corner was empty and the rest of the building sealed up. I jammed my fists into my pockets, put my head down like a gofer on a rush-job, and stalked across the street, trying to keep focused on where I was going rather than the flashing from my blind side.

It fooled the onionheads long enough for me to get across the street and it might have fooled them even longer if I'd been able to resist sneaking a glance at them to see if they were watching. They were, and I must have looked like the main attraction in a fox hunt. They let go with something that sounded like a cross between a scream and a yodel and I was off in an unsteady sprint with the couple pounding after me, howling for reinforcements.

I passed a doughnut shop just as someone was coming out; a whiff of appetite gas hit me right in the face and the blast of hunger pangs almost knocked me sideways. It mixed with the nagging, repetitive music from the soundtrack joint next door. I stumbled into the gutter, through several occupied parking places and then into the middle of the street, barely missing the front of a van. Through the windshield, the angry driver looked green, but it might have been a trick of the light, the real light or the strobing light from my blind side.

In the next lane, a taxi screamed to a stop several feet in front of me and flipped on its for-hire sign. I ran past it and hit the opposite sidewalk. By the sound, two more onionheads had joined the chase, though they weren't any faster than the first two. But sooner or later, they were going to pick up a pair who could sprint faster than I could even chained together, and my chest was burning so badly that the bile was coming up out of my throat.

I swung around the next corner thinking that the next time I saw a taxi, I wasn't going to be so panicked that I ran past it instead of using precious seconds to open the passenger door. If I ever spotted another one that would stop for me.

And then it was too late even for that, because they'd

finally gotten smart instead of fast. The sidewalk ahead of me was clearing in a hurry to make room for the pair running at me from the other end of the block, chain held at neck level and no breath wasted on scary howls.

The pawnshop sign seemed to jump out of nowhere. I hit the door at a run. It stuck for one horrible, endless moment and then gave, dumping me on the floor inside just as the onionheads reached the spot on the sidewalk where I'd been a moment before.

They didn't even bother screaming in rage. I lay on my belly, trying to breathe, listening to the rest of them congregate outside behind me. They couldn't come in and get me and I couldn't leave; I wondered how the pawnbroker was going to take that.

The door swung shut, muffling the sound of onionhead grumbling and chain-clanking. After a while I raised my head and looked around.

What's the good word?

The flash from my blind side filled my head, overwhelming everything else. I couldn't feel the pain in my chest or the hardness of the floor under me; there was only the bright white light. As I watched, it began to pulse, brightening and then dimming, and in between, I could see the pictures, like small, sequential chunks out of a holo show. Or maybe an outdoor soap opera.

. . . pull free for a moment, two moments, three, and hold on tight, hold on, because this can't last long . . . the overdose of memories has disoriented her and while she's too lost to be conscious, there's time enough to step inside here . . . the pawnbroker thinks I'm her on a bender, good . . . one fast transaction, please . . . yah, in trouble again, Ofrah, yah, shouldn't have this one but I can't go purge it, what a waste . . . right, you take it for now, lock it up and I'll come back,

*but don't give it to me, no matter what, unless I tell
you . . .*

". . . the good word?"

*She's bent over me, hands on her knees, white hair
fallen to one side and looking like this is the most
amusement she's had this week . . .*

The voice in my head faded as the mirror fragment
fell into place. The mirror wasn't completely reassem-
bled yet but there were plenty of pictures running on it,
from all of us, Marceline, both Marvas, the one with all
the memory and the one Sovay forced to existence. And
me. Whoever I was.

I held out my hand and the pawnbroker helped me
up. "Thought you'd never get back here," she said con-
genially. "You *do* have the good word this time, don't
you?"

"Yah," I said. "I've got the good word this time." I
glanced toward the door. "For all the good that'll do me
now."

She smiled. "Well?"

"The good word for today is *forget*," I said, watching
the scene from that night replay again on the mirror in
my blind side. Had that really been *me* that night, I wondered as I followed the pawnbroker into the back room;
had that been *me* pulling out of dormancy in Marceline/
Marva long enough to stash the one thing that would
positively identify me as Brain Police? Funny, I didn't *feel*
like Brain Police. But I didn't feel like Marva anymore,
either. Not that I really had since I had come up six
months before, but I'd thought that might have been
because of all the direct memory I was missing. After all,
the Brain Police officer was gone, I'd watched her go,
washing out through the hole that had opened up in
Sovay's sad imitation of a mirror—

She's coming back.

Marya?

The pawnbroker paused as she pulled the connections out of the system and looked at me. Had I spoken aloud?

All those little memories you left lying around . . .

Some in a pawnshop, too, I thought.

. . . and we'll see if you want to be a cop again.

Ofrah reached for my eye and I put up a hand. "I think I'm changing my mind," I said.

She let out an exasperated breath. "Not here, you're not. You can change your mind if you want, but you're taking this with you. Dump it on some other unsuspecting jerk if you want, but I'm not keeping it and I'm not flushing it for you."

"But I don't want to know," I told her.

"You don't? Too bad, tough stuff. Somebody's got to know and you're elected, not me." She pushed me down on a well-beaten pad that might have been a mattress once. "Everybody's got some information they're responsible for. This is yours." She stuck her thumb in the corner of my eye and pushed.

At first, I thought the connections for my eye had crumpled up somehow, but after a moment, I realized that feeling of a hard painful lump in my eye socket was purely psychosomatic. The body can be as fond of symbolism as the mind.

"Is that it?" I said, sitting up.

"Didn't take a minute, if that," Ofrah said.

Maybe it hadn't, but that had been time enough for more onionheads to join the mob out front; I could hear them. It sounded like hundreds now.

"Can I go out the back way?" I asked.

"They'll have that covered. Your best bet is the roof. They don't like heights since it's never just one of them that could fall."

"What's on the roof?"

Ofrah blinked at me. "Nothing."

"Then why should I go up there?"

"Are you crazy, or just stupid? To get away. You can go rooftop to rooftop until you get to a freebus depot or an air-taxi stand."

I laughed a little. "You mean, I wouldn't just happen to find somebody up there with an illegally parked air vehicle for a convenient getaway?"

The pawnbroker's expression was unreadable. "Do you think you're in some kind of long-playing soap opera, or is it just a dose of reverse-paranoia in your property? Maybe now you think you're after somebody and the world is out to make you happy?"

The pain behind my eye was receding as the information she'd given me was absorbed.

"Why didn't you just call them," I said. "Tell them it was here and they could come and get it."

"Call who?"

"The Brain Police."

"I don't mess with the Brain Police. I don't want to end up in a rehab ward with a bib and a diaper. Whatever you did is your lookout. If I'd known what you had when you dropped it on me, you'd have never have gotten out of here by the back door *or* the front."

I nodded. "Who am I, Ofrah?"

She roared with laughter. "You think you're a hundred people, but that's typical of any memory junkie." Her laughter wound down and she frowned at me, warily. "You're Marceline, okay? What's the matter, you lose your rudder when Bateau took his fall?"

"How do you know I'm Marceline?"

"You gave me the good word," she said, her voice cracking with annoyance. "How else would I know?"

"Maybe Marceline gave *me* the good word."

She shook her head. "Jesus save me from memory junkies. Why don't you just go get yourself a new life from some persona mill if you're so hot to be somebody else? Why do you have to come around here bothering me and then acting like I'm doing something to you? I did you a favor that night. Return the favor now and get the hell out of my store. And don't ever, ever come back, okay?"

The database in my mind revolved, delivered the code sequence that would have shut Ofrah off and brought up the Brain Police officer underneath. I wasn't authorized to do that; not that I cared much for things like authorization at the moment. But it would have been a dirty trick. The cop wasn't expecting to come up now and even a fast memory fill wouldn't help the resulting shock and disorientation. It might even hurt, depending on what memory the cop was supposed to use on the missing time—a love affair, a vacation, an illness. False, of course, but you can't maintain a functional person unless you cover up those long periods of dormancy and the person in question would never know the difference.

"Well?" she said impatiently.

I gave her a salute and headed for the front door.

She ran after me. "What do you think you're doing?"

"Getting out." I pulled her hand off my arm. "And never coming back."

"They'll stomp you into the sidewalk!"

"Will they?" I smiled. "Maybe they'll feel sporting and let me have a head start so they can chase me first."

A multitude of expressions flashed over her pale face. It was just the automated program of emergency procedures for when something went wrong during some operation but she didn't know that, of course. "You can't go out there."

No, I couldn't. I was supposed to go up to the roof and get picked up there. I glanced up at the ceiling and for a moment I wondered if maybe I *wasn't* just being paranoid.

Then I opened the door and stepped out into the middle of the onionheads.

They froze. Every last one of them froze, unable to move or shout or, by the blank looks on their faces, even think. I had to press my fist against my mouth to keep from laughing out loud.

"It's not her," one of them said suddenly.

Like that, they were unfrozen, echoing the words as they fell back, giving me a wide berth. Onionheads giving someone a wide berth—was anybody *seeing* this? I looked around. No, of course not—the sight of an onionhead mob is better than a meltdown siren for clearing an area of innocent bystanders. And not-so-innocent bystanders.

"You're wrong," I said to the mob, which was still backing away from me in an ever-widening circle. "I *am* her. I deliberately violated marital territory. At least a dozen people saw me do it."

"Whose?" someone shouted. "Whose territory did you violate? Show us! It wasn't ours!"

"Not ours!" someone else called out, and then they were all yelling it at me, over and over: *Not ours, not ours!*

I ran out into the street, trying to look at them all, but

it was hopeless. They were onionheads and one onionhead looked pretty much like another. Which was the whole idea.

Even after they dispersed, the street remained empty and quiet for a long time. Except for distant traffic noise, the only sound came from a vehicle lifting off from where it had been illegally parked on the pawnshop roof.

There was nothing to do but go home. Not to the midtown efficiency I'd been treading time in, but to Marceline's place in the Downs. As I'd expected, she was still in residence. By remote control, of course, maintenance automatically deducted from an ever-dwindling bank account that somehow never quite dwindled to nothing. The feeling of familiarity was very slight; in a less aware state, I'd have passed it off as nothing, minor déjà vu, if that.

Had it been mostly Marceline's mistake? Or had she just been the trigger for the unfortunate conjunction of Marva and Sovay? Or had they been the trigger for **her**? The database I'd gotten back from Ofrah couldn't tell me; it wasn't geared for explanation.

Unlucky combination, I decided. Three people who should never have gotten together. And perhaps most of the blame was Marceline's. She'd been allowed to collect too many memories in the course of feeding her habit, and when she had made mind-to-mind contact with Marva, it had filled in too many blanks—those that had not been filled in when Marva and Sovay had gotten too close in the course of a love affair they had erroneously assumed was just them leading their own lives.

Or maybe it was really all Sovay's fault for being the

way he was: *They all became* me. Yah. Sure did. When he had realized he was Brain Police, too—had that happened when he'd discovered me dormant behind the Marva facade, or had he discovered me because he realized what he was?

If that had been me he'd found. My head began to ache; strictly psychosomatic. I went to the one window in the apartment, over the futon, and opened it. It looked out at the side of the building next to it, but if I leaned out far enough, I could see a slice of the street, vehicles and pedestrians passing by. I had the mad thought of running downstairs and stopping people randomly. *Do you know you're an operative for the Brain Police? Do* you? *And* you? *And* you?

I put on the dataline, flipped through the channels. News reports, sitcoms, talk shows, documentaries, commercials—I paused at one for something called The Nicer Person. They'd reworked the old melty animation from Some Very Nice People.

Ah, yes. We were all Some Very Nice People, or The Nicer Person, or Power People. Maybe that had been how it had started, a decoy operation set up as a persona mill. And everyone who came in got indoctrinated —or maybe *contaminated* was a better word. And all of them mindplaying after they left, thrillseeking, buying neuroses, selling their dreams and buying others, and the contamination was spreading like some weird mental variation on a social disease. One day the sun came up and *everybody* had joined the Brain Police.

And maybe a few people found out once in a while, they would wake up and say, *Wait a minute here, what's this doing in my life?* And the Brain Police would pay them off, give them a contract, and promise that they'd never notice the missing time. *We'll only use you when we need you; then we'll deactivate you and leave you alone, and you never even have to know if you don't want to.*

Quite a generous contract.

Don't worry about whether your life has a purpose. It does . . . now.

I shut off the screen.

How'd you get so genius, figuring stuff out like you got a sherlock circuit.

Paid for it, Coney. It was very expensive information.

It would be even more expensive if the Brain Police caught up with me now. They couldn't come right out and *do* something to me—I'd give the whole thing away. Instead, they'd sent Rowan to put me on a fool's mission: find the Sovays. Yah. Thinking Sovay would trigger the reemergence of that upstanding Brain Police officer Mersine, who would go trotting home with the database intact, unscratched, and uncomprehended, so that the secret could be reburied with no muss, no fuss, and life would go on. After all, the show *must* go on, especially when it's all theatre anyway.

Was it like this everywhere? I wondered. Or had things just gotten out of hand—achieved escape velocity—here in this one city?

I already knew the answer to that one. How long would it take? Another century, or just another couple of decades? Would anyone be spared? And if not, what would happen when we reached full . . . saturation? Would we all just come up simultaneously, spontaneously, exploding in a surge of unity?

Or would we just explode?

And had this always been the point that mindplay had been leading us toward, from the very beginning? Whether we'd known it or not?

I turned to look at my own system, sitting next to the futon.

The cliff was still there. Sometimes it looked like the open panorama window of a sky-island, but mostly it was a cliff overlooking a blank nothing of a landscape.

Standing next to me, Marva wanted to know why. Both of her.

Because one individual can make a difference. And that's not any of us.

Marva said it wasn't Marceline, either.

It wasn't once, but it is now, I told her. *The fragmentation of being a memory junkie—that's what made it possible for me to merge with the remains of the Brain Police in her. Without us, she's cut off. She'll be the only person in town who isn't on the team. And they'll never know.*

Marva wanted to know why it mattered, then.

Because it does. Because there should be at least one other person in the world. Someone to Escort the Brain Police out of this world and leave it to people *again.*

But would she, Marva asked skeptically.

She'll try. And now, let's go. All of us. I turned to Sovay, standing a little ways behind us, faint and not very well developed, but there nonetheless; he had come with his part of the database. *You, too.*

He didn't want to, but he wasn't strong enough to resist. When we went, the database would go with us. The Brain Police didn't really need it for their own information, but it would rob them of an easy entrée to Marceline. Which would increase her chances of survival as an individual.

Don't take any wooden memories.

She was too dormant to feel me but with any luck,

she might be more cautious about what she did with herself when she came up.

The mirror shattered again when I threw it over, the pieces flying around as if in a high wind. But I'd figured it would take the combined weight of all of us to drag them down.

You know it's going to be a bad day when you wake up and the last year of your life is gone. Naturally, the first thing I do is panic.

This, they say, is the lot of the memory junkie: bad cess, bad living, tough stuff. I am not exactly in a position where I can complain to karma-rama. But who ever sets out to be a memory junkie, anyway? Ten thousand people buy memories every day but you, you ducky luck-off, you get the thunderbolt in the head. Little lucky number ten thousand, this is your life and this is your life, and *this* is your life, and this, too, could be your life, if you could afford to feed your habit that well. Most can't, and don't kid yourself, you won't be able to, either. Wouldn't be so bad if you could just get out and make a few memories by original recipe, but it's never your own memories that junk you up. That's the one sure mark all memory junkies share: None of us are particularly memorable citizens. If we were, maybe I'd know what happened to me.

Could be I got a nasty sclerosis grinding away from whatever I been doing during the missing time, in which case I got to hie my bad old self to a clinic for a retread. That's about as much fun as getting trepanned, with the added attraction of having the meds bitch to a fair glow for doing shit I can't even remember I did, and getting bitchier because I can't sound sorry enough.

Or it could be I been done out by the last pawnshop I went to. Happens—you get an inexperienced operator who doesn't know the difference between *clean* and *wipe*, or you get a very experienced operator who's booked on the next flight out and doesn't have to give a shit about what the carriage trade will say. You'd think I'd have a lawsuit coming for that, and if I'd been some safe-sex day-wage priv from uptown with a receipt from a Commerce Canyon salon, there'd be no question. But someone from the Downs suing a Downs pawnshop—double zero. There wasn't an eagle in the immediate world who'd even take a call about it. That's technically discrimination, but find somebody who gives a fuck.

Could also be that I made someone mad at me, which means I'm lucky I got off this easy, and I can just get on with my life as it is now and hope it doesn't happen again.

Or I coulda been rousted by the Brain Police. In which case, I should probably just stand in the middle of the Downs with a "Suck Me" sign on my forehead and get it over with.

All this goes through my poor old tampered-with mind in double triphammer-time, so even in my panic, I know I can neg sclerosis. The general rule is, if you know the word "sclerosis," you ain't got it. So there's a little relief, no bitchy what'd-you-expect-you-bad-girl lectures to sit through while I'm getting a fresh coat of myelin.

A pawnshop fuck-over is still a definite maybe. I'll have to get back to that one.

Making someone mad is also a maybe, but there's usually a few tokens of their disaffection to go along with the memory loss—shaved head, broken nose, and two black eyes. My face doesn't feel like anybody did the fandango on it, but there's something wrong with the panorama of the cracks in my ceiling. I climb out of bed and check in the bathroom mirror.

Still got all my hair. Looks like a wild animal had a

restless night in it and I forgot—ha, and ha—to take the
combs out. My nose *has* been broken, but not in the last
twenty-four hours. It's that missing eye that tips me off that
everything isn't like it should be. I squint on the trouble-
shooter, checking for any misalignment in the connection
that would mean something had been yanked against my
will. I wish they were the fancy kind with the auto-log
feature so I'd know when I'd had them out last, but for
what I can pay, I'm lucky I get the whole visible spectrum.
They're not even biogems, just government-surplus brown.

I'm so glad I didn't make anybody mad, I could almost
face the Brain Police, except that's the worst way to make
everybody mad, even if it's not my fault. But if the Brain
Police have been at me, there should be a copy of the
warrant on the dataline screen, where I'd see it first thing. I
stump over to it, but it's blanko on the lousy little built-in.
Except for the blinker in the corner. Message waiting. I
punch for it.

> *Q-up and calm down—a million strung-out hypeheads can't be
> wrong. Carefully, now: you're not a memory junkie anymore.
> Before you run out the door, consider two things:*
>> *The future is already set, only the past can be changed, and
>> If it was worth forgetting, it's not worth remembering.*
>
>   *Your fairy godmother*

I read it over twice. The kind of life I live, I'm liable to
wake up to anything, and I accept that. Like I say, I don't
have a leg for a complaint with karma-rama. But apparently I have a fairy godmother and I can *almost* remember
her . . . certain associations are still there, like ghosts,
even if the memory itself is gone. That happens, no memory ever stands completely alone. All I know is, I can trust

her to give me not only the truth, but right information as well, and if she tells me something's not worth remembering, I'd do worse than to let whatever stay where it is.

She's even right about me not being a memory junkie anymore. I got no craving at the very moment and with a six-month hole, I ought to be tearing my own ratty hair out. This doesn't mean it's not gonna jump up on me never again. Unless one of us really did change the past . . .

I touch the patch over my eye. Now, I'd rather have two eyes but one feels . . . I don't know, *right*. I sure hope it's because it was *my* idea and not, say, Bateau's. One eye and a memory loss is something he'd do to teach somebody a lesson. But I don't feel punished and Bateau never lets anybody go without feeling punished; it's part of the fun for him.

I start to punch in a phone number and something makes me stop, some kind of bad feeling I can't quite get ahold of to look at. Yah, but shit, what am I supposed to do, watch six months of archives and try to figure out my place in the universe from that? I'm nothing and nobody, and with my memory gone, I could be looking at the story of my life and not know it.

It almost makes me sick, but I get the number punched in. The screen lights up on the seventh ring.

"You look like a bad year in hell," I say. "This got anything to do with something I misplaced?"

Anwar's got this look like I'm the last person on earth he ever expected to hear from. "I don't know," he says, finally. His voice sounds like his throat's full of slow-hardening glue. "What did you lose?"

"I don't know," I say. "Can I come over and look for it at your place?"

"Sure," he says. "Sure, come right now."

I break the connection. Just as I'm getting up, some

glitch throws the message from my fairy godmother back up on the screen instead of blanking it.

The future is set, only the past can be changed, and if it's worth forgetting, it's not worth remembering.

Okay, so I'll remember it anyway, and if I don't like it, I'll just forget it again. Ofrah'll always do business with me.

And I really want to see Anwar. I could have seen him just yesterday, but as far as I know right now it's been six months. If that's closed and done with because the past got changed and I forgot, then that's how it is, but I got a right to know.

I mean, it's my life, isn't it?

ABOUT THE AUTHOR

PAT CADIGAN is the author of two previous novels, *Synners* (a finalist for the Nebula Award) and *Mindplayers*, as well as a short fiction collection, *Patterns*. She is a winner of the World Fantasy Award, and has several times been a finalist for the Hugo Award as well as the Nebula. She lives with her husband and son in Overland Park, Kansas, where she is working on her next novel.

S|Y|N|N|E|R|S

Pat Cadigan

*"Ambitious, brilliantly executed...
Cadigan is a major talent."*—William Gibson

To be a Synner is to join the on-line hardcore, an outlaw band of video hackers, simulation pirates and reality synthesizers—hot-wired socket-jockeys hooked on artificial reality and virtual space. Now you can change yourself to suit the machines—jack into cyberspace dreamscapes and leave the meat behind. All it costs you is your freedom—and your humanity.

But something new is loose in the network, a wildfire virus with a mind of its own that can crash the system and trash your brain. The Synners created it. Now it's up to them to stop it.

"Synners is a knock-out. Witty, rude, and rich with ideas."—Ellen Datlow, fiction editor, Omni

A Nebula Award Finalist

On sale now wherever Bantam Spectra Books are sold.

AN 438 11/92